God Killer

By the same author

The Tenth Circle Of Hell series:
The City Of Weeping
The Banners Of The King Of Hell
The Kingdom Of Eternal Pain
World Without End
Darkness Made Visible (in preparation)

The Book Of Neferusobek series:
Standing On The Edge Of Forever
God Killer
Book Three (forthcoming)

The House Of Altimsah series:
Altimsah
We Are All Stardust
Song Of The Universe

Divergence series:
Shambhala
Pangea
Al-Marrikh (forthcoming)

Möbius Strip
Queen Of The Uzbeks

Martin Dench

GOD
KILLER

The Book Of Neferusobek

Copyright © 2023 and 2024 House Of Altimsah/Suchos Corporation/Martin Dench

Martin Dench has asserted his right under the Copyright, Designs and Patents Act 1988 to be identified as the author of this work.

www.martindench.com

The author would like to offer his sincere thanks to the Suchos Corporation, without whose support and generosity this book could not have been published.

For Emilija, the perfect collaborator

Chapter One

As I entered the room, I noticed my mother sitting in a chair in front of me. She seemed somehow older and more frail than I remembered her. She opened her mouth, as if to speak, but no words came out. Only the empty silence of the long centuries that separated us. I walked towards her, feeling unsettled, wanting to hold her close, feel the warmth of her skin on mine. It had been so long that I had forgotten how that felt.

I heard a sound on my left, and turned to see what it was. A figure was approaching me, a figure that transformed into my father as he was bathed in the morning light that was streaming through the large window opposite. It was my father, and yet it wasn't. He seemed so much older than he had been when he'd died, a fragile and weak shadow of the strong man I had known. And yet, he was no different. He was my father and he was my rock.

I glanced to my right, towards my mother, but, to my surprise, and my dismay, she wasn't there. It was as if she'd simply vanished.

I turned back towards my father, and I suddenly realised he was covered in mud. There was a desperate look on his face, and he appeared to be struggling to say something to me. His mouth opened and shut, but, like my mother, no words would come. He stared straight at me, his eyes transfixing mine. I was certain there was something important he wanted to tell me, but I couldn't work out what it was. He simply stood in front of me, a frail and delicate old man covered in mud.

I felt helpless, powerless and I could do nothing more than cry. I felt the tears start to fall down my cheeks and I could hear the deep, desperate sobbing that burst out of my lungs. I felt to my knees at his feet, and simply wept.

And then, suddenly, it all stopped. I woke with a start. The sun was streaming through the half-closed blinds, bathing me in the glorious light of a Caribbean spring morning. I listened carefully, to see what might have woken me, but the palace was still, the only sounds coming from the distance; housekeeping and grounds work, part of the natural ambience of the early morning.

I glanced at my phone. 7.30am. I wondered why my body had decided to wake me up so early. Sleep was still a new innovation in my life and I had been taking every opportunity to experience it. I hadn't slept since 1802BC, had been cursed by narcissistic Anubis to spend every moment of every night witnessing the slow progress of Ra on the Mesektet, restoring Ma'at to the Duat, if I closed my eyes. Keeping them open for 24 hours was no easy task. Even when you don't physically need to sleep, the desire to rest and simply shut your eyes remains strong. For 3,826 long years I had endured this nightly torment, a mute witness to the Duat, close enough to touch Ra, but, at the same time, far enough away for him to appear merely a speck on the horizon. It was a curse upon a curse.

But now I had been freed from that part of the curse. Miraculously, it might appear. However, I had lived too long and witnessed far too much to be able to believe in miracles. The only miracles that existed in my life were the ones that I fashioned. No-one, not even a god, was going to do anything miraculous for me. Except by accident, of course. And that is what had happened.

Less than two weeks ago, I had attempted to fuse the Kemet of 1799BC to the Los Angeles of 2024AD. My plans had been meticulous and, as I had expected, everything had proceeded according to plan. Senusret had been restored to life, and I had avenged myself and reclaimed my throne. But then came the unknown variable. Although, of course, if I had been less arrogant and had thought more holistically about the whole process, rather than simply focusing on what I intended to achieve, it would have been neither unknown nor variable.

It was too late for recriminations now. Everything that had happened was now part of the tapestry of the past, the only practical direction was forward. Although, perversely, the way forward involved the past. Senusret was lost somewhere between 1799BC and 2024AD and I had to locate and save him.

The two time zones had been within minutes of being locked down when Horus had appeared in my apartment in the Suchos Building and had done what the gods did best. Their arrogance and narcissism were more human than human, and Horus had dared to try to stop me. Although, of course, unwittingly, he had. His hubris had been his downfall, as it would be for any of his fellow gods who tried to interfere with my plans. He had tried to intimidate me with violence, but had failed spectacularly. For a god, like Anubis before him, he was monumentally stupid. They had cursed me with immortality, filling me with microscopic machines that self-replicated and constantly repaired my body, and had been doing so for nearly four thousand years. They, however, were mortal. I had killed Anubis and then I had despatched Horus, although in his death throes he was able to disable the process that was under way. It had occurred to me on many occasions to wonder why the gods had not made use of their own technology. They appeared to have long life cycles, but they were clearly mortal. However, I always put these thoughts to one side. It wasn't important to me and I had long ago stopped trying to understand the thought processes of these creatures. One thing I did know was that they most certainly were not gods. Not as anyone in the modern world understands the concept, anyway.

The fallout from Horus' actions were immense. Bigger than immense, in fact, and utterly catastrophic. The particle accelerator at La Misión, my particle accelerator, had exploded with a force that this world had never seen. It was a detonation with a blast wave the likes of which had never even been dreamed of. The resultant devastation was shocking. The Suchos Building, some twenty miles away from the epicentre of the event, simply disintegrated, collapsing in on itself. Los Angeles was mostly destroyed, although some would argue that this was no bad thing. The blast also triggered the San Andreas Fault and caused a large part of the Pacific seabed to collapse. As a result, San Francisco was wracked by the worst earthquake in its history, and a tsunami swept across most of the Californian coast, causing not just enormous damage, but actually sinking much of the coastal plain below sea level. As a result, about a third of what had been California was now seabed. Most cities and towns in California had been affected, although the damage varied from total obliteration to minor structural damage, depending on the proximity to La Misión. The death count was not even mentioned by the media. My information suggested the figure was far in excess of a million.

The political fallout was at least as great. The investigation into La Misión was going to be the biggest such event in the history of the USA. Scapegoats were already being prepared, although not a single person had any idea of what had really happened. The head of the project, the inadequate and ineffectual Dr Simon Stuart was being groomed to take the fall, although he would no doubt try to lay the blame elsewhere. Probably in my direction. Unfortunately for him, I was far too well connected and had too many people of influence on my payroll to be any sort of meaningful target. Even the morons in Homeland Security were powerless to act against me.

The world was suddenly scared of science, and the Hadron Collider in Europe had been ostentatiously taken off line and shut down for the foreseeable future. This didn't affect me, but it did mean that I would need to find an alternative method of reaching into the past. Fortunately, I was resourceful and Plan B was already being put into effect.

After my men and I had taken stock and debriefed at The Tower, we had all left for my private island in the Caribbean, 70 miles off the east coast of Nicaragua. I had bought Isla de Gran Esperanza in the seventeenth century and had slowly built up the resources there, so as not to draw too much attention to myself. It was now a relatively small, but thriving and self-sufficient, community. My Royal Palace, although it was far smaller than those I had known during my all-too-brief time in Kemet, was at the heart of the island, which was a careful mix of modern urban and native jungle. It was, essentially, a modern outpost of Kemet, and as the sole surviving monarch, this was my kingdom. This was where my M'sha were trained, where our children were taught the values of the world that had been lost to me so long ago, where so many of my loyal subjects lived out their lives.

I wasn't sure why I was now able to sleep. I presumed that the trillions of bosons, mesons, quarks and anti-quarks that I had been exposed to when the rain had started falling on the car park in the ruins of the Suchos Building had done something to the micro-machines inside my body. I had long ago come to the conclusion that my night-time visions were not real, but the product of some form of visual programming incorporated into the tiny machines. For whatever reason, that part of their programming no longer worked and I was able to sleep. It had been both a shock and a revelation the night after we returned to The Tower to find myself feeling both tired and sleepy. I had not slept for so long that I actually didn't realise what was happening. And then I woke up the next morning. Despite all the misery and heartache I felt, there was some small joy in my heart at this turn of events. I had not slept for 3,826 years, and it felt somewhat bizarre to wake from a dream. I had truly forgotten the power of dreams.

Since then I had embraced the pleasure of sleep. It is impossible for anyone else to appreciate the tedium that comes with immortality. Whereas before I had to find ways to fill my time, ways to distract myself from the obvious and the painful, I could now sleep. And I did, to the exclusion of most other things. I had a lot of sleep to catch up on. However, with sleep came dreams, and mine seemed to project the deep inner torment that I felt. This dream about my parents was new, but no more distressing than so many others I had experienced, many of which focused on the death and subsequent loss of Senusret. I often woke to find my pillows wet with tears, my eyes raw from weeping. I supposed I had a lot of pain and suffering to catch up on. Ironically, the best dreams I had were the ones in which I died.

As I lay in bed, having this silent monologue, wanting to return to the world of dreamless sleep, there was a firm knock on the door of my bed chamber. I recognised the knock. There was only one person who had permission to enter my rooms anyway, so I didn't even need to recognise it. I sat up, pulling the sheets around me in as demure and as dignified a manner as I could.

'Enter,' I called out, moving a strand of hair that was hanging over my left eye out of the way.

The door opened and Nedjes entered. Loyal, steadfast, dependable Nedjes. I owed him so very much.

'Good morning, my Queen,' he bowed, entering, but staying by the doorway.

I said nothing, but inclined my head slightly, quizzically, silently inviting him to continue. I was certain he hadn't come in this early just to wish me a good morning. I detected a slight smile of satisfaction on his face as he spoke.

'I have news.'

Chapter Two

Extract from the unpublished memoirs of Ceryse Tabrizi:

I still don't know why I tried to save that bitch's husband. I shouldn't have bothered, for all the good it did us both. But I felt sorry for the poor bastard. He'd been dead for 3,826 years, was brought back to life in a world he had no clue about, and then found himself being thrown about by a falcon-headed Egyptian god. If you think that sounds crazy, then you should have tried being there. A queen who was immortal, a bunch of animal-headed gods and a bridge back to 1799BC. I guess that crazy doesn't quite tell the story.

I'd tried to save that bitch's husband. Nawal, Neferu, whatever her freaking name was. Egyptian history wasn't my thing. I could have coped with Benedict Arnold, but I was out of my depth with King Tut's world.

I'd rushed onto the bridge, or whatever it was. It wasn't real, but it felt like it was. It was solid under my feet and Senusret was hanging on to its edge by his fingernails. I grabbed his hands to try to help him up, although I knew I probably wasn't strong enough to haul him up on my own. And then that animal-god-thing, Horus, or whatever his name was, pushed me. I fell over the edge, and we both fell into what seemed like an abyss. It was like falling into the darkest, deepest sea you could think of. Only it wasn't wet. But it felt like I was drowning.

We fell and fell into nothingness, and then everything went black. I felt certain we were dead. I think that was a highly logical conclusion. As Rich would have put it, no doubt.

Poor, sweet Rich. I was so angry with him. I still am so angry with him, all these years later. Although, the person I was really angry with was, of course, me. It wasn't like Rich was the be-all-and-end-all. But he was fun, and kind. A nice guy. Even if he was white. My mom wouldn't have liked that, and maybe that was what stopped me from making any moves. But, at heart, I'm a little old-fashioned, being African-American, and I believed it was his place to make a move. I knew he liked me, and wanted to ask me, but was scared I'd say no. I don't really know what else I could have done to make it clearer that I wanted him, other than jumping on him and ripping his clothes off. Maybe I should have tried that. But I should have realised that sooner or later, some man-eating goddess would come along and steal him away. Well, of course, how could I have realised that? It's not like Rich was man-eating goddess material. I was biding my time, quietly confident that it was just between us, that at some point something would happen and we would wake up together after some great, or not-so-great, sex. How could I have realised that a 3,854 year old Ancient Egyptian queen would step in and steal him away? And simply to get a skull. A very dead skull. Her husband's skull. This world is fucking crazy.

And you know what? The thing that made me so angry was that I couldn't even blame him. She was something else. Even I, as a woman, could feel the power she had. She was drop-dead gorgeous, elegant and sophisticated, always immaculately and stupidly expensively dressed. She carried herself with such grace and style; she really was the epitome of beauty. But she had more than just that. There was a power that emanated from her, a dynamic magnetism that made her hard to resist. Probably one of the reasons I gave her such a hard time was because I could feel myself being sucked in and wanted to fight it every inch of the way.

That sap Rich hadn't even bothered to try, although, as I said, I couldn't really blame him. To be enslaved by someone like Neferu wouldn't exactly be a hardship. Certainly not for a man.

The problem for Rich, though, was that he was sucked in, became addicted to his Queen, and then she spat him out. Quite forcefully. Once she'd got the skull, she no longer needed him, although he'd managed to hang in there, like a raccoon around garbage. She even took him back to Ancient Egypt with her. He witnessed her revenge. The real tragedy, I guess, was that she wasn't a monster. She was arrogant, possibly the most arrogant person I'd ever met, although with good reason; she was supremely self-confident, and also obscenely rich. But underneath it all, she was simply a wronged woman trying to get her man back and make things right. The problem was that she'd had nearly four thousand years to think about her revenge and she wasn't going to settle for anything less than absolutely everything. But she wasn't a monster. Although I tried to give her hell, and hated her for spoiling what Rich and I never quite had, she tolerated me. She could have killed me, both of us, in fact, but chose not to. She didn't even kill that animal Curtis, although I probably would have done in her place. She had the ability. That was evident when she cut out the heart of that dog-headed thing. Anubis, or whatever he was called.

That was truly shocking. I don't think I'll ever experience a weirder or more surreal day than that one. But she carved out the heart of a god and stamped on it. So, she could walk the walk and talk the talk. And she left us alive, so she still had some sort of a heart. And, whatever I thought, she clearly loved her husband. That really was a love like no other, a love that spanned four thousand years. Whatever anyone says, she was hard evidence that love is stronger than death.

But it seems that even she couldn't cheat death. What I witnessed all those years ago still traumatises me when I think about it. After everything that has happened since, all the wonderful times and happy memories, I still can't get those images out of my mind. It's ironic that death walked so close behind someone who is, or was, immortal. Senusret was a nice guy, not that I could understand a word he said, but he was like a rabbit in the headlights, transported directly from Ancient Egypt to the hell on earth that was the twentieth century. And you know what? I tried to protect him, I really did. But, in the end, I was helpless. Helpless to save him. But so was she. His wife. The great Queen. She failed. In every way. I will never forget those moments, no matter how long I live. Some things just don't leave us, no matter how hard we try to ditch them. If I close my eyes, it's the easiest thing to bring back those memories, even though it was now over forty years ago. I remember Senusret, so excited to see her again, so happy and relieved, gunned down as he stood next to her, dead for the last time. He was lucky, I suppose. Most people only die once. And, of course, somehow he hadn't really died at all.

And then it was her turn. Nawal El-Karam as I once knew her. Neferusobek, 3,854 year old Queen of Egypt. No stranger to death herself, but deaths she always returned from. But this time it had been different. I had watched her die. Really die.

Chapter Three

From the Los Angeles Chronicle Online, Tuesday 12th March 2024

'California Catastrophe: The Latest News.

'By Kalandra Straub, Senior Investigative Reporter.

'Although it is now just over two weeks since the devastating catastrophe that has brought the Sunshine State to its knees, there seems little progress has been made in identifying both the cause and those responsible.

'On Saturday 24th February, life changed for everyone in this state, if not the country. Changed irreversibly and tragically. The explosion that ripped outwards from the tiny settlement of Northwood, just outside LA, was like nothing ever witnessed before. Scientific experts from all around the world are agreed that the scale of this explosion dwarves anything previously experienced, and made the A Bomb that fell on Hiroshima in 1945 seem as innocuous as the bursting of a balloon.

'What is known is that the particle accelerator at La Misión imploded, causing something like a black hole to be generated, which led to the cataclysmic explosion. The arguments about what led the particle accelerator to melt down look set to continue for some considerable time, with congressional hearings already mired in the red tape of bureaucracy and the chaos that has engulfed the entire country. It seems that Dr Simon Stuart, the Director of the Project, is being lined up as the fall guy, although he has claimed, off the record, that he and his staff were not working that day, it being the weekend. However, the destruction of the site was total, and no records remain, not even staffing ones. As many of the staff and their families were killed, it will be no easy task for Dr Stuart to disprove any of the allegations that are due to be made against him.

'The patron of the project, Ms Nawal El-Karam, has publicly expressed her shock and distress at the event, and has pledged whatever funds are needed to help continue with the rescue and salvage operations.

'Her own consultant, Dr James Curtis, a shadowy and dubious figure, seems to have also fallen victim to the destruction. No trace of him remains anywhere. Dr Stuart has suggested that what happened may have been a result of an unauthorised project being run by Dr Curtis, but there appears to be no evidence to support this assertion.

'The relief services operating across what remains of California continue to do what they can to help, but the number of survivors being found is reducing dramatically day by day. Although official sources are highly reluctant to put out numbers, an unofficial source I spoke to suggested that the victims of this totally avoidable tragedy may be as high as three million souls; men, women and children.

'And that is just the cost in terms of human lives. The number of homes, businesses, and other properties that have been destroyed runs into the millions, although, these, of course, can be rebuilt, unlike irreplaceable human lives. However, what is beyond dispute is that many of these buildings and properties are forever lost, because a third of the state is now below sea level.

'The full scope of this catastrophic tragedy is beyond the ability of words to adequately describe. What was one moment a thriving and bustling state was instantly transformed into a war-torn wasteland. Added to this is the real fear of the outbreak of disease as a result of the intolerable conditions the majority of Californians are currently being forced to live in, akin to refugee camps previously only seen in the Third World.

'As you would expect, the usual conspiracy theories abound, with the lunatic fringe proposing that we have been the victims of our own government, the Russian government, or that it signals the beginning of an alien invasion. Whatever the truth, there were some curious events that occurred near Northwood and in Wilshire immediately prior to the explosion. If you cast your mind back you may remember the bizarre murder of Professor Marcus Fraser, whose body was found mutilated in West Adams, a long way from the Institute of Ancient and Classical History in Wilshire, where he was the Director. The same Institute whose car park was the scene of a brutal shootout between police and unknown gunmen a few days before the cataclysm. The police had stated this was a gang battle, but it was odd that it took place in the car park of a museum whose senior academic had recently been murdered according to Ancient Egyptian tradition.

'And, only the day before the explosion, there had been another gun battle just a few miles from the site of La Misión, one that had involved a helicopter gunship of unknown origin. The police remain tight-lipped about this, but an insider has stated that this was not a gang battle, although no-one seems to have any idea who was responsible. All the evidence is now dust.

'These are probably simply random coincidences, but the destruction of much of our state has left many painful questions to be answered. And while we search for answers that will probably never come, the victims continue to suffer and die.'

Chapter Four

I shut the laptop and took another sip of my coffee. It seemed disappointing to me that despite the vast number of lives lost, journalists had survived. They were widely touted as proponents of free speech, but, in my experience, were uncaring of the impact of their allegations and only really interested in self-aggrandisement. Their art, if you could really call it that, was one of verisimilitude and dissimulation. Kalandra Straub was no exception, and she was in danger of becoming a major irritant. It was annoying that she had somehow linked the events involving my M'sha and the Guardians to the destruction of La Misión. It had been she who had perpetuated the ridiculous urban legend of the undead monster stalking the streets of LA after the death of Fraser. I had not met her, but had spoken to her via videolink to provide my public statement. She had seemed mostly unexceptional, although there was something about her that seemed slightly incongruous. I couldn't say in what way, it was just something in her eyes that seemed somehow at odds with her outward presentation. However, she was a journalist and if her inner self projected a different message to the insincere and vacuous words she spoke, then she was hardly unique.

I sat back and drank more of my coffee. It tasted good, even better than it actually was thanks to the welcome news brought by Nedjes. After only two weeks of searching, Ceryse had been located. And located alive. Little surprised me anymore, but that had. What were the odds of her falling into a maelstrom containing four thousand years of the past and emerging recently enough to still be alive? And it meant that Senusret might also still be alive, although Nedjes had found no record of him. However, even if he was alive, he would be significantly older, and I would still need to go back and rescue him.

My poor husband. I had lived through every year since 1802BC; the bizarre and degenerate world that surrounded me was one I had grown into over the natural course of time. He, however, had died and been reawakened some 3,826 years later. I couldn't even begin to imagine how mind-numbingly overwhelming that must have been. At least when he awoke, I was at his side. Outwardly unchanged, one constant that he could hold onto.

Thrown into the past, maybe without Ceryse, I was scared to even contemplate what might have happened and how it would have been for him. My heart ached for him in ways I couldn't even describe. I had held him, had kissed him, had felt his life-affirming warmth pressed close up against me. And then that monstrous creature Horus had thrown him into the Well Of Time. Horus had paid the price, but I needed to rescue Senusret, nullify whatever pain and suffering he had experienced.

And the task had to start with Ceryse. I hoped, however old she was, and whatever had happened to her, that she would be more amenable and less irritating. I didn't think I had met many people as annoying as she was, and that really was saying something. Maybe age and bitter experience would have mellowed her. I hoped so. Nedjes had located her in Charleston. She appeared to be married, with children and grandchildren, and living reasonably comfortably. Although the records for her were a little vague, it would appear that she was now around 70, maybe slightly older.

It was going to seem a little strange meeting her when only two weeks ago she had been somewhere around 30. I was used to the people around me ageing and dying whilst I remained the same, but it had never happened over the course of two weeks.

If she was now in her 70s, then that would seem to indicate that she had wound up in the 1980s. That had been a strange decade, a time of increasing global violence, and spiralling human ostentation and vacuity. I had a sudden vision of shoulder pads and hideously permed hair. I sighed. Sometimes I disappointed myself with my ability to remember even the most trivial of details.

The morning sun was streaming through the windows; it felt good to be bathed in the life-affirming light. I had always loathed the darkness and dampness that coincided with winter in so much of the world. I came from a world where even the rain was warm. I looked out through the window nearest to me; on this side of the Royal Palace there was nothing to see beyond the garden leading to the golden beach, and the distant blue sea, which casually merged into the equally blue sky at the horizon. In the distance I could hear the sound of children playing and other voices engaged in a variety of exchanges, none of which I could discern, even if I'd been interested enough to. It was almost idyllic, it was relaxing, it was comforting, and it was mine. Unlike the jarring, decadent and degenerate sounds that had constantly bombarded the Suchos Building from all sides. All of that was gone now, of course, the surrounding streets as dead as the rest of the city.

I sipped some more of my coffee and continued to study the vista outside. I heard the sound of rotor blades approaching. I got up and crossed to my chaise longue, making myself comfortable with my half-full cup. I would soon be off to South Carolina, so I wanted to make the most of the home comforts available to me while I could. I tried to empty my mind, but it wasn't possible. The same constant worries kept surfacing, all focused on Senusret. I felt so helpless, and useless. I had failed him. I vowed that this would not happen again. I would find him and we would have our life together, whatever the cost, financial or human. I owed him that, at least. The gods owed us that.

As I contemplated these gloomy thoughts, there was a knock on the door.

'Enter,' I commanded, and the door opened to reveal Nedjes. I noticed he had a large brown envelope in his hand.

'Is it time to go already?' I asked him, hoping to have time to finish my coffee.

'Not yet, my Queen. We'll be ready in about 30 minutes. But this came with the helicopter.' As he said this, he came further into the room and handed me the envelope. It was unaddressed, with the words 'Private and Confidential' stamped on the front. There was a small logo on the back; one of my forensic laboratories.

As Nedjes bowed and left the room, I stood up, putting down my coffee cup and opening the envelope.

There were several documents inside, containing some graphs, charts and a long covering letter. I started with the letter, and as I read it I returned to the comfort of the chaise longue. I was soon glad that I had sat down, because, as I got past the opening platitudes, what I read made no sense. Not at first, anyway. I have lived so long, seen and experienced so much, that almost nothing can shock or surprise me anymore. But the contents of that letter rocked me to the very heart of my being. I admit that I was totally unprepared for what I was reading, I had never even considered the possibility of what was laid out in black and white in front of me. I briefly glanced at the accompanying diagrams and images, all of which corroborated what the letter had already stated very clearly.

I put the papers down and got up, crossing to my desk. I opened one of the drawers and pulled out a similar envelope, taking out the letter it contained and reading it, probably for the hundredth time.

Obviously, I knew what it contained, but I needed to read it again, just to make sure that I hadn't, in some delusional way, misunderstood or misread it. No. It was all there, also in black and white; a mirror to the letter just handed to me by Nedjes. I put it back in the drawer and returned to the chaise longue, picking up the letter and reading it yet again.

I was absolutely, totally, shocked. Shocked? That word seemed so tame, not even touching the surface of the emotions that began to flow through me. The contents of this letter turned my world and my beliefs upside down. The constants that had kept me grounded since my birth had just been crushed out of all recognition. I hardly knew what to think. I sat back and tried to reason rationally, logically, make sense of it all. And as I did so, a clear picture began to swim into view. Although this was completely unexpected and more than distressing, it did make sense of much that had never made sense. Calming myself down and thinking more clearly, I could begin to see the connections. As I did so, an overarching truth finally dawned on me. The last veil had been lifted from my eyes. Now I could see everything, although much of what I could see was, at best, slightly paradoxical.

I put the letter back in the envelope and retrieved my now-tepid coffee, putting the documents in the desk drawer with the others as I did so. Returning to the chaise longue I felt a terrible hardening in my heart. Where before I had felt hatred and injustice, I now felt consumed by revulsion and an overwhelming desire to destroy. The anger swelled up inside me like a tsunami and I threw my unfinished cup of coffee across the room, with such force that it shattered into tiny pieces on impact with the wall, some remaining embedded in the plaster. Cold coffee was splattered across the vibrant Kemetian wall paintings. I found myself screaming in a way that I hadn't realised I could, 3,826 years of pent-up anger and loathing rushing out of my lungs in the most primitive way. I couldn't say anything, I just let out a wordless scream that released so much pain and suffering. I forced myself to stop, and to breathe deeply and calm down. I slowly lowered myself onto the chaise longue, forcing the tension out of my muscles. I needed to focus on my priorities, and, right now, my priority was Senusret, as it had been since his murder at the hands of Anubis.

Anubis! After I had killed him, cut his head off and burned his body, all that remained was the finger that had worn his ring of power. His head had been left in my palace in Itj Tawy in 1799BC, but his finger had been preserved. I had kept it for a reason. I wasn't convinced that a DNA test on a god would bear much fruit, but I had sent the finger for analysis anyway. And now the results were sitting in that brown envelope in my drawer. The shocking, devastating results. I felt stupid. I really should have seen it coming. Now I thought about it, it was so obvious I felt embarrassed and remarkably idiotic. It was more than obvious, it was logical. What was it that Horus had said to Curtis? 'You have betrayed us!' Sometimes my arrogance and sense of superiority blinded me to the all-too-obvious.

This changed everything. Absolutely everything. I needed to go to Charleston and speak to Ceryse, find out exactly what had happened, whether Senusret had been with her in the past. But, whatever the outcome, before I ventured anywhere in search of my husband, I now had another journey to undertake.

Chapter Five

Ceryse had done well for herself. She now lived on James Island, one of the most desirable locations in Charleston. Nedjes had not been able to find out much beyond the fact that she had retained her own names, had appeared in Charlotte, as if from nowhere, at the very end of 1982, and had married someone with the improbable name of Edward Stanhope. He seemed to be an unknown quantity, too. They'd had four children, and were now grandparents. At some point in the 1990s they had relocated slightly southwards to James Island. I presumed she hadn't changed her names in order to facilitate our rescue efforts.

Nedjes had scanned every possible resource available over the past 42 years, several times, but could find no trace either of Senusret or anyone who matched his description. That was disappointing. Extremely disappointing. I had hoped that he would have emerged on the other side of the Well Of Time with Ceryse, but that didn't appear to have been the case, although I wouldn't know for certain until I'd spoken to her. I hoped she would be more amenable and receptive than she had been when she was younger. I didn't want to have to use force on a woman in her 70s.

It was a long journey from Isla de Gran Esperanza to Charleston. First, we had to travel by helicopter to the small airfield near El Bluff, and then transfer to my Cirrus Vision Jet for the long trip to South Carolina. It was 3,400 miles, and we had to stop to refuel twice. I had hoped to get some more sleep on the way, but my mind was filled with dark thoughts, generated by the contents of that brown envelope.

Nedjes and I sat in silence, as usual, but he was no fool. He was sensitive to my moods and was clearly aware that my thoughts were troubled. On occasion I caught him offering the opportunity to discuss my concerns via a quizzically raised eyebrow, but I was in no mood to talk. I didn't even want to think, but it was impossible not to.

It sickened and disgusted me that although the microscopic machines in my body had been programmed to force me to observe Ra restoring the Duat every night for so many long centuries, there really was no afterlife. At least not the one indoctrinated into us from birth. I had lived through the various eras of a whole pantheon of gods, and I could now see a pattern emerging. A dark pattern of lies and manipulation. Greek, Roman, Aztec, Mayan; the list was endless. A list of dissimulation and deceit, of abuse and violation. The entire human race had been the victim of the worst fraud. It made me feel sick, physically and mentally.

I thought about Sobek, who had supported me and made possible so much of what I had done. Yet he was as much a part of this dark conspiracy as any of them. More human than human, but so much less, at the same time. He had coldly, dispassionately, watched two of his brothers die at my hands. He had talked about honour, as had Petbe, but their concept of honour was as warped as everything else about them. They disgusted me. I wanted to hurt them, to repay them for all of the suffering they had inflicted on humanity, for all the arrogant manipulation of innocent and trusting peoples, people trying to make sense of a chaotic world, eager to latch onto anything that made them feel there was a purpose and a point to all their suffering.

My people had more than two thousand gods; it would be no easy task.

As we continued on our long journey my mind remained restless, and the varied comforts of sleep eluded me. I tried to distract myself in several ways, but everything failed. So much had happened in recent times, and so much was still to happen. And it all sat on my shoulders, as ever. I suddenly wished my father was here. My father, who had left this world nearly four thousand years ago, but whose memory still burned brightly, whose righteous wisdom still guided my footsteps, and who I had dreamed about only that morning. He had been strong and highly insightful. Not a man who suffered fools gladly, as you might expect from the most powerful man in the world, but not without kindness or compassion. I could have done with his steady hand steering my ship at that moment, but I was stuck with mine, as I had been since Anubis had cursed me. If anybody on this planet was truly an island, it was me.

I tried not to think of Senusret. But how could I not? To have searched and fought for so very long to restore him to life, and to then have him snatched away again almost instantly, was almost too much to bear. Except that I had to bear it, and I had to carry on. What else could I do? I had faced the most terrible and daunting challenges and obstacles in my 3,826 years of searching for his bones. I had even resurrected him, despite this, apparently, being impossible. Now I just needed to go a step further. That seemed to be the story of my life; just one step further. Always just one more step. I sighed heavily, and I noticed Nedjes glance surreptitiously at me, trying to pretend he was just looking casually away from his book.

I closed my eyes and did my best to appear to be resting. I suppose my body was, but my brain certainly wasn't. And that was how it was for the rest of the journey. My thoughts moving in endless circles, to no great purpose, rolling and roaming through the uncertain seas that faced me. It was a long flight.

Eventually, after what seemed like a mini-eternity, we arrived at Charleston International Airport, although we landed and parked a long way from the international terminal, amongst the smaller, short-range planes, in a part of the airport that I rented for my private use. Judging from the stares as we disembarked and got into the waiting Estoque, ground staff and technicians in South Carolina were not used to either great beauty or great wealth.

It was fourteen miles from the airport to our destination on James Island, and we arrived outside the large and very white house in a little over twenty minutes. As the driver parked the car, I studied the building, wondering what I could learn from it. Not very much, it seemed. It was typical of all the houses in the street, detached, with three storeys and designed to take in as much natural daylight as possible. The grass and the flower beds at the front were well tended. A reasonably new, and very shiny, blue Chevrolet Suburban sat on the spacious driveway. Very nice, I thought. Whatever else Ceryse might have had to suffer, she seemed relatively comfortable in her older age.

Nedjes opened the rear door and I got out, making my way up the driveway to the house. He made to follow me, but I indicated he should wait in the car, with the driver. He didn't seem happy to let me enter on my own, but he merely nodded understanding and turned around. I was well able to defend and protect myself, as he well knew.

I rang the doorbell and stood back and waited. I was reminded of the last doorbell I rang, that of the Institute of Ancient and Classical History, off Wilshire Boulevard, at the time of my appointment with Marcus Fraser. How long ago that now seemed, yet it was only about a month since that night. And how much had happened since that time. Devastating and cataclysmic events, both for me personally, and also for California and its people. I tried not to think of the ever-increasing number of Californians who had lost their lives; had Horus not intervened so selfishly, they would all still be alive, albeit in a slightly different reality. One million, two million; whatever the final count, it was terrible. But, I wondered, how many people had died since I had been born? I remember reading somewhere a few decades ago that it was estimated that around 117 billion humans had been born on this planet, since the advent of humanity, so it was a big number. And many of them had died painful and tragic deaths well before their allotted time. Despite the increasingly number of unnecessary deaths, essentially at my hands, the only loss I could mourn was that of my husband. I presumed that this was clear evidence, if any were needed, of how much of my basic humanity had been stripped from me through centuries of suffering and loneliness. This world was, truly, a veil of tears.

I was, thankfully, drawn back from these nihilistic contemplations by the sound of the front door being unlocked. It swung inwards, opening to reveal a grey-haired, but still very recognisable figure. Even though I'd been prepared, it still surprised me to see someone who, when I'd last seen her two weeks ago, had been in her early 30's, transformed into what was, essentially, an old woman.

I was about to deliver some vague, empty platitude, when she cut me short.

'What took you so long?' Ceryse demanded, standing back so that I could enter.

'I'm glad time has mellowed you,' I said as I strode past her. She gestured to an open door on our right, which appeared to lead into a sitting room. I entered and took a seat on a large settee in the centre of the room. As she sat down in an armchair opposite, I glanced around, taking everything in, trying to get some picture of the past forty years. The room was large and bright, as I imagined the rest of the house was. Large windows and gleaming white paint. There were framed photographs here and there around the walls, mainly of people who I presumed were Ceryse's children and grandchildren. It was all very cosy. I wondered if it made up for everything she had lost.

'You haven't changed,' she told me, interrupting my thoughts.

'It's only been two weeks,' I replied, frowning slightly. I hadn't changed physically since 1802BC.

'I was thinking of the millions of people you just killed. It doesn't seem to be weighing too heavily on you.'

She was right. It wasn't. I thought about the dark thoughts that had resurfaced while I had waited for her to open her front door. It did occur to me that my apparent lack of compassion was possibly a survival technique. I couldn't have retained my sanity over the long course of my life if I hadn't been able to cut myself off from the suffering of humanity. Even when I was at least partly responsible for it.

'"For they sow the wind, and they shall reap the whirlwind,"' I muttered, reminded of Hosea's enigmatic, but very profound, words. I could see Ceryse looking at me quizzically. I was surprised she didn't recognise the quote.

I was wondering how to break the awkward silence that ensued when a white-haired man walked into the room holding a tray with a cafetière of coffee, a small jug of milk, and a cup and saucer with a spoon. He set it down on the table. Although he studiously avoided any eye contact with me, I, on the other hand, couldn't take my eyes off him. The shock of seeing Ceryse having aged so much was as nothing compared to the sight of this figure. I thought I had moved well beyond ever being shocked or astonished by anything, and I hoped my face didn't reveal too much, but I suspected that Ceryse was probably highly amused by the completely perplexed look that crept across my features.

'Nicaraguan,' was all he said, still avoiding eye contact.

'I'm sorry?' was all I could muster in response, utterly bemused. I intensely disliked any situation where control was wrested from me. It happened so very rarely, but this was one of them.

'Coffee. You like Nicaraguan coffee,' he clarified, before turning and leaving the room.

I looked at Ceryse, trying to compose myself.

'That was Edward?' I finally asked.

'My loving husband of forty-one years,' she smiled at me, clearly enjoying the moment.

'And these are yours' and Edward's children and grandchildren?' I asked, indicating the photos on the walls.

'They are,' she said. I couldn't help but feel a sharp pang of jealousy and resentment. This woman, a constant source of annoyance and irritation to me in recent times, had lost everything, but had somehow made a better life for herself than she would ever have had if she had stayed in the here and now. And she had a family. Senusret and I had planned for that, dreamed of the joys of children, but we had been deprived of that possibility, as we had been deprived of our life together. I had hoped that maybe, when he had been restored, that this might still be possible. But with every passing day, any possibility of what might be considered a normal life slipped further away. Family and children. Simple things, but something I couldn't buy and that the machines inside my body would not tolerate. And Ceryse had it all.

'What happened?' I asked, as I poured out my coffee. I now wanted to get the answers I needed and leave as quickly as possible. Every second spent in this house, this spacious, beautifully light family home, was like a knife blow to my heart, a constant reminder of what had been stolen from me.

For the first time, Ceryse lost her look of condescension and contempt. A look of guilt and almost shame came into her eyes. I now knew that I had been wrong to think that Senusret had not emerged with her. The look on her face told me all I needed to know. My heart began to ache and I fought hard to suppress the powerful emotions that threatened to engulf me. I realised that, despite my outward negativity, I had hoped that there might have been a different story to tell. But it was clearly not to be.

'It wasn't good,' she quietly responded, lowering her eyes. I didn't think I'd ever heard her speak so softly. I strained to take in every nuance. 'We wound up in 1982. On the 15th September. In Beirut.' She glanced at me, before turning her eyes away again. Clearly there was some significance to that. I thought hard, forced myself to focus on remembering. How ironic that they had emerged from the Well Of Time in Beirut, my favourite city of the modern world. A beautiful pearl destroyed by civil war and the politics of hatred. 1982. The civil war was in full swing at that time, the Israelis having decided to launch an offensive against the Palestinians sheltering in Lebanon. As I thought about it, the significance of that date hit me. The 15th September was an irrelevance, but the 16th was not. Quite the opposite. I began to feel physically sick as I thought about it.

'You were in Shatila?' I asked her, trying to keep my voice steady. Unsuccessfully, I think, judging by the way she turned her gaze back to meet mine.

'Shortly after we arrived, we were rounded up by the Christian Militia and taken to the camp. Because I was black and American, they were pretty much uninterested in me, but they decided Senusret was a Palestinian. I tried to tell them, but they ignored me. They threatened me, in fact. All I could do was go with him to the camp.' She paused for a moment, before adding, 'I'm sure you can guess the rest.'

I could, indeed, guess the rest. I put my head in my hands to hide my tears. I didn't want her to see my pain, my heartache. I had never wanted an audience for my pain, and certainly not this woman. All I could think was that I would get Nedjes to search through the photo archives, to see if there was any hard evidence. I had resurrected my husband after nearly four thousand years apart, and within two days he had been killed again. I wondered how much pain my heart could actually take; it felt like it was about to break in half. No-one, alive or dead, could even begin to comprehend how much I had suffered.

As I sat there, with my face hidden in my hands, I felt a gentle hand on my shoulder. I glanced up, through the tears, and realised that Ceryse had crossed to sit next to me and had put her arm around me, trying to provide some comfort. At least, I thought, I can go back and save him. It was within my power to right this wrong that Horus had set in motion.

'You were there,' Ceryse told me, her voice still soft and strangely gentle.

'You saw me?' I asked, momentarily confused by the complex paradoxes of time travel.

'Of course. You came back to save Senusret. I knew you would.'

'But you suggested that he died?'

'He did, you weren't able to save him.' There was a tone in her voice that I couldn't fathom. I looked at her, and she instantly averted her eyes.

'What else happened?' I demanded, the tears now mostly stopped.

'I saw you die,' she replied, still unable to look at me.

'I've died many times, Ceryse. It's part of my curse. But I always survive.'

'Not this time.'

'But I always return,' I insisted, frowning in irritation. Was she being disingenuous? I didn't think so, because her concern for me seemed genuine. Which was interesting, given everything that had passed between us, even though, for her, that was all around forty years ago.

Ceryse sighed, a sad, doleful sound to my ears, and then turned to face me. I was surprised to see tears in her eyes, too.

'I don't really remember much about that day. I know it was the 16th September, but everything else is a blur. I can remember the desperation of your grief after Senusret was killed. I remember you bending down, holding him, watching the life drain out of him. I remember thinking that I'd never seen such desolation and despair. It was so overwhelming that it almost felt like it was my loss. And then I remember this figure standing over you.'

'Who was it?' I demanded.

'I have no idea. They seemed somehow less than real, but at the same time more real than anyone I'd ever seen. They stood over you as you held Senusret. I remember you turning your head, looking upwards. And then you were dead. Really dead.'

Chapter Six

I felt very disturbed as we drove the short distance to Wentworth Place. Nedjes would never have asked me how I was, but I could clearly sense the concern he felt as I sat there in a far darker and more dismal silence than he had experienced for a very long time. I really couldn't understand what Ceryse had told me. I could understand the details, but not how I could have been killed. Properly killed. Who was the figure who had stood over me? She claimed not to know. And who had killed Senusret? She said she couldn't tell me that either. I knew she was lying, but there was little point in challenging her. If she didn't want to tell me, there was nothing I could do to change her mind, especially given her antipathy to me. I had told her that know that I knew, I would be able to go back and do things differently. But she had insisted that it wouldn't make any difference. I didn't see how she could possibly know that, but I could sense some truth in her words. As she had spoken I had begun to feel that I was moving inexorably towards a desperate and desolate manifest destiny.

In truth, I didn't know what to think. Shatila. Why did it have to be there? Out of all the history available, why did it have to be then and there? I didn't want to think about the horrors of what had happened at Shatila; it was even worse to consider that I would now have to experience them first hand.

We had parted soon after Ceryse had rocked me with those revelations. I had not seen her husband again. I didn't doubt that he would have wanted to see me, although I also imagined that she had probably encouraged him to bring me the coffee. I could see that sort of cruelty working wonders for her fragile ego. She had, however, made two strong requests before I left. The first was that if I was able to successfully rescue Senusret and return to the present, that I should leave her there and make no effort to retrieve her. She had seemed content with her life, and, understandably, didn't want to lose all the good things that had happened, despite the horrors of what she had witnessed over those two days in Beirut.

The second request was that I bring Richard to see her. She was very insistent on that. I failed to see the point of it, given that she had lived a full life and was no longer a slave to the disaster that had been their non-relationship in the twenty-first century. But, she had insisted, and given that she had tried to save my husband, and had appeared to be genuinely concerned for me, I couldn't bring myself to deny her. It was interesting to find so much compassion still lurking somewhere deep inside me, although it occurred to me that maybe my acquiescence had more to do with callous indifference than empathy.

As we had parted, avoiding any form of contact or even la bise, Ceryse dropped her final bombshell. Even though it had been only two weeks since the devastating events in Los Angeles, I was not the first person to visit her. I wasn't even the second. Despite our urgency and unstinting efforts, I was a lowly third. Surprisingly, the first had been some goon called Vandyke Moore from Homeland Security. Apparently, he had been highly bemused to find himself confronted with a woman in her 70s, and hadn't darkened her doorstep for very long. In their bid to find someone to blame for the disaster at La Misión they were clearly scraping the bottom of every barrel they could find.

Disturbingly, the second visitor had been that third-rate hack, Kalandra Straub. Ceryse told me that the meeting was a little surreal; Kalandra had nothing much to say and didn't really ask any probing or significant questions, but had mostly just stared at her and Edward in a manner that made them both feel a little uncomfortable. Although I had never considered Ceryse to be especially perceptive, she had echoed my feelings about Kalandra being a little 'off'. Some things are impossible to quantify, undoubtedly part of that future science that has been called 'intuition' for so long, but they remain deep inside, nagging away. It was disturbing, but also intriguing, because Kalandra had only made vague suggestions, had merely provided tantalising connections without exploring them. I wondered what was really lurking behind her faux journalism. I suspected that she knew far more than she should.

As the Estoque neared the hotel, I picked up my mobile phone and dialled. The phone barely rang before it was answered, the voice at the other end clearly in raptures of ecstasy at hearing my voice.

Chapter Seven

Extract from the daily journal of Richard Verlice, Tuesday 12th March 2024:

When the phone rang, I was just about to go home. I was still struggling to come to terms with the major upheavals that had taken place in my life. This journal has become a litany of clichéd superlatives and tortured emotional outpourings, but that had really been how my life had been for the past month. Before then, I had lived a dull life of monotonous regularity, but since the fateful day when Neferu breezed into my life, things had been a little bit hectic and unbelievable, to say the least. And since that terrible Saturday, when I had the joy of visiting Kemet in the retinue of the returning Queen, closely followed by the explosion that wiped out a third of California, things had been more than uncomfortable.

After we returned to The Tower, there was a brief lull while we all figuratively licked our wounds, and then everyone around me, and especially Neferu, whirled into action. In a matter of hours, she and most of her men were off to some island she owned off the coast of Nicaragua, while I found myself traveling under a false name, and in a very expensive-looking mini-jet, to Quito. Once there, I discovered that I now had a job in the city's most prestigious museum, although I knew very little about South American history, and could barely speak Spanish. I was very comfortably ensconced in the Marriott, but I was struggling with the whole situation. I was, at least, now able to use my real name, although explaining to my parents what I was doing working in Ecuador was no easy task. They were a little confused, although thankful that I hadn't suffered the fate of at least two million Californians. As was I. Nevertheless, I didn't really see the Marriott in Quito as my forever home. Much more than that, I yearned for Neferu, thought about her every single moment of every single day. And, when I wasn't thinking about her, I was feeling guilt and shame over what had happened to Ceryse. I presumed she was now dead, wherever and whenever she had emerged, although I was also very well aware that Neferu had a plan, as she usually did. And that plan had to involve yet more time travel.

I felt miserable, lonely and singularly unimportant, although Neferu had clearly gone to some trouble to get me to safety and had secured me a good job and was paying for a luxurious penthouse suite. Additionally, she had selflessly saved my life in the Suchos Building's car park. So, I clearly wasn't entirely unimportant, but definitely not as important as I wanted to be. To her, anyway.

So, when the phone rang, my heart had leapt. I hadn't heard anything from her in over two weeks, had watched the news from California unfold from a great distance, and had generally felt abandoned. I had wanted to phone her every single day, had even reached the point where my index finger was poised to press dial. But I had held back. If there was one thing worse than being ignored, it was being treated with complete disdain. I felt certain that if I phoned her I'd be fortunate to be confronted with anything as mild as disdain. So, I had waited. Impatiently. But now my impatience had paid off. Every time my phone had rung since my arrival in Quito, I'd grabbed and checked the incoming call. Prior to this moment it had always been a disappointment, but not now. I instantly answered, not caring how keen I seemed.

'Hi Neferu,' I said, trying hard not to sound over-excited and working, in vain, to keep my rapidly beating heart under control.

'Richard,' the yearned for voice at the other end responded, 'I hope this is a good time to talk?'

'It is,' I assured her. In truth, it would have been a good time even if I'd been lying mangled in the middle of a car wreck.

'Have you missed me?' she asked. I could sense the slight smile playing across her lips as she spoke. There it was. That cruel streak that seemed to give her so much pleasure. Maybe that was one of the ways she had learned to cope with immortality. Whatever the reason, I didn't like it; it made me feel like I was being toyed with, much like the way a cat bats a mouse around before finally finishing it off.

'No,' was all I said. I couldn't hear it, but I could sense her inner laughter. She knew better than I did, probably, that I was in her thrall, that I needed her in my life almost as much I needed my heart to pump blood around my wretched body. She had given me a lot, although she had also managed to take a lot away from me. And whatever she gave me, it would never, ever, be enough. My heart and my soul continued to yearn for every atom in her gorgeous and sensual body. I sighed inwardly. I seriously wondered how I would survive the rest of my life. Especially if it was going to be spent in Ecuador.

'How's Quito?' she asked, thankfully choosing not to bat me around anymore.

'It's not exactly LA,' I told her, instantly regretting my words.

'Neither is LA anymore,' she said. I felt a chill blow through me at those words. Such callousness and indifference, given what she had caused to happen. Yes, Horus had been the one who had caused the meltdown, but if she hadn't been so hell-bent on a more than full revenge, then at least two million people would still be alive, and a third of California would not now be below sea level.

I wondered how I would deal with being responsible for so many deaths. And death must be a difficult area for Neferu. She was the only person on the planet who was exempt from it. Ceryse would probably have rolled her eyes and told me that I always made excuses in Neferu's defence. She was right. But I loved her. What else could I do?

Ceryse. I felt a great wave of guilt wash across me. As ever, my old and loyal friend had been cast aside, my thoughts focused solely on the woman whose hooks were jammed so deeply into me.

'Have you called just to make me feel worse?' I asked her, trying not to sound too much like a lovesick teenager attempting to deal with rejection.

'I thought that there were rituals to go through when starting a conversation?' she replied, 'Empty platitudes to be exchanged. I was simply trying to be socially acceptable.' I said nothing. I don't know if she thought this was funny, or whether this was just her immortal royal arrogance.

The silence dragged on for a few moments, before she broke it. She was suddenly very matter of fact, as if she was now bored with the sport of mocking me.

'I'm sending a car for you. It'll take you to the airport. There's a plane waiting to bring you here.'

'Where's here?' I asked her, trying not to sound too pleased at the thought of being reunited with her. I was also a little surprised at this sudden turnaround. However, she was a woman who kept every card she had so close to her chest that you didn't even know she had them, let alone what they were.

'Charleston. South Carolina,' she replied, 'And stop at the hotel on your way to collect your things. You won't be returning.'

And that was that. With those fateful words, she ended the call. Not even a goodbye. As I got up and collected my laptop and papers, I realised that something must have happened. I just hoped she wasn't building another particle accelerator.

Chapter Eight

Extract from the daily journal of Richard Verlice, Thursday 13th March 2024:

A car had, indeed, been waiting for me. Not a Lamborghini, but a pretty nice Maserati. And, as promised by Neferu, it took me back to the Marriott so that I could collect my belongings, before then depositing me next to a private jet at the Marisal Sucre Airport. I'm not a plane geek, but according to the plaque secured to the bulkhead above the seating, it was a Cirrus Vision Jet. Whatever that was. I was accompanied on the journey by two people; a tall and powerful-looking male, who I presumed was one of Neferu's Ahati, and a young female, presumably of Arabic descent, who performed the role of hostess, seeing to most of my needs. She couldn't meet them all, however, because she wasn't Neferu.

I knew better than to ask either of them if they knew what had happened. In my all-too-brief experience, Neferu's subjects, for that is what they really were, rather than employees, were all steadfastly tight-lipped. The only words spoken throughout the entire ten hours of the flight were between Djedetkha, as the young woman had introduced herself, and me, specifically questions and answers about my comfort and refreshment needs.

Thankfully, the journey was almost directly north, so we didn't cross any time zones. We were travelling at night and, since I suspected I might be busy the next day, I spent most of the flight sleeping as best I could, which mostly meant dozing fitfully. I've never been able to sleep on planes, and it didn't make any difference that I was the only passenger. Even though I was travelling towards Neferu, I felt miserable, certain that this wasn't a booty call. I glanced surreptitiously at Djedetkha, casually wondering how far her orders to meet my needs extended. She was beautiful, her long dark brown hair hanging down around her shoulders, her lips slightly protruding in a sensual pout. I couldn't help but notice her enticing curves, her breasts clearly outlined beneath her body-hugging dress. I shook my head at myself, feeling shame. I was clearly in a bad way.

I distracted myself from the temptations of the flesh by considering the nature of Neferu's subjects.

They all spoke her language, which was interesting, given the fact that the language had gone out of common usage, even in Egypt, around 400AD. What was more interesting was their ethnicity. I was pretty sure they couldn't possibly be Kemetian, even though the majority that I had come into contact with did have Ancient Egyptian names. Neferu's maids Maria and Hortensia were an exception, and were clearly from Central America, but all the others that I'd encountered, including Djedetkha and the Ahati seated near her, appeared to be of Arabic descent, although, in the crazy, inside out world I now lived in, I wouldn't have bet against them being direct descendants of Neferu's people. I considered asking Djedetkha, but I guessed she would have politely avoided a direct answer.

What I was now realising, and which had not been evident to me before the destruction of LA, was that Neferu really was a queen, not just in 1802BC, but now. Today. She had a domain, somewhere in the Caribbean, and she ruled over a people who were spread out throughout the world. If she could only see the world she had created, then maybe she might become less determined to rewrite, or recreate, the past. I suppose the problem, apart from her bitter desire for revenge and redemption, was that she had created her current world in order to facilitate regaining the one she had lost. But, it seemed to me that this one, in many ways, was much better than the one she desired. She was still an absolute ruler, but the modern world had much to offer that her old world didn't. Bread without grit that, over years, would wear your teeth down to nothing, for one thing. Medical science for another. I felt fairly certain that the majority of her subjects in the 21st century lived at least three times as long as her subjects back in the 19th century BC had.

It struck me as more than a little ironic, that, whilst so many modern 'explorers' spent so long searching for any trace of will-o-the-wisps like Atlantis and Lemuria, there was a lost kingdom in plain sight all around them. I wondered how many people were subject to the Queen. It could be millions for all I knew.

The flight seemed to go on forever. I did have access to the internet, but had little appetite for anything much beyond thoughts of Neferu, and why she was recalling me so soon. I was pleased, but I was also fairly certain that it wasn't going to be good news. I did glance occasionally at Djedetkha, and was both surprised, and impressed, to see that at no point did she appear to be relaxing or doing anything other than being ready to serve.

Now and then our eyes met, and she smiled kindly, wordlessly inviting me to find something she could do. But the things I really needed could only come from Neferu. Of course, Djedetkha could provide a watered-down version of those, if she were so inclined, but I would simply be using her, much as Neferu had used me. I had come to feel low, the most base of creatures, but I had no intention of purposely abusing anyone else.

Eventually we arrived at Charleston International Airport, the plane taxiing slowly to a remote part of the airport, where we found ourselves surrounded by small planes that were mostly, I imagined, Cessnas. An orange Urus was waiting for me, although I was a little surprised when Djedetkha and the Ahati, whose name I had never discovered, followed me into the Lamborghini. One absolute positive about being part of Neferu's world was the associated luxury.

Before long, we had arrived at Wentworth Place. I knew nothing about Charleston, either, but I had to believe that this was one of the best hotels in the city. It simply wasn't conceivable that Neferu would stay anywhere that wasn't financially out of reach of almost everyone else.

As I had expected, the hotel was more than luxurious and simply oozed high class opulence and sumptuousness. I felt more than slightly out of place, entering its hallowed portals, and as I followed my two companions across the lobby, I half-expected a concierge to step out of the shadows and guide me back towards the front doors.

And, as I had also expected, Neferu had a large suite of rooms on the top floor, with a roof garden and large balcony. I wouldn't have been surprised to have found a swimming pool somewhere in the middle of it all, but that didn't seem to have been on offer. The rooms themselves were remarkable, but not nearly as remarkable as the immortal queen living in them. I hadn't seen Neferu for two weeks, but, at least to my eyes, she had grown even more beautiful and desirable in that time. That couldn't really be true, I knew, but it was a clear reflection of how little time apart had helped to break her spell over me.

As I entered the room, followed by my two fellow travellers, Neferu emerged from her inner rooms. I felt overwhelmed, as dwarfed and intimidated by her beauty and sensuality as I had been on our first meeting. She was wearing a long and tight-fitting vibrantly orange dress with long sleeves, a small slit from her neck revealing a modest amount of cleavage, and a split at the front stretching from halfway up her thighs down to her feet. And, of course, she was wearing high heels. Gold, with straps round her ankles, her lapis toenails on display. Her raven black hair cascaded around her, flowing in waves as she moved, and she was bedecked in a variety of jewellery, including two very large hooped earrings. Her Middle Eastern skintone complemented the vermilion of her dress perfectly.

'How are you, Richard?' she asked me, 'How was your journey? I hope you were well looked after.'

I glanced at Djedetkha as she said this, and noticed she had her eyes cast down towards the ground.

'It was fine, thank you,' I replied, 'Not that you care,' I added, disappointed that she hadn't even offered me her hand in greeting. She glanced at my two companions, and they took the hint, turning to leave the room.

'What a short memory you have,' she told me, sitting down on one of the settees in the room, the split on her dress parting to reveal two perfectly shaped legs that I had very fond, but now seemingly distant, memories of.

To be fair, she was right. She obviously did care in some way, otherwise I would either be dead or rotting in San Quentin. But, the real problem was that she didn't care in the way that I desperately wanted her to. I had been bathed in the most glorious, life-giving light, and then it had been ripped away from me.

'Sit down,' she told me, and I rapidly did so, taking the settee opposite to her. 'Your constancy is admirable,' she added, 'but quite misplaced.'

I frowned slightly, not quite sure what point she was making. I wondered if my thoughts about Djedetkha had actually been right.

'You're probably wondering why I brought you back so soon,' she asked, breaking into my musings.

'It had crossed my mind, yes,' I responded, trying to read something, anything in her ochre and gold-flecked eyes. But she remained inscrutable, impossible to fathom. She was the most closed book I had ever come across; all you ever saw was what she wanted you to see. She'd had centuries of practice, of course.

'I've located Ceryse,' she told me, as casually as if she was offering me a cup of coffee. All my surliness and gloom disappeared as she uttered these words.

'She's alive?' I asked, incredulous.

'Very much so, and, for some reason, she wants to see you.'

'She does? Where is she?'

'She lives nearby, just a short drive.'
'You've seen her?'
'I have.'

I studied Neferu intently, trying hard to read something into her words. I had a strong feeling that there was something she wasn't telling me, although it was impossible to tell. That was only my feeling; she only ever said what she believed needed to be said. She was hardly the greatest conversationalist, unless she had good reason to be, as when she had first seduced me. But I felt there was something she wasn't saying.

'We should go,' she said, getting to her feet. As I stood up, I realised that Nedjes had suddenly appeared, as if from nowhere, behind her. I guessed he'd been in the next room; the one she'd been in before I arrived. I should have known he'd be close by.

'How is she?' I asked, as all three of us made our way to the main door to the suite.

'She's fine, quite happy, it seems,' Neferu told me. I wondered if this was more evidence of her cruelty, although, of course, it could just as easily have been a statement of truth. 'You should prepare yourself, though,' she warned me, without turning her head as we headed towards the nearest lift, 'She's in her 70s now.'

Chapter Nine

Richard. I didn't quite understand how he had come to be a part of my life. It was interesting, and maybe showed that I wasn't as disconnected from the hoi polloi of this world as I thought I was. In many ways that thought was comforting. I had seen so much death, so much abject suffering, so much pointless banal striving for a better life that never arrived, so much futile empire building, so much lost love, that I had become purposely remote from the everyday lives of men and women. How could I have stayed sane or been able to function to any degree if I had allowed myself to drown in the cauldron of suffering and humdrum futility that was human history? There was clearly a practical reason why every man and woman lived with the same expectations; living without dying was a constant form of death. The constant pain of humanity was unbearable to witness.

I had loyalty and compassion towards my subjects and my employees, but that was not the same as being connected. I valued their service and wanted them all to feel fulfilled and to live contented lives. I never wanted to harm anyone that I didn't have to, but I couldn't allow the daily suffering of this world to impact on me. I was still human, after all.

My feelings for Richard were difficult for me to fathom. I had enjoyed the physical side of our relationship, although he was never anything more than a substitute for Senusret, but now that our position was clear to both of us, I still felt some attachment to him, no matter how vestigial. After the disaster of California, I could have just jettisoned him, allowed him to crawl away to die quietly in the shadows somewhere. But, instead, I had protected him and looked after him, albeit at a distance. And now I had brought him back, at the behest of one of the most annoying people I had ever met. Of course, part of me enjoyed tormenting Richard; he, no doubt, interpreted that as cruelty. Maybe it was; for his part he was always tediously predictable and perhaps it was that which fuelled my need to mock him.

He was, of course, a good man, albeit weak and a little like an eager puppy. But even good men have their price. It was both amusing and annoying that he was so besotted with me. If besotted was the

He went in and the door closed. And that was that. For half an hour, anyway. That was all the time they needed apparently. Just thirty-one minutes after entering, Richard then left, making his way down the driveway more rapidly than he had ascended. Nedjes graciously opened the car door for him, and he clambered in. He didn't say anything, not even thank you, which was unusual for him. These little formalities were normally important for him, but not today. Clearly the experience had been profound. I wondered if he'd met Ceryse's husband. That would have really shocked him, even more so than it had me.

I glanced at him, as Nedjes got back in and the car pulled away from the kerb. He looked very pale, ashen, in fact. I supposed it was an event beyond anything he had ever experienced. In fairness, it had been the first time I'd experienced it, too, but my relationship with time was very different to Richard's and, indeed, everyone else alive on this planet. I was more than tired of seeing people grow old and die while I stayed young. But, for Richard, this was new territory. It wasn't good, and it wasn't something that we, as human beings, were ever meant to experience. Sometimes I felt so set apart from humanity, that I had to remind myself that I was still a human being.

'How was she?' I asked him. I wasn't really interested, but I felt that offering him the opportunity to talk about it was probably a kind thing to do.

'You know. You've seen her,' he said, his eyes staring out of the window next to him, looking inwards rather than outwards.

'Did you meet her husband?' I asked him. That was the only question that interested me, although I felt certain that I already knew the answer.

'She's married?' he said, turning to face me. I saw both sorrow and despair in his eyes. Understandable, I supposed, but also a little pathetic. I wondered if he really thought she would have waited forty years for him.

'She didn't get her children in Walmart, Richard,' I told him.

'That's not funny,' he glared at me.

'It wasn't meant to be. Did you think time would stand still for her?'

'I didn't have time to think about anything. We need to go back and get her.'

'We will.'

'But how? Or have you got a spare particle accelerator hidden away somewhere?'

'You should know me well enough by now, Richard, to know that I never have only one plan.'

This piece of information, which I thought was reasonably reassuring, didn't seem to reassure him at all. I sighed inwardly, and pressed on, as he no doubt wanted me to.

'What did she say?'

'What do you mean?' he said, turning his eyes away from me, looking evasive. I said nothing, merely continuing to stare at him. We sat in silence for a moment, before he turned back to face me, and I saw that sadness and despair back in his eyes.

'She told me that when, not if, we go back to rescue her and Senusret, that I have to leave her behind.'

I leaned back into the soft contours of the seat behind me.

'Did she tell you why?' I asked him.

'No, but I guess you know.'

I said nothing, and now it was my turn to gaze out of the window, barely seeing the sights of Charleston as they flashed past the window. I sensed Richard staring hard at me.

'So, why does she want to stay?' he demanded.

'She's lived a life. She's got children, grandchildren. A husband, too. She's had some happiness. Why would she want to give that up for an uncertain future?' I felt the envy inside me as I spoke these words, which, of course, were only part of the reason she wanted to remain in 1982. I hated the fact that I envied one of the most irritating people I'd met in recent years, but there was no point in lying to myself. I didn't envy her the life she'd led, or even her happiness, which I presumed she'd had, but I was jealous of the fact that she'd had the opportunity. Anubis had stolen that from me. He'd stolen every shred of happiness that had ever been available to me, and I seriously doubted whether I would ever be able to get any of it back.

'She told you that?'

'No. She didn't have to.'

Richard then sat back as well, and turned away from me. We sat in silence for the rest of the short journey back to Wentworth Place. I couldn't see his face, but I felt certain that he was crying.

Chapter Ten

Extract from the daily journal of Richard Verlice, Wednesday 13th March 2024:

I had thought, after visiting Ancient Egypt in 1799BC, in the company of the immortal woman who wanted her crown and her long-dead husband back, that my life couldn't get any more surreal or bizarre. Even my enforced exile in Ecuador had seemed quite normal in comparison to what I had experienced after meeting Neferu. But, finding out that Ceryse was still alive, living in Charleston, and was aged over 70, was surely the icing on my proverbial cake.

When Neferu had told me she was still alive, I'd felt a thrill of hope. Despite still being under the Queen's spell, I felt tremendous guilt over Ceryse, and, to be perfectly truthful, still had strong feelings for her. I'd hoped that maybe Neferu would somehow release me, not that I wanted to be released, and that Ceryse and I might still have the chance to create some sort of life together. But, to find out that she was now an old woman was both shocking and devastating. As a result, when the Urus pulled up outside the house in James Island, I didn't want to see her.

She'd been pulled into this whole mess because of me. Because of Neferu and me. But, I couldn't really blame Neferu. If I hadn't fallen head over heels in love with her, and allowed myself to be so ridiculously used, in every way, none of this would have happened. Or, at least, it would have happened, but not to Ceryse and me. Or maybe not in the same way.

Nedjes had opened the door, and I'd clambered out, expecting Neferu to follow me, but she stayed rooted to her seat in the Lamborghini. I'd turned to her, almost ready to plead, but she'd merely told me, in a very dismissive manner, typical of her, that Ceryse wanted to see me, and not her. Nedjes had then shut the car door rather dramatically, as if to reinforce the point. The tinted window on Neferu's door had then glided upwards and shut, although I felt certain that she would continue to watch me, no doubt amused by it all.

I struggled up the driveway, forcing one foot in front of the other. As I finally reached the front door and stared at the doorbell, I realised that I was scared. Of many things. I didn't want to see an old

Ceryse. I wanted the young, feisty one that I knew. I wanted to save her and make everything right, although I really had no idea how that might work.

I glanced back down at the Urus, but could see nothing behind the tinted windows. So, I simply turned back to the door and pressed the bell. As it chimed inside the house, I considered running back to the car and hiding inside. I hesitated too long, however, and I could hear the sound of footsteps approaching, an ever-growing figure outlined through the glass panel on the door by the sun shining through from the other side of the house.

The door opened and I felt my body go slack, and every bit of air drop out of my lungs. There, standing in front of me, was an old version of Ceryse. Grey-haired, more rotund, a little stooped, perhaps, but her face was remarkably unlined. In some ways she looked no different, but her eyes told a different story. There were things in there that I'd never seen before, experiences that had changed her that I could only guess at.

'You'd better come in,' she told me, turning and going back inside, leaving me to close the door. Her voice was a little deeper, but was still substantially as I remembered it. I felt disappointed that she hadn't called me 'Rich', or even 'Dick'. Or anything, in fact. I'd thought about her so much in the past two weeks, but now that I was here I didn't want to be. It was one thing to be abused by my Ceryse, but to be facing the scorn and derision of an older version was almost too much to bear.

I followed her and found myself in a reasonably large, and very comfortable, living room. It was quite tasteful, which was interesting. Somewhere in the past forty years, her tastes had improved, unless, of course, someone had designed and bought all this for her.

She gestured to me to sit down on the couch opposite her, and I slowly lowered myself onto it, taking in the whole room as I did so. I felt a stab of pain in my battered heart when I noticed the photos of her with what I presumed must be her children and grandchildren.

'I haven't offered you tea or coffee, Rich, because I'm sure you don't want to stay,' she told me, staring sadly at me.

'Of course I do,' I lied. Badly, as usual.

'I wanted to see you young once more before I die,' she said, her eyes remaining fixed on me. I felt more than a little awkward under her intense gaze.

'Neferu and I are going to go and bring you both back,' I told her.

She snorted slightly at my words. I felt a little warmth creep back into my heart. So, the old Ceryse was still in there.

'Rich the action hero.'

'Neferu has a plan,' I told her, ignoring how clichéd that sounded.

'I know she does,' she said, and I saw a sadness in her eyes as she said this that I couldn't understand.

'We'll save you. And Senusret,' I assured her, although it was only as I said these words that the enormity of the task began to hit me. We were going to travel back to 1982, to one of the worst war zones of the late twentieth century, and find and save two people in a city buried in chaos and despair. The particle accelerator and the Suchos Building were nothing more than dust. How on earth were we going to get back there, let alone find two people in the middle of a civil war?

'They were hard times,' she said, mostly to herself, I thought. Her eyes had taken on a faraway look. 'I sometimes wonder how we made it.'

'Neferu told me Senusret was killed.'

'He was,' she replied, and her eyes now moved down to the floor. An air of terrible sadness crept over her, and I wondered if she was crying. 'There was nothing I could do to save him. Or her.'

'Do you mean Neferu?' I asked, feeling confused. We both knew Neferu couldn't die, so who did she mean?

'I need you to do something for me, Rich,' she said, still not looking up.

'Anything,' I told her, and I meant it.

'I want you to promise me that when you return to 1982, you won't try to bring me back.'

'I can't promise that!' I exclaimed. She glanced at me sharply, and I could see that her eyes were, as I'd suspected, red and slightly moist.

'You owe me,' she said. 'If it wasn't for you getting the hots for your ancient girlfriend out there in the Lambo, none of this would have happened, and we'd still be sitting in the museum, avoiding asking each other out.'

'But, Ceryse, how can I leave you in the past? In a war zone?' I demanded, feeling devastated that she had once again rejected me.

'Look at me,' she said. 'Do I look like I died?'

'Well, no, of course not.'

'Then leave me. I need you to promise.'

'But, Ceryse...' I began.

'No buts. Just promise me. You owe me that, at least.'

'I don't want to,' I told her, sighing heavily as I accepted the inevitable, 'but I will. For you.'

'Thank you.'

'But I miss you, Ceryse,' I blurted out, almost pleading with her in those few words. I'm sure she thought it was all a little pathetic. Which it was.

'I know you do,' she told me, but said nothing more. We sat in what felt, to me at least, like an awkward silence for several minutes, before she finally spoke again. 'Your girlfriend's waiting for you, Rich,' she said.

'She's not my girlfriend!' I responded angrily, instantly regretting my outburst.

'No, but you'd like her to be. If she was, you probably wouldn't even be here,' she said, getting to her feet, a clear indication that my audience was at an end.

'That's not true,' I protested, although, in my heart, I knew that it probably was. I was certain that I loved Ceryse, but that love was as insubstantial as a ghost when compared to the desire and need I had for Neferu. I was completely under her spell. She could have asked me to do anything, and I almost certainly would have done it. I accepted the inevitable and stood up, making my way, ahead of Ceryse, to the front door.

'Thank you for coming, Rich,' she said, leaning over and giving me a small kiss on the cheek. 'It was nice to see you again.' And that was that. She shut the door and I was left standing all alone in the South Carolina sunshine, my heart in small pieces all around me. I made my way down the driveway, back to the Urus.

I felt miserable, filled with abject despair. I knew that the meeting wasn't going to go well, but I could never have fully prepared myself for how I felt afterwards. I really felt like the lowest of the low, and, the sad thing was that I grudgingly accepted it. The woman who had turned my life upside down, who had dragged me into a war with the Ancient Egyptian gods, owned my soul. Unless she set me free, and I really couldn't see how that could happen, I would remain a prisoner for the rest of time. Well, the duration of my life, anyway.

Nedjes opened the door for me and I climbed in. I felt so miserable that I couldn't even bring myself to thank him, which was rude. But I didn't care at that moment. I really didn't care. I sat in silence as Nedjes got behind the wheel, and the Urus moved off, presumably heading back to our hotel.

After a few minutes of this silence, Neferu asked me how it had been. I was surprised at that. I didn't get the feeling that she really cared, and I was surprised that she felt obliged to take part in the sort of conversation that she must have long ago come to despise, if, as a Queen, she had ever even acknowledged. But she asked me, and I answered. Reluctantly, but I did answer. I felt awkward talking to her about Ceryse. I knew that Neferu had little affection for someone she regarded as a major irritant, although I was also aware that she had developed some grudging respect for Ceryse having tried to save Senusret from the wrath of Horus. Another highly surreal moment in my recent life.

We talked about it, and Neferu forced me to face some unpleasant truths. Ceryse had obviously got married. That thought hurt, although, of course, who else could I blame other than myself? No-one, obviously. The whole thing hurt so much, and the realisation that Neferu probably understood Ceryse's motivations better than I did was the cherry on top of the icing on my cake. I turned away from her, stared out of the window and did my best to hide the tears that I could no longer hold back.

Chapter Eleven

Extract from the unpublished memoirs of Ceryse Tabrizi:

It was a shock to see Rich again. It had only been two weeks for him, but I'd lived through forty good, bad and sometimes quite ugly years. I'd never forgotten what had happened. How could I? I was confronted with daily reminders. But I liked to kid myself that I'd forgiven. But every time I thought of Neferu, the words 'fucking bitch' came to mind, so I suppose I'd never really forgiven. I tried to think of her differently, focusing on Senusret and the centuries she'd spent faithfully tracking his bones. Well, maybe not faithfully, not in the marital sense, anyway. She'd suffered and endured, but she'd also made a lot of other people suffer. I didn't know that for a fact, but, if you knew Neferu, you'd believe it. And, clearly, she'd also got a lot of pleasure out of some of it. Rich was living evidence of that.

When I felt happier, I found myself removing some of the blame from Rich. After all, we'd circled around each other for years with neither of us making any real sort of move. At times, I even blamed myself for that. But, I often wondered, would he have been able to resist even if we'd been an item? That bitch had powerful claws, and she'd dug them into him really deeply. He was weak and a man, and she was all-powerful. I mean, fuck, even I'd felt the power and sensuality that she practically oozed out. She was, I supposed, some sort of living goddess.

She was the one I blamed. And it still really pissed me off when I thought about her too much. But, sometimes, when I pictured the last time I'd seen her, cradling her dead husband, and then dead herself, too, I felt pity. Pity that someone would fight so hard for nearly four thousand years, give everything they had for someone else, and then watch them die. And then die herself. That really was some shitshow.

I couldn't blame her for what had been done to her, and for being so irresistible and powerful. Those were the cards life had dealt her, just like the shitty ones I'd got. The only problem was that she'd never needed to twist, and I couldn't. Although, I guess I did, and look where that landed me. Back in a fucking war zone in 1982 with the bitch's husband.

It was bizarre seeing Rich sitting so awkwardly in my lounge, forty years down the line. He hadn't changed, but I obviously had. He clearly didn't want to be there, and seeing me so old had upset him. No doubt he was, once again, wracked with guilt. It hadn't stopped him fucking that bitch, though, had it? It upset me, too, seeing him so young. It reminded me powerfully of just how old I'd become. It was hard to believe that only two weeks earlier, that younger version of me had been running around abusing him.

I'd told Edward to stay out of sight, and not to even consider offering Rich any coffee. I'd said the same when Neferu had come, but being the jerk he was, he couldn't help but poke his nose in. But I was glad he did. It had been worth it simply to see the look of complete shock on her face. I doubted that she felt that way very often, and the expression on her face almost made all those long years of waiting worth it. I knew she'd say nothing, would keep it to herself. She kept everything to herself, so she was hardly likely to share that.

But I knew he'd stay away today. He might be a jerk, but he's not that much of a jerk. He wouldn't want to see Rich, any more than Rich would want to see him. Poor Rich would probably have had a coronary anyway, and I didn't want him dying on my time.

I saw him studying the photos of my family, just as Neferu had. I'd caught a brief glimpse of her envy and that had made me feel good. It was cruel on my part, but I was glad that there was something I had that she couldn't take from me, could never achieve herself. It made me think that falling back to 1982 maybe hadn't been such a bad thing after all. If I was honest with myself, it was one of those things in life that was both terrible and good. I've seen things that I never would have seen if I'd been allowed to carry on with my sad fucking life at the museum, but, on the other hand, I've lived a life that I never would have done had I stayed where I was. I reckon the scales are tipped slightly in my favor.

I was sure that when Rich saw those photos of me with all the children and grandchildren he would have been tormented with feelings of remorse and regret, the realisation that those could have been his children and grandchildren. Well, he'd made his choice. He only had himself to blame.

I had wanted to see him again, but once he was there, sitting in my lounge, I wanted him to go.

Having him there brought back nothing but pain and loss, and I didn't even want to be close to him. I was still human, after all, unlike his ex-girlfriend.

I only had one thing to say to him, something he definitely didn't want to hear. I knew he'd be upset, that he would take it as yet another rejection. But it was the truth, it was what I wanted. And it had been what I'd wanted back in September 1982, despite the horror and violence that had surrounded me. Maybe because of it.

I'd told him that when he came back for me, which I knew he would do, that I wanted to stay behind. He couldn't understand it, but I could hardly explain it to him. And I was sure it wouldn't have mattered if I had. He wanted to save me for all the wrong reasons.

I'd told him that he owed me. And he fucking did. More than owed me, in fact. Although, in truth, he owed me nothing. But I needed him to agree, and it seemed the only way to get what I needed without another long and painful discussion. He reluctantly agreed, and that was it. Game over. There was nothing left to say, so I goaded him about Neferu, just to piss him off, so that he would leave. He was upset, naturally, since she'd ditched him when she no longer needed him, although, for some strange reason, she seemed to have kept him dangling. Maybe she liked the sport. She did have a cruel streak, after all.

I watched through the window as he marched down the driveway, probably much quicker than he'd walked up it. I couldn't see her, but I knew she'd be waiting in the back seat of the Lambo sitting by the kerb. I watched as he walked out of my life forever. The last sight I had of him was as he climbed into the back of the Urus. As the car door closed after him, it felt like a door had closed in my life.

'Has he gone?' a voice asked from behind me, as my jerk of a husband approached from the direction of the kitchen. He stared out of the window as the Lamborghini pulled away from the kerb, heading back, I guessed, towards some overpriced and very upmarket hotel.

'He's gone,' I replied, trying to understand how I felt. A warm and old hand rested itself on my shoulder.

'It's for the best,' he said.

I looked up at him, putting my hand on top of his. I said nothing, but he was so right.

Chapter Twelve

I had much to think about as we drove the short distance back to Wentworth Place. I was, in fact, grateful for Richard's misery. He was quiet and withdrawn, so there were no distractions. It had occurred to me to wonder about Curtis' convenient appearance in my world, at just the right time, really. If he'd ended up arriving earlier, the technology required would not have been available, clunky though the particle accelerator was. I had never wanted to believe in random coincidence, and maybe I was right not to accept it in this case. But if it wasn't a coincidence, why had he arrived then, and who had sent him? Or, maybe more to the point, who had arranged for him to fall back through time. There seemed no question that he hadn't been a willing participant. He had hated the early twenty-first century, and had pursued a very self-destructive path following his arrival. It seemed to me that, if there was no coincidence in play, then he was just another pawn in someone else's game.

It probably wasn't too hard to work out whose game it was, but the question remained: why? I could think of only one way to answer that.

I forced myself not to think about the DNA test results sitting in my desk drawer back on Isla de Gran Esperanza. There was nothing positive to be gained right now by stoking that fire again. It was burning very brightly inside me as it was. One thing seemed certain, however; I needed to know more before I moved forward.

Richard remained morose and quiet even after our return to the hotel, so I left him to his own devices and returned to my suite of rooms.

'I'll have my lunch in the roof garden,' I told Nedjes, making my way to the small flight of stairs on the opposite side of the room. It was a hot southern day, and I wanted to feel the wind in my hair, and the sun on my skin. As I made my way through the large open space, past the various ferns, yuccas and other assorted foliage, which I presumed the hotel management believed to be exotic, I decided took my shoes off. My feet didn't ache, the microscopic machines inside me ensured that this would never happen, but sometimes I simply liked to feel connected to the world around me, and having the skin on the soles of my feet in contact with the concrete on the roof of the hotel helped me with that.

With every passing day on this planet I felt more and more divorced from the world and the people around me, so it felt important to be able to feel a connection, even in the most spurious and superficial manner.

So, I unstrapped my shoes and stepped down, carrying them with me to the Louis Vuitton table and chairs situated in the middle of the roof space. The roof garden was an extensive space, considered an expensive luxury by the hotel management. It was expensive, but it wasn't really my idea of luxury. However, it was a pleasant setting, with an ambience far removed from that of the Suchos Building, surrounded as it had been by the sordid squalor of Los Angeles. The sounds in evidence all around me were far more sedate and pleasing to the ear. Which wasn't to say that Charleston was heaven on earth. Far from it, but it certainly wasn't the cesspit that LA had been.

My food, a rather simple four course offering, was served by both Nedjes and Djedetkha. I enjoyed eating, although I could survive without food or drink, thanks to the machines inside me. However, when you have all of eternity ahead of you, any enjoyable pastime is a real blessing. And, for me, eating was one of them, although it was hard to constantly find fresh delights. Richard, of course, had benefited from one of the other enjoyable pastimes.

As they cleared the plates away, and brought coffee, I gestured to Djedetkha, who crossed to my side, bowing slightly as she did so.

'Richard is miserable,' I told her. 'He's just discovered his faux girlfriend is now an old woman. Maybe you could try to ease his pain?'

'Of course, my Queen,' she said, 'although,' she added, 'if I may speak openly?'

I nodded assent, knowing full well what she was going to say.

'I've seen how he looks at you. I saw how he was on the plane when he knew he was returning to you. He isn't interested in anyone else.'

She was, of course, right. I had been beautiful before Anubis had cursed me, but over the long centuries since, I had built up some form of powerful aura, almost a dynamic magnetism, that the majority of people found both intimidating and overpowering. It was, in fact, both a blessing and a curse. Yet another curse. However, it had helped me immeasurably in my quest. My power, if that was how you chose to view it, was all about me, but

I also didn't think it was surprising. It would be more surprising that anyone could live for 3,854 years and not become an all-powerful supreme being of sorts. Even Djedetkha, my faithful servant, could feel the power I emanated. That was very apparent. Sometimes I tried not to abuse it, but it wasn't easy, given how inconsequential the rest of the human race seemed to me, most of the time.

'I know, but try anyway.'

'As you will, your Highness,' she responded, bowing slightly again, and continuing to clear away the dishes. In another couple of minutes, she and Nedjes had gone, leaving me to the relative peace of a Charleston afternoon. I moved from the dining table, and crossed the roof to the comfort of a cushioned recliner. It occurred to me as I sat down that I might be able to get some sleep. After so many centuries without any real rest, it was still exciting and pleasurable to feel tired and to want to sleep. To sleep, perchance to dream, I thought. Shakespeare had no idea how precious those words were when he wrote them. He'd thrown words around as if they were simply confetti. I wondered how he'd react if he knew just how embedded in the English language his throwaway phrases now were. A little like Van Gogh, I supposed, who only ever sold one painting in his own lifetime, but whose works now changed hands for obscene sums of money. I had a few myself, although I'd bought them when they were considerably cheaper than the current market price.

I closed my eyes and felt a wonderful fatigue sweep across me. I wondered what I'd dream about. Even if they were the most miserable dreams imaginable, they were still my dreams, unlike the programmed horror of the Duat and the Mesektet that I'd had to endure every night for millennia. If there really was a god, then I thanked him, or her, or it, for releasing me from that unrelenting torture. For a moment, I thought about the carpenter. That was so very long ago. I hadn't thought about him and those days for a very long time. Maybe centuries. I wondered why he should suddenly spring into my thoughts now, after such a long absence. Modern science seemed to be of the view that if you could live for ever, or, at least, for considerably longer than most people's current lifespans, then you would lose memories, that your brain would struggle to retain old information. However, modern science hadn't accounted for the presence of the microscopic machines that constantly repaired my body. It simply wasn't possible for my brain to deteriorate or suffer any losses of memory. I remembered everything, every small detail. There was nothing that had happened to me since 1802BC that I didn't remember. Of course, some of it could be hard to get at sometimes, but like the memory of the carpenter, all those centuries ago, they were all hidden inside my brain somewhere.

That was the arrogance of modern man. The more they thought they knew, the more they thought they understood their world and the universe around it. Such conceit. And so wrong. The more they thought they knew, the less they actually understood, instead creating spurious and often nebulous theories to explain things that they couldn't even begin to comprehend. Humans were entirely finite creatures, living in an infinite universe. Only an infinite being could truly hope to gain some real understanding of the cosmos. And, of course, so far as I was aware, I was the only infinite being in existence.

As I reclined peacefully, thinking these pointless thoughts, circling the drain of sleep, I became aware of something. Something at the edge of my consciousness. And not so much a something, as a sound. A very familiar sound, that started to increase in volume as I listened. I sat up and looked in the direction of the noise, and there it was, slowly starting to form on the roof of Wentworth

Place. It was ironic that I hadn't seen one of the gods' vortexes for centuries, but in the last few weeks they'd become almost commonplace.

Nedjes had also heard it, and came rushing up the stairs, armed with an HK416, with four of my men, equally armed, close behind him. I gestured to him to stand easy. I couldn't be certain, of course, but I felt fairly confident I knew who was coming through.

As the vortex continued to swirl, translucent, almost opaque shades of blue flowing and blending through it, a figure appeared as if in the distance, slowly increasing in size as it approached, until, finally, it emerged into this world, leaving its own behind. As it did so, the vortex slowed and then faded away.

The last time I'd seen this monstrous creature, he had supported me when I'd regained my throne in 1799BC. On that occasion, he'd been flanked by a small army of crocodile warriors, but today he was on his own.

'My Lord Sobek,' I said, with mock irony, as he approached me, towering over me. I had to admit that, even given what I now knew, he was an impressive sight. He was about seven feet tall, with the body of a man and the head of a crocodile. Altimsah, I thought. He was dressed, as always, in the vestments of a god, a crown standing high on his head, with a spear in his right hand. They looked ridiculous, I thought. He was remarkably muscular, with large crocodile feet and a long and equally muscular reptilian tail dragging along behind him.

'Abase yourself, child,' he commanded, his deep and powerful voice booming out sonorously in the large open space. I had remained seated, and had no intention of either standing up or kneeling at his feet.

'I will not,' I told him, some of the anger I'd felt when I'd read the letter about Anubis' DNA test results surging to the surface.

'You disrespect me. You should perhaps remember who helped you regain your throne.'

'But you did nothing to help me keep it, Lord Sobek.'

'Remember who you're speaking to, child!' he cautioned me, his voice increasing in tone. I thought that, if he got any louder, the people on the street below would probably be able to hear him.

'I know exactly who I'm speaking to. That's why I haven't bothered to get up.'

'You have become arrogant, child,' he boomed, now towering over me, no doubt trying to intimidate me. 'You think that because you have those tiny machines inside you that you are now a god.'

'No, Sobek, I don't think I'm a god. I think I'm a god killer.'

He hissed as I said this, and I wondered if he was going to lash out at me.

'You already have many enemies. Do you wish to make more?'

'You are all my enemies, Sobek. I know that now. You only ever used me for your own personal gain.'

'If you continue to provoke me, you will regret it!'

'I'm not provoking you, I'm just telling you the truth. If you choose to be provoked, then that is your choice. My Lord.' I stared hard at him, offering him nothing but irony and contempt. His eyes remained focused on mine, cold and hard. It was actually very hard to read much into a crocodile's eyes, I realised.

'I will give you one last chance to make obeisance. You are a Queen of Kemet. You were brought up in the old ways. Respect me!'

'Respect is not a right in this world, Sobek. You have to earn it. And you're not worthy of my respect. Now go, and leave me to my rest.'

As I leaned back onto the recliner, his temper finally got the better of him, and he brought the spear down on the concrete surface of the roof with all his might, which was considerable. The object shattered into at least a thousand tiny fragments.

'I hope you have another,' I told him, my eyes now closed. 'I shouldn't imagine something like that is very easy to come by.'

'I have warned you, daughter!' was all he was able to say, blustering all the while.

'Just go please, you're standing in the light.'

I forced myself to keep my eyes shut, but it was easy to hear what was happening. Sobek wasn't exactly light on his feet. He noisily turned around and headed back the way he'd come. As he did so, I could hear the sound of a vortex forming. In a few moments the sound had gone. I opened my eyes slightly, peering around to make sure he'd gone. I waved my hand dismissively at Nedjes and his men, and then returned to my hard-earned rest.

Chapter Thirteen

Extract from the daily journal of Richard Verlice, Wednesday 13th March 2024:

    I felt about as miserable as I'd ever felt. I'd plumbed the depths of darkness when Ceryse had been lost into the Well Of Time. That had been a desperate time. I'd been exiled from the woman I couldn't live without, and had lost the woman I felt so much guilt about. But, it seemed that seeing her again and knowing she had lived a life full of a husband and children, not to mention grandchildren, sent me to an even darker place. I was, in truth, in a personal maelstrom of despair and confusion. My entire being, body and soul, yearned for Neferu, but on some level I wished that none of this had happened and that Ceryse and I were still in our elephant in the room relationship limbo. Seeing her as an old woman had brought home to me very harshly the fact that I was in danger of not living at all, not in the sense of being fulfilled and having any sort of meaningful relationship. I'd believed for a couple of weeks that the most beautiful and desirable woman in the world was in love with me; a complete delusion, it had transpired. For some reason I couldn't fathom, she hadn't completely jettisoned me, which was probably even worse. A bit like being able to see through the toy store window without being able to get inside. I wished she'd pulled the shutters down and thrown the key away. It would have been painful, but not as painful as this living hell of seeing her, knowing she was there, and wondering if anything was going to happen. My underlying belief was that she enjoyed the sport of tormenting me, although why she would, I have no idea. But then again, how could I possibly hope to understand the mind of someone who had lived for nearly four millennia, with no end in sight.

As I sat there, ruminating on my miserable thoughts, there was a knock on the door. My heart leaped slightly. I'd been thinking about her, maybe the power of my thoughts had forced Neferu to come to my room. If only.

I got off the bed, rushed to the mirror and checked myself out, just in case. I looked passable, so I smoothed my hair a little and crossed to the door. I opened it eagerly, but my hopes were instantly dashed. It wasn't Neferu, and, of course, it was never going to have been her. I sighed, angry with myself at having raised my hopes so stupidly, and made my way back to my bed.

As I sat down, I realised that Djedetkha was still standing in the doorway, a look that I took to be bemusement, on her face. I felt an instant pang of guilt, yet another one, for having so obviously shown my disappointment at her presence.

'I'm sorry,' I said to her, 'I didn't mean to be rude. I was expecting someone else. Please come in.'

'Thank you,' she said, shutting the door behind her. She crossed to where I sat and remained standing, a little awkwardly, in front of me. I was struck again by her beauty. She was really remarkably striking, her olive toned Arabic skin glistening in the sunlight that streamed through the window. Her long hair, which swayed almost in slow motion around her head and shoulders as she walked, was a dark brown color, but appeared almost golden in the glare of the sun's rays. She was wearing a knee length tight-fitting black dress, with short sleeves, which further accentuated the sensual body that I'd guiltily observed on the flight north from Quito. Like her queen, she was accessorised with beautiful Ancient Egyptian jewellery, gold, carnelian and lapis lazuli earrings, necklaces and bangles. Additionally, she had lapis nail varnish on her fingernails, and on the toes that emerged gracefully from her black high heeled shoes. Her soulful brown eyes were fixed on me as I sat looking up at her from the luxurious double bed, and her full lips pouted slightly, in a way that I found highly provocative.

It was crazy, I thought. Here I was, alone in my room with such a sensual and beautiful woman, and all I could think about was Neferu. I was crazy. More than crazy. I was pathetic, and I'm sure those were the thoughts going through Djedetkha's mind as she studied me intently.

'Would you like something to drink?' I asked her, feeling I should offer some hospitality, but not really sure what I could manage, given that we were in a hotel room.

'Yes, please. Coffee,' she told me. Her voice was pleasantly rich and dark, with the merest hint of a Middle Eastern accent buried somewhere. 'May I sit down?'

'Of course. I'm sorry, I'm being so rude,' I blustered, getting to my feet, and offering her one of two couches next to the small table on the other side of the room. I went in search of a kettle, coffee and cups.

'Not at all,' she replied, far too kindly. 'I understand it's a difficult time.' As I turned on the kettle and lined up two cups and saucers, I could hear the sound of her heels on the floor as she crossed the room.

The kettle seemed to take forever to boil, and I hovered around the kitchen area feeling more than a little awkward waiting to make our drinks. Eventually, I crossed to where she was sitting and put the two coffees down on the table.

'Would you like milk or sugar?' I asked.

She shook her head, picking up the cup and having a sip of the drink. I was quietly impressed that she was able to drink it when I'd only just poured it out. It was still far too hot for me.

I sat down on the couch next to hers, and tried to look casual. It was no easy task. I felt uptight and uncertain. I had no idea why she was here. I hoped that Neferu had sent her with a dinner date or something, but she could equally be a harbinger of doom.

'So,' I asked, wanting to fill the silence that had lasted far too long. 'How are you? You must have been tired after that long flight.'

'I'm fine, Dr Verlice,' she said, once again smiling kindly as she did so, a gesture that might have appeared sweet, if she weren't so sensual. 'I'm used to it. And I got some rest after we arrived.'

'Richard, please,' I told her. 'Or Rich, I don't mind,' I added, thinking briefly about Ceryse.

'The real question, Richard, is how you are?' she asked me.

'How do you mean?' I responded, wondering, despite my misery, exactly what she was alluding to. In truth, it was hard to maintain a state of despair and misery in the company of someone like Djedetkha.

She didn't respond at once, instead drinking more of her coffee. I noticed that she poked out her little finger while holding the cup. She'd obviously gone to a good finishing school.

'You've been through a lot. Your world has changed out of all recognition. There are things you know now that you never would have thought possible. And I believe you also had an upsetting morning.'

Her kindness and compassion were a little overwhelming. I realised that I'd been bottling up how I felt for some time. Since the destruction of the Suchos Building, I'd pretty much been on my own, away from Neferu and everyone else who I cared about. She was right about what I'd experienced, and the morning's revelation had really been the final straw. I'd cried in the Urus on the way to the hotel, and now, in the face of her gentle sympathy and concern, I found the tears building up again. I had become a little cynical, though, and in the midst of the onset of this embarrassing emotional outpouring, I couldn't help but wonder if she had been sent to offer a shoulder to cry on.

'I'm sorry,' I said, wiping slightly at my eyes, 'I just feel a bit hopeless.'

'It's alright,' she said, offering me an understanding smile, 'there's a lot to take in. Some things take a while to process.'

'Can I ask you something?' I said. Although I felt as low as I could remember feeling since Neferu had thrown me out of the Suchos Building, some four weeks before, I still had many questions about the world I now lived in. Neferu either declined to answer questions, or simply avoided them. I hoped that Djedetkha might be a little more forthcoming.

'Of course. I may not be able to answer, though.'

'Were you born into this world? Or did Neferu recruit you?'

'My family have served my Queen for a very long time. Only she probably knows how long.'

'So, are you actually Ancient Egyptian? Sorry, Kemetian?'

'The blood runs thick in my veins.'

That really was interesting, I thought, my interest overtaking my misery for the moment. So, Djedetkha was part of a race that was generally assumed to have disappeared nearly two thousand years ago.

'And Nedjes and the others? Are they also Kemetian?'

She nodded assent. 'We all have similar bloodlines. Some are not pure, that has been hard to maintain over the centuries. But the other bloodlines are mostly Arabic. We're as pure as we can be.'

So, I'd been right. All those adventurers and romantics seeking out lost civilisations were blind to the most obvious one of all, the one that existed in their own world.

'How many of you are there?' I asked her.

'We are many,' she told me, 'but only our Queen could tell you the exact number.'

Very diplomatic, I thought. Still, she'd shared something very precious with me. It was incredible to think that Neferu's world still existed, through her single-minded determination and obsessive resolve. It was truly remarkable and a testament to her strength and dynamic power. I was reminded of my earlier thought, that she was so preoccupied with what she'd lost, or believed she'd lost, that she failed to see what she actually had. Did she really need an Ancient Egypt when she had a modern Kemet all around her, serving and worshipping her as the immortal Queen she so desperately wanted to be?

'Kemet is here,' I said, 'it's everywhere.'

She said nothing to this, merely finishing her coffee. As silence fell between us for a moment, it occurred to me to consider how she'd described her race. She'd used the word pure more than once. With my twenty-first century sensibilities, that felt a little uncomfortable, although it seemed that she was merely reporting what she knew to be a fact.

'Tell me, Richard,' she said, obviously deciding to change the conversation. 'How do you feel after this morning? That must have been devastating.'

Was this what she'd come to do? Offer me some comfort? And, if so, had she come of her own volition? Or had her Queen sent her? I knew she wouldn't tell me, even if I bothered to ask her.

'Devastating?' I repeated, weighing up the word as I spoke. California had been devastated. Could I really apply the same term to myself? But, seeing Ceryse as an old woman had been devastating to me, personally. As well as terrifying and horrifying. And distressing. It really brought home the reality of what I'd experienced, much more so than anything else I'd seen. Ceryse was real, grounded in my world. And seeing her suddenly in her 70s made everything suddenly very real, in a way that seeing Anubis, Horus, Sobek and Itj Tawy in 1799BC hadn't. That had seemed more surreal and unreal than anything else I'd ever experienced, a bit like a virtual reality console game. 'It was,' I finally agreed, feeling the weight of my emotions beginning to press down on me again.

'I'm sorry,' she said. 'I'm aware of how much you care for Ceryse. But our Queen has a plan to go back and bring her and our Lord Senusret back to us.'

'But she told me she doesn't want to come back,' I told Djedetkha, focusing my eyes on hers, feeling the pain of that rejection threatening to burst my heart.

'She must have her reasons. Did she say why?'

'No, she didn't really tell me anything. But I could see that she'd had a happy life, full of children and a man who must have loved her.' I hung my head as I said these words, the power of my despair now filling my entire being. I'd failed her. Even before Neferu had appeared and destroyed our non-existent relationship, I had been unable to bridge the divide between us, had never managed to even ask her out on a proper date, even though I had desperately wanted to. The fear of rejection had always stood in the way like the most insurmountable wall, and now it was all too late. I felt the tears building up again.

I also felt something else, as Djedetkha got up and moved the short distance to where I was seated and lowered herself next to me. I found myself awash in her sensual perfume as her body moved up close to mine, and she put her arms around me, pulling me in close, cradling my head against her chest. She said nothing, but I could feel the power of her reassuring comforting as she wrapped her arms around me.

I hated myself for it, but I couldn't help but be aroused by her presence, by the closeness of her warm and soft body. She was pressing my head against her breasts, which was powerfully distracting. Although I felt miserable and desperate, I also began to feel other, equally powerful emotions, specifically desire and longing. I had missed Ceryse, although there had never been anything remotely physical between us, and I had missed Neferu, whose body I had drowned in, and whose soft and gentle curves had taken me to a whole different plane of existence. Now, being held so close by Djedetkha that I could feel her heart beating, could hear the soft susurration of her breathing, I was almost overcome by my need to share with another human being.

'Djedetkha,' I said, raising my head from her chest, staring into her soulful brown eyes. She raised a finger to her lips, to indicate I shouldn't say anything, before she slowly and very seductively lowered her face towards mine, her full and inviting lips meeting mine in a soft and lingering embrace. I sat up and pulled her close to me, our lips still as one, and prepared to drown in a different sea.

Chapter Fourteen

It was interesting trying to sleep on the roof of a hotel, in the middle of a busy city. I was very unused to the process of sleeping, having only been reintroduced to it two weeks earlier after a gap of nearly four thousand years. Up to this point, my sleeping had been done indoors and mostly in seclusion. So, reclining and dozing in a roof garden with the constant noise of traffic and people going about their tedious daily lives far below was surprisingly distracting. Nevertheless, I was able to fitfully doze and lose myself in a few quite surreal dreams, although none were as surreal as the life I actually lived. I wondered how many people down below were aware that a god of Kemet had just appeared in the roof garden of Wentworth Place? None, obviously. No-one believed they existed, or, indeed, had ever existed. But I was living evidence that they were not a figment of anyone's imagination, although I also now had evidence that they were not gods. At least, not gods as anyone in either the present or the past understood the term. They were an abomination, of that there was no doubt. An offence against humanity and nature. How had it happened, I wondered? Was it born out of necessity, or simply amorality? It was important to know before I took any further steps into the past.

Sekhemrekhutawy had dared to call me an abomination, the last pathetic insult of a coward and an insect, but the truth was that these creatures were the real abomination. I was merely a human being held in a stasis of perfection, they were the apotheosis of man's inhumanity. And I needed to know why.

I lay still, trying to bring on a deeper sleep, but my brain was too active now. So, I simply rested, my eyes shut. That was quite a nice pastime, too. However, as I reclined, trying to find some calming inner place, I became aware of a sound. The same sound I'd heard earlier. The sound of one of the gods' vortexes forming somewhere on the other side of the roof garden. I sighed. Had Sobek thought of some more interesting insults to hurl at me? I kept my eyes shut, hoping to express my utter contempt for him by completely ignoring him.

The sound stopped, and I could hear feet marching towards me. They didn't sound quite as heavy or graceless as Sobek, but I paid little heed to that. The walking sound continued, and finally stopped somewhere near me.

'If you came back for your spear, Lord Sobek, housekeeping are busy making beds for paying customers. You'll have to pick the pieces up yourself,' I said, trying to sound both ironic and patronising.

However, as I uttered these insulting words, all hell seemed to break loose from the floors below. Gunfire and screaming started in equal measure, and I could hear the sounds of my M'sha shouting orders. In that instant, I realised that this was not Sobek, and opened my eyes. A shudder ran through me as I saw the beast that was Set towering over me. The lord of chaos, disorder and violence in person. He was possibly the ugliest of the gods, his tall body essentially human, but his head that of some nameless canine creature. Historians referred to it as the 'Set-animal', but I could see that he was simply a hybrid-hybrid. How ironic was that? In the instant that I opened my eyes I realised that I could see aspects of many creatures in his face, including aardvark, donkey, hyena and who really knew what else. I'd shuddered because his reputation for violence and aggression was unmatched amongst the gods, and his name had been used in my childhood in much the same way that children of the twenty-first century were threatened with the bogeyman, or similar hideous constructs. Only Set was no construct, as his towering, intimidating and very threatening presence indicated.

'My brother Sobek may be happy to be insulted by you, but you will speak to me with respect, Neferusobek!' he boomed. His voice was loud and menacing, the tone a little like gravel being scraped across glass.

'Respect needs to be earned,' I responded, sitting upright and preparing for both fight and flight.

'We have earned your respect!' he shouted at me. I wondered if he had any mode other than angry.

'By lying to us, manipulating us, killing us?' I asked him.

'We are your gods!' he declared, 'We do not have to justify our actions!'

'If there's one thing you're not, Set, it's a god,' I said, swinging my legs over the side of the recliner, away from him.

He raised his mighty fist, and brought it crashing down on the recliner. I jumped out of the way just in time. The chair shattered into several pieces. I looked around, and saw where I needed to go, on the far side of the roof. I began to run, but as I did so, I felt a monstrous fist pile into my back, and I fell to the ground, tumbling as I went. The pain was immense and agonising. I knew my micromachines would be working overtime to repair all the damage, but that didn't stop it from hurting while they did so. At times like this, I wished Anubis had cursed me properly, in a magical way, so that I didn't have to suffer every time I was hurt. But maybe that was also part of the punishment. Nobody on the entire planet had any concept of what it was like to die and return even once, let alone repeatedly.

Set kicked me hard as I lay sprawled on the floor and I couldn't stop myself crying out in pain as he did so.

'The mighty Queen Neferusobek!' he roared with laughter, not a pleasant sound. 'That is the best place for you, humbled at my feet.'

'The best place for you, my Lord, is hell,' I told him, grabbing the foot he'd once again extended to kick me, and pulling it forward with all my strength. In his arrogance he hadn't expected any resistance, and he fell crashing to the floor. I clambered to my feet, wishing that I'd changed out of my orange dress and into something more practical, and running as fast as I could across the roof of the hotel.

My thoughts had become focused on Set, but as I ran I became aware, once again, of the sound from below. There seemed to be a number of running battles going on, with gunfire apparently coming from several directions. I could still hear voices shouting instructions in Kemetian, as well as the screams of the wounded and those who had unwittingly been caught up in the battle. I could also hear the sounds of sirens in the distance. I briefly wondered what the press would make of this, especially when the news broke that I was staying in the hotel. At some point someone other than Kalandra Straub might start to make some connections.

Set roared with an almost molten fury as he got back to his feet and came sprinting after me. For such a big creature, he was surprisingly nimble and fast. Unlike that lumbering leviathan, Sobek. He was taller than me and faster, and he caught up with me before I could reach my target. He had picked up a chair on the way and swung it into the back of my head as hard as he could. The chair shattered and the pain from the blow erupted like a volcano, and it felt as if every single nerve-ending in my head and neck screamed in agony. I fell to my knees, crashing into a small dinner table as I did so, trying hard to remain conscious and to hold onto my wits. I knew that if I passed out, Set could then do whatever he wanted with me. Which would not be good.

As he towered over me, his jaw clenched in anger, I reached out my right hand for something that I'd seen glinting in the sunlight as my head had exploded in pain.

'You are an insect, Neferusobek!' he roared as he bent down over me. 'You will suffer as no-one has ever suffered!'

'I already have,' I told him, as I grabbed the fork and rammed it as hard as I could into his right eye. Set screamed in agony, flailing around with the silver handle sticking out, the tines embedded in his eye, blood dribbling down his hideous cheek. I leaped up and ran over to the table by the stairs. I reached under it, grabbed and pulled hard at the object I'd had Nedjes put there earlier.

Set had finally pulled the fork out of his eye, and now ran towards me, his pain pushing his anger to some level well past incandescence. He couldn't even speak now, he was simply screaming in anger.

As he approached, I slipped off the safety catch, aimed at him and squeezed the trigger on the HK416. The assault rifle spewed bullets. To his credit, Set kept going for a few seconds, before collapsing in a pool of not so very divine blood. I changed the clip and walked over to him, emptying the new one into him, just to make sure. I kicked him with my bare foot, but there was no response. I knelt down next to his right hand, and pulled the thick black ring off his index finger.

'Thank you, my Lord,' I said, getting back to my feet. The sounds of the battle down below remained as strong, and the sirens were now much louder. I ran over, picked up my shoes, and made my way back down the stairs, the HK416 levelled and ready. The sounds of battle were far louder down there, and I went in search of Nedjes. I had to use the automatic rifle a few times as I searched for him. There seemed to be Guardians everywhere, and I felt my anger rising to almost unbearable levels as I found myself stepping over fallen Ahati.

I found Nedjes with a group of M'sha, finishing off a small squad of Guardians.

'My Queen!' he exclaimed, a look of relief crossing his usually calm face.

'I'm fine,' I told him, 'I've just had an argument with Set. He lost. I need someone to go up to the roof to bring his head back. When these cowards see their god's head severed from its body, they'll lose the will to fight.'

'Yes, my Queen,' he nodded, and spoke briefly to two of his men, who ran off back the way I'd just come. I turned back to Nedjes.

'We need to get out of here before the police arrive. Get everyone and everything together and let's go.'

Chapter Fifteen

Extract from the daily journal of Richard Verlice, Wednesday 13th March 2024:

I woke to find Djedetkha had gone. She'd taken her clothes, too, unsurprisingly. I turned over, feeling some new and not very interesting forms of guilt moving through me. Djedetkha had been kind, gentle, attentive, receptive and completely sensual. I was tempted to think she'd taken advantage of my vulnerable state of being, but that would have been completely disingenuous. If anything, I had taken advantage of her, although not in any negative way. At least, I didn't think so. However, I now felt tremendous guilt at having put my thoughts of Ceryse, and my desire for Neferu, so easily to one side. It seemed that I was, after all, just like all the other men on this planet. As Ceryse had told me. Neferu had known that when she'd seduced me, and Djedetkha had obviously known that when she'd offered herself to me. I hoped she wouldn't think too badly of me, or despise me for my weakness. I felt weak right now. Weaker than at any time in my life. It occurred to me that I was possibly always weak.

I rolled over, seeking out some memory of my time with Djedetkha, and was pleased to find some traces of her musky perfume on one of the pillows. I nestled it, breathing in the faint smell, picturing her naked body still next to me. A sudden thought thrust itself into my mind; Ceryse would now be even angrier with me. I thrust it back down where it had come from. Right now, Ceryse was a presumably happily married woman in her 70s. She couldn't have any complaints about my behavior.

As I lay there, trying to recapture the feeling of Djedetkha's soft and very smooth olive skin pressed hard against mine, I realised I could hear something somewhere nearby, inside the hotel. I knew the sound, and it completely shattered my thoughts about Djedetkha. The last time I'd heard that sound had been in the Suchos Building, some two weeks ago, when Horus had come to piss on Neferu's party. And, unwittingly, he'd done more than that. He'd pissed all over California. However, the crucial thing was not that Horus had been responsible for the negative feedback loop that had led to the implosion of the particle accelerator at La

Misión, but that the sound heralded the arrival of the gods and their Guardians.

I leapt out of bed and started pulling my clothes on. As I did so, all hell seemed to break loose in Wentworth Place, as gunfire, shouting and screaming began to fill the air. I suddenly felt very scared. It reminded me of that fateful night in the museum car park, when Nawal had died and been reborn as Neferu. Of course, she'd always been Neferu, but I hadn't known that. I was stupid and naïve, but I couldn't be blamed for not realising that the woman I'd thought was my girlfriend was actually an immortal Ancient Egyptian queen. Even if Ceryse had actually found evidence that suggested she might have been.

The sounds from the floors above and below me were terrifying. The screams, I presumed, were either of the dying, or of innocent bystanders confronted by all-out war in a luxurious and very expensive hotel. I wondered if one of the gods had come with the Guardians, and, if so, I wondered which one it might have been. There were plenty to choose from, but I knew for certain it wouldn't be Anubis or Horus.

As I pulled on my shoes, the door crashed inwards. My heart nearly exploded with the shock and the fear, and I made to dive behind the bed, but a familiar voice stopped me.

'Richard! Come on!' Djedetkha shouted at me. She was still wearing her figure-hugging dress and her high heels, but had put a Kevlar vest on. She was also toting an assault rifle. She threw another bullet-proof vest at me. 'Put it on,' she commanded, 'and follow me.'

I did as I was told. I wasn't going to argue with what seemed to make perfect sense, given the situation. As I followed her down the corridor, I was struck, despite my fear, by her poise and her movements. She was clearly trained in many arts, including combat. Neferu really did think of everything.

There were footsteps from behind us, and Djedetkha whirled around, shoving me forcefully out of the way and firing indiscriminately down the corridor. Two men, presumably Guardians, fell dead to the ground. I ran over and picked up one of their guns. Djedetkha arched an eyebrow at me as I did so. She was clearly under no illusions as to my fighting skills.

'If you're going to use it, remember to make sure the safety catch is off,' she said, over her shoulder, as we moved forward again. 'And don't shoot me.'

That was sound advice, although it was probably safer for me to leave the safety catch on.

We reached a bend in the corridor. As Djedetkha turned to face me, the butt of a large weapon crashed around the corner and into her face. She fell to the ground, momentarily stunned, a deep cry of pain forced from her lips. I glanced at her, could see blood everywhere. My first thought was to help her, but as I vacillated over what to do, a burly Guardian stepped into view. He was tall, taller than me, anyway, and dressed in a nondescript black uniform from head to toe, just like the ones at the museum had been.

He looked at me in a very contemptuous way, and I'm sure he was completely unimpressed by the awkward way I was holding my gun. He turned his eyes to Djedetkha, still dazed and only now back to her knees. He raised his gun and pointed it at her head, smiling darkly as he did so.

'Die, bitch!' he spat, as he began to squeeze the trigger. The sound of automatic gunfire filled the corridor, but Djedetkha stayed on her knees. Instead, the Guardian fell to the ground, his body riddled with bullets, his torso gushing blood. I was shocked, and looked from his now dead body to Djedetkha, who slowly got back to her feet.

'Thank you,' she said, wiping away some of the blood from her face. It appeared to be coming mostly from her nose, although I suspected she was going to have some horrible bruising, if we survived.

I said nothing. What could I say? I was in shock. I'd not only fired a gun, something I'd never done before, but I'd killed someone. I had never imagined, even in my darkest dreams, that I would be standing in a hotel corridor holding an automatic rifle, having just shot someone.

Djedetkha put her hand on my arm. 'Come on, Richard. You did well. We can talk about it later, but if we don't get out of here, it will have been for nothing.'

I simply nodded, and followed her up the corridor, heading for the central stairwell. I felt completely numb. The young Ceryse might have been impressed that I'd killed some 'bad ass motherfucker', as she would probably have put it, but I felt very unimpressed. But, if I hadn't shot the man, he would have killed Djedetkha, and then, presumably, me. It wasn't like I'd had a choice.

The sounds from all around us remained as intense and scary as before. However, there was now another sound, in the far distance. I could hear sirens. I was reminded of the police arriving at the museum and the bloodbath that followed that. Mostly the blood of the police, it had seemed.

These Guardians were a constant thorn in Neferu's side. Aside from the shootout at the museum, they had ambushed her near La Misión, killing Meryamun, one of her most trusted Ahati. And, of course, the man I had long considered to be a friend, Professor Marcus Fraser, had also been a Guardian, and had been executed according to traditional Ancient Egyptian laws, after attempting to kill, or at least, incapacitate and capture, Neferu. I had no idea who the Guardians were, other than the fact that they were men, unlike the gods and many of their servants. Sobek's troops, after all, had also been crocodile-men, but the Guardians seemed quite human. There seemed no clue as to whether they were from the past or the present, but I guessed that, if the one I'd just killed was anything to go by, they were at least brought up in the modern world. I couldn't imagine anyone from Kemet referring to Djedetkha as a 'bitch', and certainly not as an insult.

As we reached the stairwell, I headed towards the lift. Djedetkha grabbed my arm, and pulled me towards the stairs.

'Never use a hotel lift in an emergency,' she told me.

We could hear a stampede of feet coming down from above us, and Djedetkha went into a crouch, her gun at the ready. I paused for a moment, before copying her. I could see the sense of providing as small a target as possible. I'm ashamed to say that I took my position to her right, behind her in the context of the line of sight from the stairs. It wasn't very alpha male of me, but then I wasn't an alpha male. And she was clearly the one who could fight and knew what to do in a combat situation. I might have just killed someone, but that was simply blind instinct, and my desire to protect Djedetkha.

The sound approached, and feet came running down the stairs. I could see the tension in Djedetkha as we waited expectantly, and I could obviously feel it in me. It was almost unbearable. At that moment, I couldn't understand why or how anyone could do this sort of thing for a living. Lying naked next to Djedetkha was much more fun than crouching next to her clutching a gun.

I could hear the sound of my relief, withheld air launching itself out of my lungs, as I recognised the sight of Neferu and Nedjes reaching our floor, the fourth. I could see the tension drain from Djedetkha, too, as she recognised her Queen. We got to our feet and rushed over to them, a group of about twenty men and women.

Neferu was still wearing her orange dress, although it looked a little the worse for wear, with blood spattered on it. She herself, of course, looked unharmed, and as wonderful and desirable as ever. She had an assault rifle in one hand, and her shoes in the other. That, I thought was the first amusing thing I'd seen since I'd heard the vortex arrive. In the midst of all this carnage and violence, she was holding on to her personal priorities.

I glanced at Nedjes, and felt instantly repulsed. I hadn't noticed when he'd first appeared, but he was holding a severed head in his left hand. And not just any head. It certainly wasn't human, although I wasn't really sure what it was. It looked like some sort of absurd hybrid creature, a bit of a mix of a lot of animals. And then I realised who, or what, it had belonged to.

'Is that Set?' I asked Neferu.

'The great Lord paid me a visit,' she responded, her voice tinged with bitter irony.

I couldn't help but be impressed, despite the horrible sight of the disembodied head. Set was the god of chaos, violence and disorder, amongst other things. The Ancient Egyptians had many terrible stories about him, although they weren't all bad. However, he had killed Osiris and had tried, unsuccessfully, to rape both Horus and Isis. And yet, the human queen had not only tamed him, she'd killed him.

It occurred to me that these gods were actually very stupid. They had cursed Neferu with immortality, made it impossible for her to die, and yet they kept trying to kill her. I presumed that they could turn off the nanobots inside her, but they would need to capture her first for that to happen. And they didn't seem to be having much luck with that. I couldn't quite understand why they, who were clearly mortal, had chosen to make someone immortal as a punishment. However, Anubis had alluded to others, who had been equally cursed, and who had begged for release. It seemed that he and Sekhemrekhutawy had completely underestimated Neferu. She had not only completed their challenge, over the course of nearly four millennia, she had now taken the battle back to them. And all because of her love for one man. Anyone who believed that death was stronger than love should meet Neferu.

'We need to go,' Neferu stated, breaking into my reverie. 'We've set up roadblocks to hold off the police, but they'll be here soon.'

'What about the Guardians?' I asked her, gazing up the stairwell, half expecting a group of black clad thugs to appear, guns blazing. However, I realised that the sound of gunfire and shouting had now stopped, replaced instead by the simple and awful sounds of people screaming and crying.

'They've gone,' Nedjes told me. 'When they saw Set's head, they showed their true colors and fled.'

We made our way down the stairs to the ground floor, and then headed for the rear of the hotel. I was impressed to find a whole army of Lamborghini Urus' and, also, what appeared to be Becker JetVans, waiting for us. Some of Neferu's M'sha were already there, loading equipment and luggage on board.

Neferu climbed into the lead Urus, and Nedjes followed her. I simply stood still, not sure what to do, but Djedetkha grabbed me by the arm, once again, and pulled me into the vehicle. As we took our seats, the driver, the same Ahati who had flown up from Ecuador alongside Djedetkha, put the vehicle into drive and we pulled away from the kerb. As we drove off into the urban jungle of Charleston, I could hear the sound of police sirens angrily swarming towards the front of Wentworth Place.

I felt a hand on my left arm, and turned to face Djedetkha.

'Thank you,' she said. She looked a mess, and there was another look of something midway between frustration and disappointment on her face, a little different to the one when she'd stood in my doorway. That look, I thought, had been a little dramatic, but this one was genuine, and possibly represented a belief of failure.

'There's nothing to thank me for,' I told her, 'You saved me. I was just returning the favor.' She seemed ambivalent about this view, but I simply felt numb. I'd killed a man, albeit one who was about to kill a woman I'd just made love to, and who would have happily then killed me, but I'd killed him nonetheless. When I'd left Ceryse on James Island, I'd felt miserable and wretched, but at least I'd only been a betrayer, not a murderer. I had sunk so low, and in so short a space of time.

Chapter Sixteen

After our departure from Wentworth Place, we went straight to the airport. However, when we arrived, a fleet of black SUVs, with an accompanying force of black-suited and well-armed men, awaited us. Out of the corner of my eye, I saw Nedjes place his hand on his HK416. I reached over and placed my hand on his arm. He glanced at me, and I gently shook my head. I had no objection to killing US government agents, but this wasn't the time or the place. Not yet, anyway.

As our convoy slowed to a halt, just in front of the army of Homeland Security agents, and only a short distance from my Cirrus Vision and the Airbus A220-100 that the rest of my M'sha and their equipment had flown in, I checked my appearance in the mirror on the nearest sun-visor. I didn't look great, but I teased my hair back into some semblance of order. Someone's great-coat was on the floor, so I picked that up and pulled it on, hoping to hide the bloody mess that was my once beautiful dress. I also put my shoes back on, fastening the straps around my ankles as quickly as I could.

Satisfied that I looked better than any of the faceless agents blocking our path, I got out of the Urus, Nedjes close behind me. I'd indicated that the rest should remain inside, especially Djedetkha, with her injured face.

I slowly approached the line of fifteen black-suited men, walking gracefully and slowly, wanting to appear unhurried and disinterested. One of the men, the squad leader I presumed, detached himself from the others, and walked to greet me.

'Ms Nawal El-Karam?' he demanded.

'And you are?' I responded, using the most imperious and contemptuous tone I could manage.

'I'm Agent Vandyke Moore, Ms El-Karam. We're from Homeland Security, and we have a warrant for your arrest, along with all of your, um, staff.' He spoke with an indelicate southern accent, although I had no idea which part of the south he might have hailed from. I had never taken any interest in American accents, and had little interest in the country beyond its resources and its capacity for corruption. I resented everything about him, and especially his clumsy insinuation about my

M'sha. I particularly resented the fact that he had located Ceryse before we had.

'On what grounds?' I demanded, continuing to project contempt, disdain and disinterest in his direction.

'My superiors are concerned about your involvement in the explosion at the La Misión particle accelerator. We were also just alerted to a battle at Wentworth Place that you and your staff appear to have been involved in.'

'Has anyone determined the cause of the explosion yet?' I asked him.

'No, ma'am.'

'And do you have any direct evidence of our involvement in any sort of violent affray?'

'Well, no, ma'am.'

'So, on what grounds do you propose to arrest us?'

'On the grounds of protecting national security interests, ma'am.'

'Please don't call me 'ma'am'. It's very disrespectful. I have a name, agent.' He simply glared at me as I said this. 'And precisely what risk to national security do I and my staff represent?'

'We'll explore that, ma'am, Ms El-Karam, when we have you in custody.'

'May I see your warrant, agent?' I demanded. He seemed taken aback by this. I wondered if he was aware of the fate of the last two Homeland Security agents who had made the mistake of trying to interfere in my plans. They had truly incurred the wrath of the gods.

He turned to one of the minions behind him and shouted unnecessarily loudly, given that the man was only about six feet away. 'Martinez. Give me the warrant!' The other man reached into his pocket and pulled out a brown envelope, which he passed to Moore. He opened it, pulled out a few sheets of white typed paper inside, and handed them to me.

I took them from him, and simply tore them up, without even bothering to glance at them.

'What the fuck are you doing, lady?' he shouted at me. I sensed Nedjes tautening behind me, so I gestured behind my back for him to calm down. The situation was completely under control. 'Ripping up our warrant won't stop you getting arrested.'

'Agent Moore, swearing is the last resort of the intellectually challenged,' I informed him, although I was well aware that he would almost certainly have no clue that I was calling him a moron. 'And, for your information, your warrant is worthless.'

'What do you mean?' he demanded, the first look of doubt crossing his face. I suspected he had never been confronted with such an indifferent response to an arrest warrant before. He believed that he was going to rendition me to Guantanamo Bay, or somewhere equally disgusting, but he was going to be hugely disappointed.

'Agent Moore, with people like you at the helm, I'm not surprised that this country is in the state it is. You people are barely competent to tie your President's shoe laces, let alone protect your citizens from the real criminals.'

'You're beginning to piss me off, lady!' Moore exclaimed, his voice rising in concert with his anger. 'You are under arrest!'

I turned to Nedjes. 'Do you have that envelope that I gave you this morning?'

He nodded, and reached into the inner pocket of his jacket. He pulled out a brown envelope, almost identical to the one that Moore had been handed, and passed it over to me. I opened it, took out the two sheets of paper inside, and handed them to the agent.

'What's this?' he demanded.

'Why don't you try reading it?' I suggested. 'I suppose they taught you to read at school?'

He scowled angrily at me, but began to read the documents in front of him. As he did so, his face darkened even more and I noticed his hands beginning to twitch slightly.

'I don't understand,' was all he could say, as he finished reading. I reached out and took the papers back.

'It's very straightforward,' I told him, smiling patronisingly as I did so. 'My staff and I have been granted diplomatic immunity by your government and you have no power to arrest any of us. Please go away and leave us in peace.'

'But that's not possible,' he blustered, clearly very confused.

'It's not only possible, Agent Moore, it's true. Perhaps you'd care to phone someone to find out? I'm sure the Secretary of the Department of State would be able to set you straight. I'm certain he'd be delighted to be interrupted by you to talk about it. Would you like his number?'

Moore looked at me with a combination of anger and confusion, obviously conflicted, before taking out his phone. 'What's the number?' he demanded. I was impressed that he was willing to take the risk. I told him the number and he dialled it into his phone, and held it to his ear. He walked away slightly, no doubt not wanting his conversation to be overheard, just in case it went the way he feared it might. I followed him, wanting to share in his humiliation.

'Mr Secretary?' he said, as the call was answered at the other end. 'My name is Agent Vandyke Moore of Homeland Security. I'm currently at Charleston International Airport with a warrant to arrest Ms Nawal El-Karam and her staff. She's just shown me a document suggesting that she has diplomatic immunity, which I know can't be right because....'

At that point he stopped talking. I couldn't hear what was being said at the other end, but I could imagine the tirade of abuse coming back towards Moore. Sometimes it was worth paying over the odds. The results were usually worth it.

'Yes, sir. I understand, sir. I'm sorry for having troubled you, sir. Agent Vandyke Moore, sir.' As he said this, the call obviously ended, and he lowered the phone. I hoped that he had some backup skills, because I suspected his days in Homeland Security were now numbered. He glared at me viciously for a few moments, before clearly making a decision. A very stupid one on his part, but maybe he felt that he had nothing to lose. He reached into a holster and pulled out his gun and shot me.

The crack of the bullet being discharged was shockingly loud at such short range, and the projectile tore into my collar bone at around 1,800 miles per hour. I screamed in agony as the bones shattered and blood began to pour from the wound.

Moore simply stood and watched while I bowed my head, willing myself to endure the unbearable pain for the few seconds it would last. I didn't need to see Nedjes to know that he was incensed and wanting to act, and I forced myself to indicate with my right hand that he should hold off for the moment.

After about thirty seconds, the pain began to subside as the microscopic machines inside me began to do their work, and I slowly raised my head and stared at Agent Moore, my gaze so fierce and angry that he had to turn his eyes away.

He couldn't hear it, but the sound of my collar bone being healed was almost deafening to me. I reached up to where the bullet had entered, and waited for the lump of metal to be ejected. I took it, held it up for him, and his men, to see, for a moment, and then lobbed it to him.

He caught it and simply gazed at it, then at me, and my perfect collarbone and I saw a look of fear cross his face. He had been so certain of himself and of his mission that he had decided to cross a line, believing that it was all in the cause of national security. But, he'd now witnessed something that had turned his structured, rigid world view upside down.

I was furious that he'd shot me, and had not appreciated the agonising pain he'd inflicted on me, but I was now amused by the look of horror and fear on both his face, and that of his men.

'I don't understand,' was all he could say.

'There are some things, Agent Moore, that you were never meant to understand,' I told him. I turned my back on him, nodded at Nedjes and made a small gesture to my M'sha waiting in the vehicles.

In a matter of moments, the field was bathed in the sound of gunfire, as the Homeland Security agents were riddled with bullets from HK416s. Still in shock, they'd had no time to prepare themselves for the bloodbath that followed. It was all over in moments.

'Let's go,' I said to Nedjes, making my way to the Cirrus Vision. Nedjes, Richard, who looked like he was in shock, Djedetkha and Shoshenq, who had been driving, followed me. The others, all thirty-one of them, stowed our equipment, our dead, and themselves on the Airbus A220-100. We wasted no time in getting off the ground and into the air, heading out to sea as fast as we could to leave US airspace, just in case anyone else in Homeland Security decided to try to stop us.

After take-off, I got Nedjes to have a look at Djedetkha's face. She wasn't badly hurt. There was more blood than damage, but I was angry with her. She knew better than to let her guard down like that, even if she was protecting a hopelessly inept white man. I valued her many skills, and her natural and easy way with people, but such negligence was not acceptable. On the other hand, I'd been quite impressed by the news that Richard had killed someone. Of course, he'd done it as the ultimate chivalric sacrifice on his part, shooting some brutal Guardian to protect Djedetkha. Richard was definitely old school. It was sweet, quite endearing really, but it also made him very malleable. And he knew it.

'Why did you do that?' Richard asked me, his face a curious mixture of horror and despair.

'In case you hadn't noticed, they shot me,' I told him.

'But you didn't have to kill them all,' he protested.

'How do you think that was going to go down?' I demanded of him, irritated by his naïve and childlike view of the situation. 'They'd ignored our diplomatic immunity and then shot me, and seen the results of that. They weren't just going to pack up and go.'

He nodded at that, could at least see the sense in it. Agent Moore had sentenced his men to death by not accepting the inevitability of the situation. Human nature was remarkably consistent. There was nothing on this planet that could not be bought. Except me.

I turned away from Richard, and thought about everything that had just happened. The gods seemed to be upping the ante. I felt pretty certain that Set would not have turned up in person if they weren't worried. That pleased me. I wanted them to be worried. They had controlled mankind for so long, now it was their turn to be manipulated and abused.

What I didn't know was why they feared me so much. No doubt it was something to do with those DNA tests, but I needed more information. And that was the next step. Finding out more. And the only way to do that was to go to the source.

'As soon as we return, I want updates,' I told Nedjes, who was sitting beside me. 'We need to be ready to move as soon as we can. There's no time to waste.' Time? Well, actually we had plenty of that, but, also, not enough. For the human race, time passed, but I simply straddled it. I understood time as no-one else could or did. And that made it the best weapon I had. It had always been so.

It was a long trip, and we had to stop to refuel twice, before we finally reached the terminus at El Bluff. From there, we transferred by helicopter to the welcome sanctuary of Isla de Gran Esperanza. We were the last to return, the Airbus not having had to stop on the way back.

As the helicopter brought us in to land, soaring over the beautiful white neo-Kemetian buildings and the large open squares, Richard was clearly unprepared for what awaited him, his face reflecting the awe and shock that he obviously felt.

'What is this place?' he asked me.

'This is the heart of my kingdom,' I told him, unable to suppress the pride and satisfaction that I felt at the thought. For so long, I had simply been a woman with a small group of followers. It had taken a long time for me to accumulate any serious wealth and influence. The world, until relatively recently, had never been a kind place to women, and certain states had actually embedded laws that disenfranchised women and prevented them from owning anything beyond makeup and a hair brush. But, when faced with eternity, you needed to be patient, more patient than any other human being could even begin to comprehend. And, after many centuries, my patience finally began to pay dividends.

In 1608 I had been able to buy this island from Spain, via male intermediaries, of course. The transfer had been signed over in perpetuity, and it became my safe haven, a place where I could begin to rebuild my Kemetian Kingdom, surrounded by my loyal subjects. From here I had been able to continue to teach succeeding generations the learned wisdom of the ages, and to ensure that they were all brought up, in every way that mattered, as citizens of Kemet.

The island was big enough to house almost everything that I needed to maintain my kingdom throughout the world. Recent years had seen the addition of such things as research laboratories and small-scale industrial plants. There were certain things I needed, which were now scientifically possible, that I didn't want the rest of the world to see. Part of the purchase agreement with Philip III had been that the island had been granted sovereign status. Philip had not initially been keen on such a radical agreement, but my money and personal charms had eventually changed his mind. His wife had been a very pious woman, and, it went without saying, that a husband, and especially a king, needed certain outlets that a devout and highly virtuous wife denied him. He was not an unattractive man, especially considering the inbreeding that later tainted the Habsburg family in Spain, although it was, of course, demeaning for a queen of the most powerful nation that ever existed on this planet, to have to lower herself in this way. But it hadn't been the first time, and it certainly wasn't the last. In order to survive eternity, you either adapt and thrive, or you suffer and fall into the slough of despond. I've never been ready for that dark pit, even in my darkest hours, of which there have been more than most humans could cram into their pathetically short lifetimes.

Philip duly granted Isla de Gran Esperanza sovereign status, and, as a result, the island existed in its own right, separate to all other nations, and was out of bounds to everyone, including Homeland Security and the CIA.

'It's incredible!' Richard exclaimed, as the helicopter settled down into the central square, surrounded by some of the finest modern examples of Kemetian architecture. As I glanced around, trying to take it in from his perspective, I became aware that there were many monuments to the gods, and especially Sobek. I no longer needed these constant reminders of the duplicitous creatures who had duped mankind for so long. What made it worse was that I, obviously, was the one who'd had them all constructed.

As we descended from the Airbus H225, I turned to Nedjes.

'Please remove every statue of the gods.' He looked at me with some surprise, but said nothing. 'Destroy them. Reuse what can be recycled. Grind the rest to dust.'

'Yes, my Queen,' he responded.

I saw Richard looking at me, having overhead this command. He looked surprised, and a little confused.

'Things have changed,' I told him. 'Even you must have realised that these creatures are not gods.'

'Yes, well, not as I understand the term,' he said. And, of course, he meant from a modern perspective, where gods are truly divine and all-powerful, and don't take physical form or directly intervene in anything.

'They're not gods as anyone understands the term,' I told him, unable to avoid the bitter tone in my voice. I felt so betrayed, so used, and so violated. These creatures had controlled my world for nearly four thousand years, both directly and indirectly. There was no word in any language, even mine, to adequately express the anger I felt towards them. 'I will kill them all, one by one, if necessary.'

'There's a lot of them,' he told me, as if I didn't know that better than him.

'I've got all of eternity,' I reminded him, as if he needed reminding.

'Queen Neferusobek the God Killer,' he said, 'it's got a ring to it.'

'I'm Neferu. Sobek is no longer welcome in my world,' I told him. However, he had amused me. It was a suitably grandiose and arrogant title for the greatest queen of Kemet. I had to admit, although I didn't want to, that there were things about Richard that I liked. Maybe he deserved a reward. After all, I had turned his world upside down and inside out, beyond all recognition.

'We'll have dinner later,' I told him, offering him a gentle smile, which I thought he might value. I turned to Djedetkha, whose face was now beginning to show the bruising that her negligence had invited. 'Can you show Richard to his suite? Make sure he's comfortable and has everything he needs.'

'Yes, my Queen,' she responded, taking Richard by the arm, and leading him away towards the far side of the square, where most of the accommodation was situated. There were no hotels or guest suites available on the island, since there were never any guests or visitors, but we did have residences set aside for returning Kemetians who lived abroad. She would take him to one of those.

I hadn't spared any expense in creating the towns and villages that existed on my island. Apart from the fact that I now had so much money I could do exactly what I wanted to, regardless of the cost, I also wanted my people to live in luxury, to appreciate the value of being Kemetian, and as a reward for the centuries of loyalty they and their families before them had provided me. I could not have achieved what I had without them. As a result, whatever suite of rooms was assigned to Richard, he would discover a luxury and opulence that he would never have seen in his own world. I hoped he would appreciate it.

'I want updates as soon as possible,' I reminded Nedjes, as we walked towards my palace, a vast single-storey building, decorated with frescos, mosaics and Kemetian art and statuary, all of which reflected the munificence of my rule and portrayed both myself and Senusret. He was never far from my thoughts, and it was my only goal in life to have him share this world with me. Well, it had been my only goal, although it now seemed I had another, which I might need to attend to first.

'Yes, my Queen,' Nedjes responded, although I knew he wouldn't have forgotten.

'I'm going to rest, but wake me up when you need to,' I told him, as we entered the vast entrance hall of my royal palace. I wanted to get some sleep, and I hoped that, in amongst all the other dreams, there might be one with Senusret.

Chapter Seventeen

From the Los Angeles Chronicle Online, Thursday 14th March 2024:

'Terror in Charleston. The horror that now haunts us all.

'By Kalandra Straub, Senior Investigative Reporter.

'Two new terror attacks yesterday sent the hearts and minds of all decent American citizens into yet another tailspin. Hot on the heels of the devastating catastrophe that has destroyed so much of California, and which still claims lives on a daily basis, a terrorist attack on a luxury hotel in the heart of leafy South Carolina, followed by the brutal slaughter of a group of Homeland Security agents, has underlined the terror that stalks our streets on a daily basis.

'The reassuringly expensive Wentworth Place hotel, only a stone's throw from the suburban haven of James Island, was yesterday thrown into chaos and anarchy by a horrific terror attack. The sound of automatic weapons gunfire and the screaming of innocent victims was clearly audible throughout the neighboring blocks.

'Nobody is quite sure exactly what happened, but eye witnesses report that shortly after 3pm local time, a group of armed men, clad entirely in nondescript black uniforms, began attacking another group of people in the hotel. The people they were targeting are reported to have been resident in the hotel, and all appeared to be of Middle Eastern origin. The battle, for that is what it was, lasted for little more than ten minutes, and by the time local police finally arrived, all the combatants had miraculously disappeared. However, it wasn't as miraculous as it seemed, since it would appear that the police were hindered in their attempts to reach the hotel, several roads being blocked by impassable vehicles as they approached. This delay clearly gave combatants on both sides the opportunity to slip away virtually undetected.

'Three residents of the hotel were wounded, and are currently in hospital receiving emergency treatment. None are reported to be in a life-threatening condition, although one has sustained potentially life-changing injuries. Of the dead and wounded on either side, there was no sight. There was plenty of blood, but no bodies were left behind. It would seem that both sides were unwilling to leave their battle dead behind, which, obviously makes the job of identification that much harder.

'Even more frustrating is the news that the hotel's CCTV cameras were out of service for the duration of the battle, although it appears they came back online when the police arrived.

'A little later the bodies of fifteen Homeland Security agents were found on a secluded section of Charleston International Airport. Information is sparse, but my informants advise me that they were brutally shot. It remains to be seen whether these two events are linked, but it would be a remarkable coincidence if this wasn't the case.

'You may be wondering what these outrageous assaults on American civil liberties and peace-loving freedoms has to do with either California or the devastation recently experienced, but there is a common denominator in all of this. The group under attack in the hotel would all appear to have been employees of Ms Nawal El-Karam, who was also resident, and who, you will be well aware, was the philanthropic benefactor of the ill-fated La Misión particle accelerator. It would also seem that the shooting of the Homeland Security agents took place near a part of Charleston Airport which Ms El-Karam rents for her private planes.

'Violence seems to follow Ms El-Karam around. You may recall that there was a helicopter battle near La Misión a few days before the explosion. Additionally, you may also remember that I had reported on a supposed gunfight between rival gangs in the car park of the Institute of Ancient and Classical History in Wilshire Boulevard. Both of those opposing groups also vanished into thin air, despite a SWAT team being involved and suffering heavy casualties.

'No-one is suggesting that Ms El-Karam is anything other than an innocent victim in all of this, but there are significant questions to be answered around who was fighting who, why they were fighting, and why Ms El-Karam thinks it is appropriate for her employees to be armed to the hilt with semi-automatic weapons, which, incidentally, are presumed to be the same ones used to gun down the Homeland Security agents. I have contacted her office for comment, but she would appear to be unavailable at this time.'

Chapter Eighteen

I was woken by a steadfast knocking on the door of my bed chamber. I recognised the rhythm, and, of course, it could only have been one person anyway. I forced myself up from the depths of the abyss, feeling the dreary numbness of fatigue dissipate almost instantly, thanks to the machines inside me. They really were very attentive.

I called my maids and had them get me dressed. They quickly tended to my hair and make-up and found appropriate jewellery. It was important that I always looked my best, which, of course, was somewhere close to perfection, and I also always needed to look like a Queen.

As I entered the Meeting Room, which I had come to use for informal audiences, I noticed two things. Firstly, Nedjes, thoughtful as ever, had provided fresh coffee. He really did know me as well as anyone could. Secondly, standing a few feet to his left was Psusennes.

'You may be seated,' I said to them both, indicating the chairs around the central table. 'Help yourselves to coffee,' I added, as Nedjes poured me a cup.

As we all took a seat, I glanced at Psusennes. His father had served me faithfully for a happy lifetime as groundsman and principal maintenance engineer for the royal palace. He was no intellectual giant, but he was good with his hands and, from what I had seen, a kind and gentle man. However, from an early age it had been apparent that his eldest son was very different. Psusennes was constantly exploring equipment and devices, often incapacitating them with his desire to know how they worked. But he didn't just have an enquiring mind, he also designed and built things. It was my job to be aware of the potential within all those around me. I hadn't survived for as long as I had without recognising the latent qualities embedded in those who served me. Over the years, as he had grown from child to young man, I had met with him on occasion, explored his interests and his knowledge. And, when he was old enough, I did what any sensible person in my shoes would have done, I sent him to MIT. In those days, before those morons in Al-Qaeda launched their futile attack on the USA, it was a relatively easy task to send someone of Middle Eastern stock to study nuclear and particle physics. Nowadays, I had to make use of less prestigious institutions in countries that were friendlier to people without white skin.

Psusennes had not disappointed. He had come top of the class in almost everything he had studied, and had graduated with first class honours. After his PhD, many private and governmental institutions from around the world were desperate to head hunt him, but, like the faithful Kemetian he was, he duly returned to the fold. No-one else could ever pay him what I did. And what need did he have for money when he lived in a virtual heaven on earth?

The only real problem for him had been that his knowledge was, unsurprisingly, constrained by the world that he had been brought up in and which had educated him. That was why I'd needed Curtis. But Psusennes had recently been given some tools that had enabled him to move far ahead of his contemporaries, and I was hoping that he was about to bring me the news I desperately wanted to hear.

'Well?' I demanded. I was their Queen; there was no need for pleasantries.

'It's good news, my Queen,' Psusennes told me, his white hair glistening in the sunlight that was streaming through the windows. 'The device is fully operational. And with the third ring, we have enough power to reach wherever you want.'

'You've tested it?' I asked him, not prepared to allow myself to be a guinea pig.

'Yes, thoroughly. And it works.'

'For how many?'

'Ideally five, but possibly six.'

'Is that because of power constraints?'

'Yes. If we had more rings, we could send more people, but five, or maybe six, will give us the perfect balance with power and output.'

I sighed inwardly. I almost felt like hugging him, but I couldn't do that. Not as his Queen. But it was a tremendous weight off my shoulders. Now, at last, our fate was in our own hands. We no longer had to rely on the resources and limited goodwill of others. My M'sha had spent days combing the wreckage of La Misión, searching for Anubis' ring, and they'd found it. That was a significant achievement. Losing that would have set us back, and there was also the danger of government forces finding it, which was completely unacceptable. I'd also sent some men to dig Horus' body out of the Suchos Building and dispose of it properly. It wouldn't have done for anyone to find him, either.

I turned to Nedjes. 'Get the team ready, prepare them. Get whatever we need ready. We'll leave tomorrow morning.'

'Yes, my Queen,' he replied, finishing the last of his coffee.

I poured myself a fresh cup, and sat back. I had felt excited at the thought of being able to move forward at last. But, as I thought about it, I felt some anxiety. It wasn't like me to feel anxiety, but then again, I usually had complete control over most situations. Tomorrow morning, five of us would be stepping into the complete unknown.

'There's one other thing, my Queen,' Psusennes ventured, and there was something in his tone that instantly drew my attention.

'Which is?'

'We ran some tests on the DNA and tissue samples you provided, and we think we understand why the gods are mortal.'

'Go on,' I urged him, wishing he would simply tell me what he had to say. I was so tired of this game that so many people seemed to enjoy playing.

'The nanobots function perfectly in the human body, but they will almost certainly fail, in very dramatic fashion, in theirs.'

'They can't tolerate them?'

'Apparently not. We can't know for certain unless we have a live specimen to test, but it seems fairly conclusive.'

'Do you know why?'

'It would appear to be the DNA itself. They would appear to have successfully merged the incompatible, but the nanobots won't recognise it.'

I thought about that. It certainly made sense of why they had inserted the tiny machines into me, but hadn't done so for themselves. On the face of it, that seemed an act of extreme stupidity, not even worthy of a fake god. But, maybe, when they did that, they had no idea that they couldn't use them. The irony was precious. Truly precious.

'You may go,' I said to them both, sipping some of my coffee.

Nedjes got to his feet, Psusennes following his lead. They crossed to the door, and Nedjes opened it, letting the physicist out. However, instead of leaving with him, he then closed the door and walked back to where I was sitting, deep in thought with my coffee.

It took me a moment to realise he was standing over me.

'Yes, what is it?' I asked him. If he felt there was something he needed to say without Psusennes being present, then I needed to listen.

He took a USB stick out of a pocket and handed it to me.

'Our last team brought a lot of material back with them. Most of it wasn't very interesting, but this is. You need to read it before the morning.'

'I will,' I said, 'thank you.' He nodded, and made his exit. As he left, I finished my coffee and crossed to my desk, turning on my laptop and inserting the memory stick. There had been something in his tone that made me think that I didn't want to read whatever it was he'd given me. I sat down and waited for everything to warm up. I scrolled to the USB stick and opened it. There was one document on it, a PDF simply titled 'document 1'. I double clicked on it and impatiently waited the few seconds it took to open.

It was a book, intriguingly entitled 'The Global Crisis and its Resolution: How Humanity Was Reinvented'. The author was an R.A. Kaddo. I glanced briefly at the publishing details before I started reading, but there was nothing there that was particularly interesting. However, once I got past the foreword, which was a tediously unhelpful piece of self-aggrandisement by another apparently undistinguished geneticist, I found my heart sinking. Every successive word I read confirmed my worst fears.

Chapter Nineteen

Extract from the daily journal of Richard Verlice, Thursday 14th March 2024:

Neferu's island was incredible. It was like something out of a Victorian adventure novel. I was reminded of all those old books I'd love to read as a teenager, stuff like L'Atlantide and She. It really was surreal, landing slap bang in the middle of a modern outpost of Ancient Egypt. And yet, it also seemed so modern. Neferu had clearly gone to great lengths to hold on to the trappings of her ancient culture, while at the same time modernising it all to fit in with the tastes of the times she lived in and had, at least to some extent, come to enjoy. Or, maybe, she had simply evolved with the world around her. Either way, it was something else. The architecture was stunning; fantastic modern revisions of buildings that I'd only ever seen in ruins, or in artistic recreations in books. Even the clothes people wore were obviously Ancient Egyptian, but at the same time undeniably 21st century. The entire place was a masterpiece of reinvention and synthesis.

It was also extremely bizarre to hear Neferu's supposedly long-dead language being spoken by everyone I encountered. I was reminded of Neferu's anger at Ceryse's assertion that her language was dead. The whole experience was so outlandish and unreal that if I'd been told I'd been slipped a shedload of LSD, I probably would have believed it.

Djedetkha was amused by my response to a world that she clearly took for granted. She told me that she'd been born there, but had been sent overseas when she was aged twelve to be educated. She'd studied law at Harvard, before returning to take up a relatively senior position in Neferu's personal retinue. I'd asked where she'd learned her combat skills, but she declined to answer that question. It wouldn't have surprised me, though, if she'd told me she'd interned with FARC or Hezbollah.

She had a horrible looking bruise emerging on her face, although she played down any pain she might have been experiencing. I got the distinct feeling that she felt she had dishonored her queen in some way by being injured. She was dismissive of my concern for her, and it was clear to me that, although she was very grateful that I'd saved her life, she was considerably embarrassed, if not humiliated, that I'd had to.

'You're in my debt now,' I'd joked, but her reply had unsettled me slightly.

'I know,' was all she'd said. It was a good thing I wasn't quite the bad guy that Ceryse thought I was, given that statement.

She had led me halfway across the city, which was how she described it, to where I was due to stay. It seemed a little grandiose to me to describe something that seemed little more than a small town as a city. However, it did occur to me that in Neferu's time as queen of the real Kemet, Itj Tawy probably wasn't much bigger than this place, so maybe calling it a city wasn't completely ridiculous.

The house I was assigned was bright and light, a one storied affair with everything I could have hoped for, except cable or satellite television. There was a fully provisioned kitchen, a bedroom with an immense and very comfortable looking double bed, a vast bathroom with power shower, bath, bidet, and much more, and two separate living spaces, complete with couches, chairs, tables, and other assorted furniture. The walls were decorated with modern renditions of ancient Egyptian art, most of it, I felt certain, depicting Neferu and Senusret. I had mixed feelings about living in a house with artistic interpretations of her husband. While I felt a large amount of sadness for his plight, I also resented him. Massively. What man who had been ensnared by Neferu would really feel well disposed towards the true object of her desires?

Djedetkha told me that the wardrobes and bedroom cupboards had been stocked with clothes for me, that the kitchen had food and drink, but that if I needed anything else, I should call her. She gave me her mobile number, which felt like an odd touch in this sort of land-that-time-forgot.

'I'm sorry that you had to do that,' she said, and for the first time she looked a little awkward. I'd thought that looking uncomfortable was my role.

'Do what?' I asked, although I knew exactly what she meant.

'You shouldn't have had to,' she told me.

'I couldn't let you die, could I?' I said, not really sure what else I could say. I didn't feel great about what I'd done, but there hadn't been any choice, and she would clearly have done the same for me.

She said nothing, instead pulling me in close and holding me tight for a few moments. I was drawn back to our time in my room at Wentworth Place as I felt her breasts pressed hard against my chest and her soft breath on my cheek. She was very sensual and I found that both exciting and intimidating, a very heady combination, especially for a man like myself, who hadn't even managed a partial launch with Ceryse. Ceryse. I dreaded to think what she would have said if she could have seen me at that moment, wrapped in Djedetkha's strong arms, a happy smile on my face.

She finally let me go, said goodbye, and left me to my devices. I sauntered around the house for a while, opening doors here, cupboards there, until I finally ran out of things to investigate. I then made a coffee and went and sat down in the living room that faced into the city. I spent a little bit of time simply savouring the view and the coffee, indulging in some unique people watching. It occurred to me that if I tried to write a paper about this, I'd probably find myself institutionalized.

After about an hour or so, I began to feel a little tired, so I made my way to the bedroom and threw myself onto the vast bed, which was every bit as comfortable as it looked. As I drifted off to sleep, I briefly wondered whether I would ever want to leave here. Why on earth would I want to return to the dog eat dog world of the USA when I could live on an island with Neferu and Djedetkha? And, I might even find myself becoming best buddies with Nedjes. As that ridiculous thought faded away, I fell asleep.

At some point I found myself in a strange and scary world. Rockets flew overhead, crashing into and destroying buildings all around me. The sound of gunfire and shouting was incessant, accompanied by the regular deep booming of artillery shells being discharged. The sky was grey with dust and smoke. I was standing in the middle of a street, surrounded by wrecked cars and rubble. At the far end of the street, about twenty feet away from me, was Ceryse, as I remembered her, not as she'd been when I'd last seen her, yesterday. At least I thought it was yesterday. I had no idea of time right now.

'I'm not coming with you,' she said to me. Somehow, despite the infernal noise all around us, and her distance from me, I could hear every word she said without her needing to shout.

'Ceryse, you must!' I responded, unable to get my head round what she was saying.

'I'm not. I'm staying here. I've got no future in the future. At least I can make a new life now.'

'You have me. We can work it out together,' I implored her.

'Stay here then,' she responded.

'I can't,' I told her, although, in truth, I didn't know why I couldn't.

Suddenly, she was right in front of me. I had no idea how she'd managed to move so quickly, but there she was. She grabbed my arm and starting shaking me.

'Wake up, Richard,' she said, more softly now. She kept saying it, over and over. 'Wake up, Richard.' It was odd because she'd never called me Richard, other than to mock me about the fact that Neferu called me that. What was also odd was that her voice had changed, and she sounded just like Djedetkha. The Golden Falcon.

I opened my eyes. Of course, it was Djedetkha. I'd been dreaming, a very odd dream. I suspected my subconscious was trying to rationalise the shocking news that Ceryse had presented me with. I hoped it wasn't precognition.

When she saw me open my eyes, Djedetkha stopped her gentle shaking and imploring, and stood back slightly. The bruising on her face was now much darker, and I hoped, for her sake, that this meant it would pass quickly. It was, I supposed, a constant reminder to her of her perceived failure.

'It's time for dinner,' she told me. 'You don't want to keep our Queen waiting.'

Our Queen? That was an interesting thought. It hadn't occurred to me that she was my Queen, other than in the sense of being the woman I adored and worshipped. I had become one of her subjects, albeit not from choice, so I supposed this had to be true. I certainly didn't want to keep her waiting, but not because she was the Queen. Simply because I wanted, needed, to be with her.

However, I was curious about something. I hoped she might have the answer.

'When I was just coming out of my dream, when I realised it was your voice, the words Golden Falcon appeared from nowhere. I can't think what it might mean. Do you have any idea?' I asked her.

'I've looked out some clothes for you,' she told me, ignoring my question in typical Kemetian style. 'I'm sure you want to look your best.'

'Thank you,' I said, putting the Golden Falcon to one side for now, and, instead, wondering if there were any things this young woman didn't, or couldn't, do, at least in the name of her Queen. I did want to look my best, although I'd never felt that my best was particularly great. But if Neferu wanted me to look good, then that made me feel good.

I glanced at Djedetkha. I realised that she also looked good, more than good. She was once again dressed in a figure-hugging knee length dress, and was as accessorised as her Queen, although, no doubt, her accessories were not quite as priceless. Her dark brown hair hung loose, and she looked beautiful, even with the ugly bruise that marred her face. I didn't exactly feel conflicted, but I felt a stirring as I gazed at her.

She handed me a shirt, a jacket and a pair of trousers. I noticed the labels read 'Boss'. Not bad, I thought. I'd try not to get food on them.

'Have a shower and get ready,' Djedetkha told me. 'I'll be back in an hour.' And with that, she left. I watched her languid hip movements as she walked away from me, a sight that I thought I could probably never tire of. She carried herself with the same grace and poise as her Queen. In fact, as I watched her leave, it occurred to me that she and Neferu were remarkably similar, in many ways. It seemed ridiculous, but I wondered if there was some connection that linked them, no matter how tenuous it might be. I knew it couldn't be possible, so I put it out of my mind and focused on the task in hand.

I showered and shaved first, and then I took some time moisturising and doing all those things that I thought might make me desirable. Desirable? Who was I kidding? Not even myself. However, a bottle of Clive Christian No. 1 had been strategically placed in the center of the washing area of the bathroom, so I hoped that some of that might make a difference. I knew that it retailed at over two thousand bucks a bottle, so some of that might help me transcend my stunning mediocrity. At least in the eyes of the Queen who'd obviously had it put there.

True to her word, Djedetkha reappeared an hour later. She smiled at me and nodded her head appreciatively as she took in my rather unusual appearance. I was normally an adherent of the smart casual look, not the over-smart over-smart look.

'You look good, Richard,' she said, 'Who would have guessed?'

I threw a hurt look at her, and she simply laughed.

'I'm teasing,' she told me. 'I thought you Americans did humor?'

'Only when it suits us,' I said. She laughed a little more at that.

'Come on,' she urged me, turning for the door. 'We don't want to be late.'

No, we don't, I thought. And I was also certain that her Queen would not look favorably on her for delivering me late. I had nothing that I needed to take with me, and I presumed that security was not an issue on the island, so I followed Djedetkha out of the house and into the square outside.

It took us about fifteen minutes to reach the Royal Palace. It was a cloudless night, and the clear skies above the island were filled with brightly shining stars. The air was dry and warm, but not overly hot. It was, in fact, a beautiful night for a walk, and it was refreshing to hear the quiet sounds of people living their lives all around me. There was none of the noise that went with big cities in the modern world, like the cacophony of pre-disaster LA, or the relentless traffic of Quito. The island felt like a safe haven from the insanity that existed everywhere else. It was also nice walking with Djedetkha, who kept up a constant stream of conversation with me, asking me about my family and my interests outside my work. Like everyone else I'd met from Neferu's world, she was good at deflecting attention away from herself. I supposed they were trained to give away nothing of the secret world that they'd been born into.

The Royal Palace was a sprawling one-storey building. It wasn't like any palaces I'd seen in the ancient world, or the one we'd visited in Itj Tawy. It was smaller and more understated, but, nevertheless, everything about it spoke of power and authority. It had been designed to make a statement, to reinforce the almost divine nature of the Queen, but at the same time it had a subtlety that marked it out from the ostentatious statements of wealth that shaped most royal and imperial palaces throughout history. I didn't think it represented any great showing of humility on Neferu's part, because I knew she was almost certainly the least humble person I'd ever met, but it did show a desire to dominate without the need for justification.

The exterior, like all the other buildings I'd seen in the city, was white. The building was spacious and, like everything here, designed to be well ventilated and to repel heat, as much as possible. Inside, it was even more impressive, as I discovered after entering through the large, vaulted portico that served as the main entrance. The ceilings were high, and the walls were filled with murals and paintings representing Neferu and Senusret in the many aspects of a royal couple: fighting wars, blessing crops, accepting gifts from their subjects, and a myriad of other scenarios. These works of art were faithful to the style of ancient Egypt, but, at the same time, were definitively modern, a sort of reinvention of a classic form of art. It was all, quite simply, beautiful. It was a tragedy that the world was deprived of such art, I thought, and I felt privileged to be seeing it, to almost be a part of it.

I did notice that there were some marks on the floor in places, suggestive of something having stood there at some point, but having since been removed. I guessed that these had been statues of their gods, which Neferu had ordered Nedjes to remove and destroy. I didn't really understand why she had suddenly decided to do this now, given that she'd fallen foul of some of them nearly four thousand years ago, but had continued to venerate them in the interim. In fact, Sobek had been there when she'd killed his brother, Anubis, and both he and Petbe had marched with us on her triumphant return to Itj Tawy. I didn't get it, but I knew there would be no point asking her. She'd tell me if she wanted me to know. She certainly wasn't one for idle conversation. I could understand that. Over the course of four millennia, I could well imagine that any desire for small talk would quickly wither and die.

I thought about the last time I'd shared dinner with her, the night before she reclaimed her husband and her throne, then lost them both again, thanks to Horus. The late Horus. Ceryse had been there then, as well as Nedjes, and it had been a brittle affair, mostly thanks to Ceryse's sharp and acerbic tongue. However, what had happened afterwards had been very nice, and I wondered if tonight might follow the same pattern.

Djedetkha led me through various hallways, until we reached two large wooden doors, ornately carved with Kemetian sigils, and seemingly made out of something like oak. She didn't knock, but simply pushed the doors open, and they swung smoothly inward to reveal a reasonably large dining room. I say reasonably, because it was on the same scale as the rest of the building. Impressive, but not overly grandiose. It was my guess that there was little in the way of formal or state dining on the island.

Neferu was standing by the table when the doors opened, and she turned to face us as we entered. I was immediately overwhelmed and intoxicated, as always, by her sensuality and her dynamic, all-powerful, beauty. She was dressed in the most exquisite dress. The underlying material was cream, but it was inset all over with what appeared to be amber stones. It had a halter neck, and her delicately shaped shoulders stood out enticingly, her long black hair cascading down in slight waves over them. The dress was long, but I could see her gold shoes poking out from underneath. High-heeled, of course. For once, she wore little jewellery, beyond some earrings inset with more amber and some simple gold bracelets. I noticed that her toe and finger nails, which were so often painted with lapis, were currently gold. But what struck me the most were her beautiful gold-flecked ochre eyes, which were fixed intensely on me. It was intimidating and overwhelming, but it was what I wanted. Being in Neferu's presence, having her full attention, being awed and intoxicated by her, made me feel more alive than I'd ever felt in my life. I'd come to realise that this was an essential part of the power she held over me. She was remarkably sensual and beautiful, and also sexually enticing, but, of course, she had such a powerful presence that to have all of this directed at me was more invigorating and seductive than anything else that I'd ever experienced. Even Djedetkha, beautiful as she was, paled into insignificance in comparison with her Queen.

Neferu glanced briefly at Djedetkha, and she immediately retreated, closing the doors behind her. The Queen sashayed over to me, and, I have to say, her sashay was truly a joy to behold, even from the front, and ran a finger down the lapel of my blue suit jacket.

'That looks good on you,' she told me, momentarily closing her eyes and arching her head backwards. 'You smell good, too,' she added, although I presumed she already knew that I would, since she must have chosen the aftershave.

'You look stunning,' I told her, although there weren't really any words I could think of, in any language that I knew, that did justice to her immortal beauty.

She bowed her head slightly, in acknowledgement of my praise. Knowing her, she would probably have called it encomium. She loved language and its proper and correct usage. I knew she found many of my American idioms irritating and disappointing, and I tried not to use them when I was in her company, although it was hard not to, simply because of habit. There was no question that she knew more about language than anyone alive, or dead. Like everything else, really.

Two women and one man entered the room holding trays and plates. I hadn't seen any of them before, and I thought briefly about Hortensia and Maria, who had served so faithfully in the Suchos Building. They were possibly the only non-Kemetian people I'd seen in her employ. I hoped that they were okay, and had survived the destruction of LA. If they had, I felt certain that their Queen would have taken care of them. Despite her arrogance and disdain for most things around her, she obviously valued her loyal staff very highly, and rewarded them appropriately. The luxury and opulence of the settlement that lay beyond the royal palace was clear proof of that. A benevolent tyrant. Who would have thought it? However, I was fairly certain that Neferu would not appreciate being referred to as a tyrant. She was a dynastic Queen. I felt confident that she would describe this as something entirely different.

'Sit down, Richard, dinner is here,' she said, moving to take her place at the head of the table. A place had been set next to her, on her right. It would have been nicer to have sat opposite, but the other end of the table was about twelve feet away, so at least I was close. I felt encouraged, in fact, that I wasn't sitting all that distance away.

It was another eleven-course meal, a remarkable expression of ancient and modern cultures, a thoughtful and quite wonderful fusion of traditional Ancient Egyptian foods with modern tastes and styles. And, I was pleased to note, the bread had not been ground using traditional Kemetian methods, which meant that my teeth were safe. I couldn't imagine that Neferu would tolerate grit in her bread if she didn't have to.

The food was excellent, and the wine, which was chosen to match each course, was equally delightful. I found myself transported back to those early days in the Suchos Building, when I had simply believed, very stupidly, that I had landed myself the most beautiful and wealthy girlfriend in the world. I'd been right about everything except the girlfriend part. There was no doubt in my mind that those were the best few days of my life. I wouldn't ever tell that to Ceryse, since it would only confirm what she already thought, and would no doubt lead to even more verbal abuse. However, I had to remind myself that I couldn't tell her, even if I wanted to, because the Ceryse I'd known was now in 1982, with Neferu's husband.

'What do you think of my island, Richard?' Neferu asked me.

'It's incredible. Really incredible. You're a woman of amazing vision.'

'Thank you,' she replied, not looking up from her food. 'Vision is one thing. Being able to afford your vision, and having the opportunity to create it, are something else entirely. It wasn't easy.'

'That must make it even more satisfying,' I said.

'Of course. Although, it would have been better if it had never come to this.'

She was right, of course. If Anubis and Sekhemrekhutawy hadn't usurped her throne and damned her with this immortality, then she would have simply continued on her happy way as Queen, opposite her royal consort, Senusret.

'Neferu,' I began, changing the subject. I didn't think there was any value in leading her down that road. It would only lead to misery. 'The last time we had dinner together, I asked you about Haggard. You avoided answering, but, now I'm here, it's obvious that he knew you very well.'

She laughed, a sound that filled my heart with joy. I loved the sound of her laughing, not the least because it happened so rarely, at least, in my experience.

'Henry,' she said. 'He was obsessed with me. But you already knew that.'

I knew it, partly because of Ayesha, She-Who-Must-Be-Obeyed, but also because I couldn't imagine a man spending time with Neferu and not falling hopelessly under her spell.

'I wondered, but seeing your kingdom made it very clear. He couldn't have you, so he wrote about you.'

'He said that having me live in his dreams and his writing made it easier to cope with the devastating loss of not being able to possess me.'

I could completely relate to that. He wrote four books about Ayesha, even bringing her back from the dead. I thought about the crappy films that had been made of what were, actually, pretty good books, and I laughed inwardly. Every single film maker had completely missed the mark. Neferu was not only infinitely more beautiful than any of the actresses cast in the role, she was also not blonde and white.

'I'm sure he was right,' was all I said.

'It hardly matters,' she responded. 'And he never really understood anything. As his books made very apparent.'

We lapsed into silence for a short while, both of us focusing on our food, which was now up to the ninth course. As I sipped at my wine, I decided to try to make the conversation a little more serious.

'So, what is your plan?'

'My plan? It's simple. We go back and rescue Senusret. I would have saved Ceryse, too, but from what you said it seems she wants to stay in 1982.'

'But you don't have a particle accelerator,' I countered. 'Or do you? Is there one hidden here somewhere?'

'I wouldn't put my kingdom at risk by building one here, Richard. You should know me better than that,' she responded, her eyes intently fixed on mine. 'But I don't need a particle accelerator.'

'You don't?'

'No, I don't.'

'So, what have you got?'

She sighed, and clearly made a decision. I knew she liked keeping all her cards close to her chest, and didn't believe in sharing anything she didn't have to, but maybe she was feeling well disposed towards me, or maybe she just wanted to share her genius. Either way, for once, she took the time to actually explain something to me.

'When Curtis arrived in 2017, he brought with him the device that had enabled him to travel through time. However, it was damaged in the process, and he believed it had been destroyed.' She paused to sip some wine, although I also expected it was to add to the effect of her story. 'But it wasn't. My people retrieved it, and we've been working to repair it and make it functional ever since.'

'So why did you use Curtis to help you go back to 1799BC then?'

'His device wouldn't have been able to transport all the people I needed. And it could never have forged the bridgehead. Even with the power rings we have from Anubis, Horus, and now Set, this device can only cope with transporting six people, at the most.'

I was a little bit shocked by this news, that Neferu had her own time travel device. The whole concept of travelling through time had seemed utterly absurd to me only two weeks earlier, but now I had to accept that it was possible. I knew because I'd gone back with her to reclaim her throne. However, it did mean that many of my worries about Ceryse were instantly eased. I felt certain that when I met up with her back in Beirut in 1982 that she would agree to return to 2024. I couldn't really imagine why she wouldn't, despite what Neferu had said. After all, back in 1982, Ceryse would have had no idea of the happy life that lay ahead of her. I thought about that, and realised that I was now sounding even more selfish than ever. I seemed damned if I did, and damned if I didn't.

'So, when are we going back to get them?' I asked.

'Very soon, Richard, but there's somewhere I need to go first.'

I looked at her, hardly believing what I'd just heard. Her face had taken on a familiar look, unreadable and giving nothing whatsoever away.

'What could be more important than your husband?' I demanded.

'Nothing is more important than Senusret,' she replied, icily.

'So why are you delaying?'

'It doesn't matter to him, he's safe.'

'But he isn't. He's dead!'

'Richard, you don't understand time. Senusret is safe in the past. He is dead right now. However, when we go back, he will be alive and I can save him. But, for the present, nothing is going to change for him.'

'I don't understand,' was all I could say. She was right. And the paradoxes inherent in it all were making my head spin.

'Don't try to. It's not worth it. I have somewhere to go and then the time will be right to save him. And Ceryse, if she wants. And, for you, I'll only be gone for an instant, anyway.'

'But what is so important that you need to do it first?'

'I need to go to the future,' she told me. I was a little shocked.

'The future? Why?'

'I can't tell you that.'

'But why not?'

'I can't tell you, and I won't tell you. You simply don't need to know.'

'You don't want me to know the future?'

She said nothing, merely continuing to stare at me with an expressionless look written across her face.

'Take me with you,' I said. I didn't really want to go, but I also didn't want to be left behind while she disappeared, possibly never to return.

'I won't do that. You need to stay safe here.' For a moment I saw something in her eyes, something that expressed concern and worry, but then it was gone, replaced once again by the empty mask she'd been wearing.

'Safe? Is it dangerous, then?'

'Everything's dangerous. Haven't you seen that yourself?'

'Yes, but....'

'It's not open for discussion. You'll wait for me. I'll be gone for just a few moments as far as you're concerned. And then we'll go back to Beirut in 1982.'

There was something in the way she spoke, something in her matter of fact tone, that worried me. But what could I do? What possible leverage could I bring to bear on her? And, to be honest, what possible use would I be in the future? If she could only take five or six people with her, then she needed to take people she could rely on, not a mediocre academic who struggled with even basic DIY.

'Where are you going? Surely you can least tell me that?' I asked.

'2105,' was all she said.

'Curtis' time?' I said, now confused.

'There are some questions that I need answers to, and which will make traveling into the past safer,' she told me, as if that explained everything.

'What questions?'

'You don't need to know, Richard. When you do, I'll tell you.'

I bristled a little at these patronising words, but, what could I do? She was probably right, and maybe I really shouldn't know about the future. The Romans had passed a law making the predicting of death days illegal. I could see the wisdom in that, and there was no question that their augurs had no meaningful insight into the future. Neferu did, or, at least, would have.

'Would you like some coffee?' she asked me, her expression subtly changing, some warmth creeping back in, with a general softening of her body language.

'No, I want you,' I told her, deciding, against my better judgement, to be bold. I knew that Neferu preferred plain speaking, so I hoped she might be receptive to my bluntness.

'Do you?' she asked me, as if she didn't know, her face softening further. 'Then you'd better come over here.'

I didn't need to be asked twice, and I got up from my chair. As I did so, she also stood up, crossing the short distance between us. As usual, with her heels on, she was slightly taller than me, which I enjoyed. She leaned down ever so slightly and kissed me on the lips. It felt like I'd been electrocuted, the power that ran through her and into me was overwhelming. Of course, there was no real shock or power, but the effect of her lips touching mine, of her body now pressing up hard against me, was electrifying.

I kissed her back, and pulled her as close to me as I could. The hairs on the back of my neck stood up as I felt her fingers slowly move under my shirt and up my back. Once more, and with a happiness that I had not known for two weeks, I prepared to drown in her passion.

Chapter Twenty

Abridged version of Chapter Three, The Global Crisis and its Resolution: How Humanity was Reinvented. Kaddo, R.A. Damascus. 2106:

The signs were there for all to see. The fact that they were largely ignored is completely irrelevant. The global crisis of the late twenty-first century was apparent from as early as 2036, as has been clearly documented in the seminal works of both Duncan and Miller (Duncan 2096; Miller, 2097). As has been demonstrated (Zhang, 2065), governments are not especially proactive in terms of global problems, instead focusing on their own issues in isolation. This is, of course, a gross oversimplification of a very complex set of variables, but the point is a good one. It was evident in 2020 that the response to the so-called 'Covid Crisis' was patchy and inconsistent. And much of this patchiness and inconsistency enabled the pandemic to spread further (Zeaman and Gabrisch, 2089). Of course, there was a later argument put forward that many governments tolerated Covid-19 simply because they believed it might seriously decrease their elderly populations, which were becoming a significant burden on the developed world's welfare states (Irving, 2048).

In 2026 the coming crisis was first widely detected, although, in hindsight, there was clear evidence that it had already existed, in some form, from 2025 onwards (Asalanka and McMillan, 2078). Of course, as the authors noted, the human race has always been prone to many genetic aberrations, so even if anyone had attempted to read a pattern into the early cases, they would almost certainly have been disregarded by those who held the purse strings.

It was not until 2036, when the World Health Organisation met for a routine health conference in Vaduz, that the many worldwide strands of this impending global catastrophe were brought together into a coherent whole. As noted in their own documentation of the conference (WHO, 2037), what had previously been considered by individual states to be an unusual pattern of genetic anomalies, suddenly represented a global situation of alarming proportions. It was considered alarming, even though there were still relatively few cases, taken as a percentage of overall population sizes (around five per cent globally, at that time, allowing for regional variations), because even the most optimistic forecasts indicated that the 'infection' rate would hit around 90 per cent by the start of the twenty-second century.

When distributed to the world's governments, these figures were generally disputed and ridiculed. However, it was only politicians who downplayed the coming crisis. Their advisors, both in healthcare and the economy, were less cavalier, although, initially, they were rarely listened to.

The condition under discussion was first discovered, as already noted, as early as late 2024, although it wasn't possible to trace its routes back any further. No similar cases were identifiable before then, and there remains some uncertainty over what may have caused it. Significant research (Dyer, 2059; Jones, 2065; Simonez, 2067; et al.) has attempted to locate a single source, and, although no-one has yet succeeded definitively, the likeliest source was the catastrophic event that happened in Northwood, California, in early 2024. What is apparent, regardless of cause, is that the locus of the first cases was, indeed, California, and it would appear that it was spread from there by the simple method of human movement and transition (Al Bacha, 2058).

As noted, governments were slow to act, and this helped to hasten its spread. Although, in hindsight, and knowing what we do about Zvidsai-Charig Syndrome, there was probably little governments could have done, in terms of reducing infection rates. What was needed was significant investment in research, and, in the early years, only China, possibly stung by global criticism over the Covid affair, ploughed money into this area. As the size of the catastrophe slowly became apparent, many more governments around the world began to invest heavily, some, with fewer available resources, joining together. Some progress was made, but, because it had been left so late, the whole process was essentially a 'firefighting' task (Lake and Springer, 2071), and, therefore, under the most burdensome pressure imaginable to produce results.

There is no need here to document the political, economic and social chaos and disorder that occurred as the situation worsened, with no obvious hope of a positive resolution. Governments talked long and loud about their protective measures, and the money they were shovelling into research, but nothing that they did, if they, indeed, actually did anything, made much difference to the increasing spread of Zvidsai-Charig Syndrome. By 2065, it was apparent to even the most positively minded humans on the planet, that the future was now looking very bleak (Greenstreet, 2065).

This acknowledgement that the Syndrome appeared uncurable, at least in any meaningful way, led to an investment in different types of research (McPhoy, 2078). Governments became concerned with finding a way forward, a way to stabilise or modify humanity so that the effects of the Syndrome would become null and void. This led, in 2070, to the emergence of Jonathan Peiper and his so-called 'Wunderbar' Laboratory as world leaders of a new movement, a movement that he claimed would not only save humanity, but would actually improve on it (McPhoy, 2078). Situated near Gelsenkirchen in industrial Germany, Peiper posited not fixing broken DNA, but modifying it, using existing and undamaged materials from elsewhere to not only strengthen humanity, but to, supposedly, improve on it (Peiper, various).

These views were radical and were considered highly dangerous by many respected scientists and researchers (Gororo, 2082; Henry, 2084), but, as the mass of humanity became aware of its impending demise, this solution polarised opinion. Many were scared of what it might mean for humanity and its future, while others, understandably wanting to avoid what appeared to be the inevitable ending of the race, saw it as the only way forward. The latter fully embraced it, the former rejected it out of hand, feeling that it would be better for humanity to pass than to go down this route.

Inevitably, civil and global war followed.

Chapter Twenty-One

I awoke the next morning feeling a strange combination of physical and emotional satisfaction, coupled with anxiety and uncertainty. I had enjoyed my evening with Richard. He was, as usual, very serious and earnest, but also gentle and considerate. I had enjoyed his continued obsession with Haggard. That had amused me. Poor Henry had been willing to be my slave, and was prepared to give up everything simply to follow me around like an obedient puppy, happy with the occasional bone that I might throw his way. But he had been of no real importance to me, and, apart from the obvious distraction that he had provided, I had no need of him. He was an intelligent man, and had gained a significant glimpse into my world, but was at least sensible enough to realise that if he had attempted to report it as fact rather than fiction, he would almost certainly have been dragged off to Bedlam.

Richard had probed me about my plans, and I had generously explained some things to him, even though he didn't need to know. But, for him, the real stumbling block remained his ignorance of the machinations of time. It always came back to the same point: how could a finite being understand the infinite?

However, the crux of the evening, for us both, was what followed. Richard, despite his feelings of guilt over Ceryse, and his obvious attraction to Djedetkha, remained in my thrall, and had only really come to dinner with one thought on his mind. However, the same was true for me, too. I had complex needs in my life, and only some could easily be met. But, Richard had the skills and the tenderness to help me lose myself for a few hours in the oblivion of passion and desire. And he hadn't disappointed. It was a given that I hadn't disappointed him, either. That was never a possibility.

My body really was a temple, a place of veneration and worship, but only certain high priests, the most select and precious few, were ever allowed within the hallowed portals. And only because my heart's true desire had been so cruelly and inhumanly snatched away from me. I was not a wanton or immoral woman, but I did have needs that had to be met. How could I have survived for nearly four thousand years without some comfort?

But now it was the morning, and time to prepare for the next phase of my plan. This was undoubtedly the least certain and most nebulous part of it. Going back to Beirut in 1982, saving Senusret and returning to the present, seemed fairly straightforward, although I had no doubt that, in practice, it would be anything but. However, traveling to the future in search of clarification, understanding and a resolution, was anything but straightforward. I had sent out reconnaissance missions, and they had provided some useful information, such as the e-book I'd read yesterday, but there was only so much they could discover and usefully pass on. The future remained an unknown country, a place of dark secrets and even darker motivations.

The book had been a revelation, but not in a good way. As I'd read it, my heart had continued to sink, until there was no deeper level for it to descend to. The global crisis had clearly been the most dramatic and catastrophic in mankind's history, and it explained so much of what those DNA tests had hinted at. The more I had read, the more I had desperately wanted to find myself back in the much simpler and far less degenerate days of ancient Kemet. I had yearned to be back in Itj Tawy, surrounded by nothing more than the simple needs and desires of my time. But I realised now that I could never go back there, and I had to work with what had been put in my path. It made me think about God. Not the old, fraudulent and deceitful gods, but the all-powerful, omnipotent being that Christians, Muslims and so many others believed had created the world they struggled to survive in. Unlike anyone else alive in this world, I had known the carpenter, seen his works at first hand. But even I struggled to understand the presence of God in the face of the future that was about to come. However, a human being, even an infinite one, could never hope to understand a truly divine creature, so, for all I knew, perversity could have been part of the greater plan.

We would be traveling to Denver, Colorado. This seemed to be the centre of the world that had sent Curtis tumbling back to 2017. It was hard to know why Denver, hardly the hub of anything important, should have become such a key player. However, I supposed that, in the context of continued global warming, it could be strategically important, situated as it was, one mile above sea level. The sea level in 2024, of course.

We had posted instructions for my future generations of M'sha, who, I believed, would be able to provide us with significant support. I also didn't want to find myself facing myself. That would have been wrong on every level, and might even cause some catastrophic physical reaction. Such was the stuff of science fiction stories, but it might also be science fact. Best not to find out, either way.

I forced myself, somewhat reluctantly, out of bed, and slowly prepared myself for the day, with the help of a few of my maids. At home, in my palace, I allowed myself the luxuries that a Queen of Kemet was entitled to, but which were harder to manage in the wider world of humanity. It was nice to be pampered, to not have to think about anything much, beyond what would follow. They knew not to rush, and the various tasks were slowly completed, culminating in my make-up and hair. For once I eschewed any but the most basic jewellery, putting on simple Kemetian earrings. I thought that anything else might be a liability if the worst came to the worst. I put on a black combat suit, tailored specifically for me, of course, and some military boots. Although having to be my true height didn't please me, I knew that anything else would have been ridiculous and stupid.

The image that reflected back from the full-length mirrors in my dressing chamber remained pleasing, although not in a way that I favoured. The important thing was that I still looked like a queen, even in my combat fatigues.

Fully dressed, and now prepared, as much as I could be, for whatever was to follow, I called Nedjes and told him that I was ready. Accompanied by some of my maids and a small force of guards, I began to make my way to the Research Centre. I felt no threat or need for concern, but the presence of an armed accompaniment was essential for any Queen of Kemet. It was different in the outside world, but in my own kingdom there were standards of etiquette and protocol that, despite the changing times I had lived through, needed to stay unchanged.

The Research Centre was on the other side of the city, set in the shadow of the mountains that rose up from the coastal plain and began to shape the rugged interior of the island. The area around the complex was green and forested, carpeted with lush green grass and thriving tropical foliage. It reminded me of the life-affirming fertility of the Nile delta after the annual inundation. I couldn't think of anything that would have made it more beautiful, other than it actually being in Kemet, rather than the Caribbean Sea, just a few dozen miles from the coast of Nicaragua.

The double doors slid open as I approached, and the men on guard inside the entrance briefly tensed, until they realised who had arrived, and then they instantly bowed, offering me their most unctuous obeisance. This part of the complex was like an over-sized warehouse, and many interesting and often bizarrely fantastic experiments and procedures had taken place here over the preceding decades. However, nothing had been more fantastic than the event about to be enacted.

The vast space was empty, save for myself, my retinue and the handful of people waiting for me. There was a small pile of equipment next to them, but, other than that, the room was empty. As a result, all our voices echoed around the walls.

'Good morning, my Queen,' Nedjes said, bowing slightly, as did Djedetkha, Shoshenq and Menkheperre. Richard, who was standing next to them all, followed suit, albeit belatedly, and rather awkwardly. Of course.

'Have you done the briefing?' I asked.

'Yes, your Highness,' Nedjes responded. That was good. I didn't want to have to listen to the same things again. We needed to get in, find what we needed to, do what had to be done, and get out again. It sounded simple, in principle, but, I had no doubt that, in practice, things would be far from simple.

'I still don't understand why you need to go,' Richard said.

'Of course you don't,' I told him, dismissively. I had no time for his constant need for reassurances today.

'We'll be back the moment after we leave,' Djedetkha told him, offering him the comfort that I wasn't interested in giving. I noticed that the bruising on her face had significantly subsided, there being mostly a strong yellow and red mark around her eye now. It was a testament to the wonders of our medical science, and Kemetian salves.

Nedjes handed out hand guns to us all, and HK416s to the other three. We didn't particularly want to look like we were ready for a fight, but, at the same time, we had to be prepared for one. He gave each of us a small device that resembled a mobile phone, computing tools that would hook into every local network that the reconnaissance teams had been able to identify, as well as helping us to keep in contact if we were separated. He passed backpacks to us all, including myself. It wasn't particularly becoming for a Queen of Kemet to be carrying anything for herself, but this was no state occasion.

'Does anyone have any last questions?' Nedjes asked.

'Only one,' Richard responded. 'Can I come with you?'

Djedetkha reached out and put what I presumed she thought would be a comforting hand on his arm. 'We'll be back before you've even had time to blink,' she told him. He looked sceptical, but said nothing more. He knew the chances of changing my mind on anything were less than non-existent.

'Let's go,' I said, and Nedjes pulled out a small black device from his backpack. It resembled a digital camera in size and shape, but had no lens. It was incredible, I thought, that such a small device could harbour and effectively harness so much raw power. The same was true of the three rings that were located inside it, and which were now going to power it. But this was technology from the future, and the power rings, I suspected, were from the far future, although I had no real way of knowing that.

Nedjes moved his fingers across it, and everything around us blurred and went dark.

Chapter Twenty-Two

Extract from the daily journal of Richard Verlice, Friday 15th March 2024:

I had given up trying to understand Neferu. She blew hot and cold in a way that no-one else could. She could move from contemptuous indifference to overwhelming passion in the blink of an eye. She was impossible to read, although, when I'd first met her, I'd arrogantly assumed I could. However, to be fair, I had no idea she was really a Queen of Kemet. In my defence, I don't think anyone would probably have jumped to that conclusion.

It was an absurd conceit on my part that I could even begin to understand her. I had lived for 32 years, with probably no more than double that time left to me, if I was lucky. She had lived for 3,854 years, with no suggestion of an end in sight. How could I possibly even begin to understand someone who had lived longer than any civilisation on this planet had lasted? Although much of what she said irritated me, and I was, in truth, fearful of her endgame, I did count myself incredibly fortunate to know her. I just wished she would be more forthcoming about the things she'd experienced and lived through. I knew very well that she despised historians, and believed that history, as documented by the modern world, was around 95 per cent lies. And I couldn't really argue with that. After all, as a historian myself, I was only too well aware that we only had the written historical records and archaeological information that had survived, or been allowed to survive. She had lived through almost all of it, although she obviously hadn't seen or experienced everything. One thing she couldn't do was to be in more than one place at any given time.

However, she was very reluctant to talk about history, other than in enigmatic and highly opaque and cryptic asides. I believed, although she wouldn't discuss it, that she was certain that knowing the truth of the past would actually disable, rather than enable, me, or others. And, I felt equally certain that she would decline to discuss any aspect of the future with me. I could understand that, it made good sense. Her disinclination to discuss the past made less sense. But, I had long ago realised, although it wasn't really very long ago, that there was nothing I could do to change her mind on anything.

She had wanted me last night. There did seem to be a slight pattern, if you could read a pattern into two events. She had done the same thing the night before she created the bridgehead back to 1799BC. It was as if she needed some human comfort, some connection to the world around her, before she stepped into the potentially cataclysmic unknown. The same was true of last night. Today she planned to step into the future, that, even for her, had to be largely unknown. And she had wanted comfort, warmth, love. Maybe she wanted to feel simply like a woman with all the human needs a woman had, to escape the constant reminders that she had evolved into something more. She was a woman still, obviously, but she had long ago transformed into something else, an infinite being for whom all things were possible, unlimited by the constraints and restraints placed on the rest of us. It sounded like she was living the dream when you thought about it like that, but I suspect that it was also the most burdensome weight that could be imagined sitting squarely on her shoulders.

We had made love, as she had clearly intended, and it was every bit as wonderful and life-affirming as every time we had in the past, even when I'd simply thought of her as Nawal. She was a sensual creature, and gave everything of herself at these moments. It was probably the only time in her life when she did give anything meaningful of herself to anyone else. I supposed that I should take it as a compliment, that it wasn't really about her using me for what she wanted. It was a shared experience, and she seemed to trust me completely in this area of our relationship. I think she needed that. I didn't get the feeling that it was ever simply about sex. I knew how desperately she missed her husband. She needed to feel that connection to the world around her, she needed to be able to drown herself in the sharing of human interconnectivity. It was about being loved, being able to love, and being a woman. To all intents and purposes, I became Senusret at those moments.

I could live with that. It wasn't really very flattering, but then again, I was deluding myself if I thought a woman who had fought and died, repeatedly, over four millennia, to restore her husband, would really have fallen in love with me. Love motivated Neferu. Love for Senusret, love for Kemet, love for being adored and worshipped, love for power. Her love was stronger than death, which, I have to admit, I'd thought was the most powerful force in existence until I met her. Death transcended everything mortal, made everything we humans strived for futile and pointless. But, in her hands, love transformed and conquered in a way that no-one else could ever manage. This love she had for her husband was beyond anyone's capacity to understand. It was possibly love in its purest form. I just hoped, for her sake, that when they were finally reunited, she wasn't disappointed. She had lived for a long, long time, but he'd been dead the whole while.

What was a surprise, and a revelation, was that, after we'd finally spent ourselves, she'd slept. As she lay asleep in my arms, I revelled in the moment. She'd only ever pretended to sleep before, and I remembered that horrible night in the Suchos Building, our first night together, when she'd been gently crying on the balcony, tormented, as she had been for every night since 1802BC, by visions of Ra and the Mesektet moving inexorably through the night air.

But now, it seemed, she could sleep. I wondered how that had happened. Had she engineered it herself? Maybe, but it could also have been due to what had happened in LA. Who really knew what effect the blast from La Misión would have on the world in the years to come? It had certainly been unlike any previous explosion that had happened, even the A Bombs dropped on the helpless Japanese in 1945.

She had been very peaceful in her sleep, and I had taken advantage of that to hold her close, and simply exist in the moment, feeling her softness and her sweet perfume so close to me. It was a joy, one that I knew would end, but which was almost as pleasurable as what had gone before.

The morning dawned, of course, and she woke to find me still pressed up close next to her. She had smiled kindly, and told me that I needed to go. I knew that she would, but it didn't make the separation any less painful. I felt fearful about what was to come, what the day might bring, and wondered if we would ever share a night like that again.

As she saw the look on my face, she crossed to where I was putting my clothes back on, and surprised me by giving me a big and very tight hug, a real pleasure since she was still naked.

'The time has come,' she said, her lips next to my ear, her voice so soft I had to strain to hear her words. 'Follow your heart.'

And with that, she let go, and turned away, heading towards her inner sanctum, and, no doubt, a posse of waiting maids.

I had no idea what she meant, but, then again, I had become used to her cryptic monologues. I simply left the palace and made my way back to my new home. I couldn't help but wonder how long I would be on the island. It was beautiful, and welcoming, and I felt certain it could come to feel like home. But, I had a feeling of impermanence, a sense of everything being temporary. However, that may well have just been the product of my anxiety over what the day would bring. I couldn't say that I was relishing the prospect of Neferu disappearing into the future. What if she never returned? And, when she did, I was looking forward to traveling to Beirut in 1982 even less. Out of one frying pan and into the worst fire I could imagine.

I had a shower, shaved, and then dressed in the black combat fatigues that had been provided for me. I hoped that Neferu might provide some more useful items, like a bullet-proof vest and a steel helmet.

I made myself a coffee, but just as I sat down to drink it, there was a knock on the door. That surprised me, although I supposed there were a very limited number of people who it was likely to be.

'Come in,' I called out. The door opened and, of course, Djedetkha walked in.

'Good morning, Richard,' she said.

'Would you like some coffee?' I asked her, admiring her black and pleasingly tight-fitting combat outfit.

'No, thank you,' she said, sitting down opposite me. 'Finish it, and then we have to go.'

'Do you know why Neferu is going to 2105?' I asked her.

'Yes,' was all she said.

'Would you like to share that information?' I persisted, certain that she would say no. I wasn't disappointed.

'I'm not at liberty to discuss that with you, I'm afraid,' she responded, as I'd expected. Studying her beautiful, but still bruised face, closely, it didn't strike me that she actually felt very remorseful about this.

'There's a surprise,' I muttered, as I sipped my still piping hot coffee.

'You have to respect our Queen's decision,' she told me, 'She wouldn't do anything that she didn't consider essential.'

I merely glanced at her over my cup, thinking about the events of last night. I knew that Djedetkha wasn't likely to tell me anything. Maybe when it was all over, and they were safely back, they might lower themselves to explain something to me. Assuming they returned safely, of course.

'How's your face?' I asked her.

'It doesn't hurt anymore,' she said, looking slightly rueful. It was evident that she didn't enjoy being reminded of what had happened. I felt certain that Neferu wouldn't have been impressed by her allowing herself to be taken by surprise. She was attempting to keep me safe, though, so I didn't think it was very fair to blame her.

'I'm glad,' I told her. 'I'm sorry you got hurt.' And I was sorry that I had to kill someone because of it.

'We need to go,' was all she said, getting to her feet. I think she'd had enough of talking about it, which I could well understand. It was history now, for both of us.

I downed the rest of my coffee and got up, following her as she crossed the room back to the front door. She led me away from the Royal Palace, towards the small mountain range that rose up from the coastal valley towards the interior of the island. In the distance, I could see a tall building, designed quite differently to everything else around us. It looked simply modern, whereas everything else had been designed to blend the old with the new. There was a lot of glass in evidence, and, unlike most of the other structures I'd seen, it was on four levels. It was big, too.

As we finally reached it, the double doors at the entrance slid open, and Djedetkha led me inside. There were two burly looking men on guard duty, who tensed slightly as the doors opened, but relaxed when they saw the two of us. I wondered why security was needed in this paradise, but then I remembered Anubis and Horus, and the battle with the Guardians at the museum and the hotel. If there was anything worth guarding in this building, then two guards seemed woefully inadequate.

We found ourselves in a small corridor, with passages leading away on either side. However, Djedetkha continued straight ahead, through another set of sliding double doors.

'The security seems a bit slack,' I said.

'There are defensive measures in place around the island,' Djedetkha responded, dismissively. It clearly wasn't something that bothered her.

'Defensive measures?' I asked, not sure what she meant.

'It's impossible to open a vortex here,' she told me.

'What about air or sea attack?' I asked, remembering that the Guardians had used a helicopter against Neferu.

'They could try,' she said, clearly completely disinterested in the subject. If she felt secure, then I supposed that I should. Although, she was the one with a big bruise on her face.

The doors opened to reveal a vast, and mostly empty space. It was a little like a warehouse, and the sound of our feet on the hard floor echoed around the room, as we crossed to where Nedjes stood. He was there, with the Ahati who had left Ecuador with Djedetkha and myself, and whose name I now knew to be Soshenq. There was another man there, who Djedetkha introduced as Menkheperre, and some equipment in a pile on the floor. I could see backpacks, some electrical equipment, and what I guessed were assault rifles. I supposed it was important to prepare for all contingencies, but the presence of guns didn't make me feel any better about what was going to happen.

As I stood there, feeling a little like a spare part, the doors behind us opened, and in strode Neferu, with a small flourish, surrounded as she was by some guards and a handful of her maids. She was dressed all in black, a combat suit very similar to the one modelled by Djedetkha. I was reminded of the night she retrieved Senusret's skull from the Institute. She had been dressed in a similar way. I remembered what happened afterwards. I hoped that today wasn't going to be like that, although I suspected that it would probably be far worse.

'Good morning, my Queen,' Nedjes said to her, as she approached. He bowed a little as he spoke, as did Djedetkha, Shoshenq and Menkheperre. I didn't want to appear disrespectful, even though I'd been in her bed next to her, completely naked, only a couple of hours earlier, so I belatedly gave a little bow myself.

'Have you done the briefing?' she demanded of Nedjes.

'Yes, your Highness,' he replied. He must have done it before Djedetkha came to collect me. Standing there, feeling a distinct outsider, I wasn't even sure why she had. Maybe Neferu wanted to see my beautiful face one more time before she disappeared into the future.

'I still don't understand why you need to go,' I said to her.

'Of course you don't,' she told me, dismissively. I don't know why I'd expected any other answer.

'We'll be back the moment after we leave,' Djedetkha told me, at least offering some sort of reassurance.

Nedjes then handed out the guns and equipment. I was surprised that Neferu took a backpack, that wasn't her style. She wouldn't even open a car door by herself. But, I supposed they needed every bit of equipment they could take, even though it probably wasn't becoming for a Queen of Kemet to resemble a pack mule.

'Does anyone have any last questions?' Nedjes asked, although I didn't think the question was aimed at me.

'Only one,' I responded. 'Can I come with you?'

I felt a hand placed softly on my arm, and looked to see that Djedetkha had reached out to me.

'We'll be back before you've even had time to blink,' she said. I wasn't sure I could believe that, but what could I say? I was no expert in time travel, although I had experienced it, so I supposed I had to believe her.

'Let's go,' Neferu said. Nedjes opened his backpack and pulled out a small device. I couldn't really make it out from where I was standing, but it was quite small, no larger than a phone or a digital camera. He swiped his fingers across it, and everything around me suddenly blurred. I looked around in shock. They'd gone. I was all alone. Well, not quite alone. Neferu's guards and maids were still there, but the five heading to the future were gone.

I blinked my eyes, deliberately. Nothing happened. I did it again. Still nothing happened.

I wondered what I should do. I felt a bit self-conscious simply standing there, waiting. I considered going back to my house, although I was worried that they might come back and go again without waiting for me. That possibly wasn't very likely, since Neferu seemed very keen for me to return with her to 1982, but it could happen. So, I decided to wait.

About two, or maybe three, minutes passed and then suddenly everything blurred again. And, just as they'd instantaneously disappeared, so they reappeared. Only, they weren't alone. And they looked different. Neferu looked tired, and their outfits weren't quite as pristine as when they'd left a few minutes before, but, significantly, the bruising on Djedetkha's face had only slightly faded, so it was apparent that they hadn't been in the future for very long.

She stood next to a tall creature with the body of a woman, but the head of a cat. Although, as I studied her, a little intimidated by the dark and vengeful look in her eyes, I realised that she actually had the head of a lioness. This was Sekhmet, the ruthless manifestation of the Eye of Ra. She was restrained by handcuffs, and Djedetkha was holding her assault rifle pressed into her side, with Nedjes and Soshenq flanking her.

I realised that Menkheperre was not with them. I hoped that maybe he was coming back separately, but I suspected he wasn't coming back at all.

Almost as soon as they appeared, Neferu moved into action. She reached into one of the pockets of her jacket and pulled out a handful of large black objects, which I realised were the gods' power rings, and handed them all to Nedjes. She then gestured to some of her guards, who rushed over to her side.

'Take this creature and secure it,' she commanded. Nodding obediently, they took Sekhmet from Djedetkha and led her away.

'You will die for this, Neferu!' Sekhmet hissed and spat at her, struggling against the guards, but unable to break free or do anything much other than be dragged away. Neferu simply turned her back on the god and ignored her, treating her with the utter contempt that she clearly felt for her. I could understand her anger with Anubis, who had cursed her so unfairly, and even with Horus, who had, unwittingly, ended her plan to fuse time, but I couldn't understand why she hated the others with such fury. However, I remembered her words after she'd commanded Nedjes to dispose of all their monuments to the gods. There was no doubting the hatred she felt for them, and her desire to destroy them all, even if it had to be one at a time.

'We need to rest,' she told me. 'We'll meet here in the morning.' She turned on her heel and marched off, accompanied by the remainder of her guards and her maids.

I turned to face Djedetkha, who also looked tired and drawn. She simply shook her head, indicating that she wasn't going to answer any questions.

'I'll take you back to your house,' she told me. 'I need a lot of coffee.'

Chapter Twenty-Three

Everything blurred for an instant, and then we were in almost total darkness. It smelled musty, dank. An atmosphere of decay and neglect. As we stood momentarily in darkness, I knew in my heart that everything I had feared was true.

We were suddenly drowned in light. Nedjes had found some switches on the far wall and had flicked them on. It was at least some comfort to find that there was power. I had worried that there might be nothing.

I looked around. We were in the basement of an office block owned by the Suchos Corporation, situated almost in the dead centre of downtown Denver. It was full of desks, chairs, office equipment of every description. And it was all covered in cobwebs and thick layers of dust. It was the basement, I reminded myself, but it wasn't how I let my buildings be maintained. I believed in order, efficiency, structure, routine and purpose. This was simply neglect.

'Go and check out the rest of the building,' I said to Soshenq, Menkheperre and Djedetkha, and they moved off, heading towards the stairwell on the other side of the room.

Nedjes had got out a small tablet and switched it on, searching for networks to hack into. Our earlier teams had identified that networks and communications systems had not changed very radically over the course of the next eighty years. Or previous, from our current perspective.

'Curtis is still here,' he said. 'He's still recording and documenting.'

I shuddered when I thought about Curtis. I'd seen so many disgusting and depraved sights in my life that almost nothing had the capacity to shock or distress me anymore. But, I'd never met anyone as disturbing or unsettling as James Curtis, and that was saying something. And, thanks to the DNA test that I'd run on him, I knew why.

I moved round the room, studying the neglect and decay as I went. It bothered me. I had no real control over what my employees and subjects did around the world, but this wasn't our culture. This was not Kemet or Suchos. As I had that thought, I sensed something. I couldn't understand what it was, but it unsettled me and I glanced up at Nedjes.

He was staring at me, with a look on his face that I rarely saw. Concern.

'What is it?' I demanded.

'Your Highness,' he began, looking a little awkward. Again, unlike him. 'I wasn't sure how to tell you this.'

'Just tell me,' I said.

'Our reconnaissance teams never found any records of you.'

'I've never been to Denver,' I told him, 'why should that have changed in the future?'

'No, my Queen, that isn't what I meant. They found no records of you anywhere.'

'I don't understand,' I said, feeling confused. The thought was a little like imagining the Earth without the moon, or the sun.

'I don't have an explanation, Your Highness. There appears to be no record of you in the second half of the 21st century. The Suchos Corporation and all its associates continued, but without you.'

'I must have changed my name again.'

'No, my Queen. You simply aren't here.'

'And the island?'

'That's beyond everyone's radar, Your Highness. It's impossible to know anything about it.'

I felt very disturbed by this conversation. He should have told me before, although it wouldn't have had any material bearing on anything. But he should have, nonetheless. I couldn't even begin to make sense of it. I'd existed in this world every day since 1830BC, without a single absence for any reason. What had happened? Maybe I'd left a note for myself to explain, or maybe I'd been incarcerated by the gods? Maybe the microscopic machines inside me had finally broken down, although I couldn't believe that for one moment. They were self-replicating, so that really wasn't likely. I felt some anxiety creeping in, and I pushed it back the way it had come, pressing against it with every metaphorical muscle in my body.

As I wrestled with these disturbing thoughts, the other three returned.

'The building looks abandoned,' Djedetkha said, 'but you should come and have a look outside.'

Glad of the distraction, I turned and followed them back the way they had come, up the dusty stairs towards the ground floor.

As we reached the top of the stairs, I gazed around at what was obviously the reception area. It was no different to the basement. Furniture and equipment were lying around in a very disorderly way, layers of dust coating everything. There were papers and booklets strewn randomly around the floor. It really didn't look like anyone had been in the building for a long time.

I glanced at the vast window that framed the large space.

'I thought we were supposed to arrive at the same time we left?' I asked Nedjes, a little annoyed that this most simple part of the plan had failed.

'We have, Your Highness. It's shortly after midday.'

I shook my head in disbelief and walked over to the glass to get a better look at the world of 2105. The sky was dark, the cloud cover one hundred per cent. A storm was raging in the distance, and rain was falling heavily everywhere. Because of the rain, it wasn't easy to see through the windows, the persistent raindrops obscuring the world outside. I crossed to the front doors and pushed at them. Nothing happened. I turned to Nedjes, and he gestured to Soshenq and Monkheperre, who ran over to the doors and studied the locks. They then straightened up and both gave them a hefty kick. Nothing happened again, although there was, at least, some movement. They kicked again, and then once more, and the doors finally flew open.

I felt my breath drain out of me as the air from the outside hit me. I hadn't been prepared for the heat and humidity that flooded in. I'd naturally assumed from the wet and stormy conditions that it would be cold, but it was actually quite tropical. I'd never been to Denver, as I'd told Nedjes, but from what I did know of the place I hadn't been expecting that.

I walked through the doors and into the world of 2105. It was remarkably underwhelming. In the open air, away from the bright lights in the building, it wasn't quite as dark as it had seemed, although it was hardly summer sunshine. But it was warm and humid. The buildings all around us, which all appeared to be offices, similar to the one we'd brought ourselves to, were dark and apparently equally abandoned. There were lights in the distance, but there seemed to be little happening where we were. No traffic, no people, not even the sound of birds or animals of any description. Just the constant pattering of rain on all sides.

'This is our future?' Djedetkha asked, now alongside me. The sound of dismay in her voice was profound.

'It's their future, not ours,' I told her.

'But we'll have to share it,' she responded. I said nothing. She was right, of course. It had seemed inevitable to me, since the earliest days of the Industrial Revolution, that humanity was on a collision course with climatic disaster. This was the problem with finite beings. All they thought about was what they could conceive of, the world in their own lifetimes. This was still the case, even though the evidence was stark and clear. Maximum profit, minimum outlay. That was how humanity worked. I had always tried to forge my undertakings on sustainability and health growth, but the difference was that I could play the long game, I could be patient and wait for a few centuries for the investment and planning to pay off. Mortal humans were only interested in today. And this was the world they had shaped.

If humanity had been a divine creation, and I had long stopped believing this to be the case, then it showed that even the most divine being was flawed and could make horrible mistakes. I wasn't sure if that was a comfort or not. It certainly didn't feel like it, standing in the doorway of my abandoned building in the middle of a tropical storm in downtown Denver.

What had God been thinking of? He'd already wiped humanity out at least once, but he'd let them return. That struck me as being the classic definition of insanity. Doing the same thing repeatedly, but expecting a different outcome. Maybe God was insane. That might explain a lot.

'Let's go back in,' I said. It was horrible outside, and if I didn't exist in this world, then maybe that wasn't a bad thing. I was reminded of what Ceryse had told me. Could it be that I had actually died?

I turned and re-entered my building, and made my way back down to the basement. Although the district seemed abandoned, I didn't see the need to draw attention to ourselves unnecessarily.

We found some chairs, dusted them down, wiped away all the detritus that had settled on them and sat down in a circle.

'The Peiper Institute is only a mile away,' Nedjes told us. 'It's a reasonably straight walk.'

'How do we get in?' Shoshenq asked. 'Is it open 24 hours?'

'No, but there is security. The plans show an old access tunnel that leads inside, from next to the underground car park. We can get in from there.'

'Surveillance?' Djedetkha interjected.

'Yes, but we can block it.'

'What about Curtis?' Shoshenq said.

I was silent for a moment. I had misled everyone, except Nedjes, about the true nature of our mission. Now was the time for them to know the truth, to know why we were here, and what we were about to do. In principle, it sounded simple, but I knew it would be anything but. The gods weren't about to give us anything for free. Other than death, perhaps. But that was what I was counting on.

Chapter Twenty-Four

Extract from the daily journal of Richard Verlice, Friday 15th March 2024:

I'd been a little surprised that Djedetkha had volunteered herself for a cup of coffee. Or several, in fact. I had no idea what they had all just been through, but they looked weary and drained. They'd also captured a god, and, judging by the evidence, killed several others. I don't know what you do after a mission like that, eighty-one years in the future, but I wouldn't have put having a cosy cup of coffee somewhere near the top of the list.

She sat opposite me, slouched on the sofa, a cup in her hands. She was close physically, but her eyes were a long way away.

'I'm glad you got back safely,' I told her.

'We didn't all make it,' she responded, her eyes still distant.

'So, what happened?'

As I spoke, she turned her head slightly to face me, and her eyes swam slowly back into focus, as if she were returning from another world.

'There was a plan within a plan,' she said.

'What do you mean?'

'I mean that we didn't go there to gather data.'

'So, what did you go for?'

She said nothing, and an uneasy silence followed. I desperately wanted to know more, but I knew there was little point in pressing her. I'd already worked out that, although she was generally far more approachable and amenable than Neferu, she was no less intransigent. If she was going to tell me, she would, regardless of whatever I might say. So, I sat back, sipping my coffee, and waited.

'Do you believe in God?' she finally asked me, her eyes seeking out mine with genuine interest.

'Do you mean the Christian God, or the ancient Egyptian gods?'

'Were you brought up as a Christian?'

'I was, although my family weren't particularly devout. We'd go to church for Christmas, funerals, baptisms, all the usual stuff.'

'But did you believe?'

'I've never really thought about it,' I told her. 'It was sort of there, in the background, but I never really knew anyone who was a strong believer. I know Ceryse and her family went to a Baptist Church, but we never talked about it.'

'I was brought up with the gods,' she said. I saw a look in her eyes that I couldn't quite work out. It was almost an angry sadness. 'They weren't like your God, but they ruled our world. After all, it was Anubis who caused all this to happen.'

Anubis, who I'd seen Neferu kill with her own bare hands. She'd carved his heart out and crushed it under her heel. I couldn't imagine doing that with my God.

'Richard,' she said, looking at me very earnestly, 'what would you do if you found out your God was nothing but a lie?'

'Plenty of people in this world believe he is,' I told her. 'There are probably more people who question God's existence than believe in him.'

'I believed,' she said, 'but it was all a lie.'

'What do you mean?' I asked her. To be honest, I didn't know what I thought of the Kemetian gods, but they weren't gods as I understood the term. According to my belief system, it was impossible to kill a divine and omnipotent entity like God.

'It was all a lie,' she said, staring straight at me, her eyes holding mine with an uncomfortable intensity. I could now see clearly that she was both angry and devastated.

'So, who, what, are they?'

'They're us. Our future.'

I was silent for a moment. This wasn't quite the answer I'd been expecting. Extraterrestrials, perhaps. Or creatures from a parallel universe, or a separate dimension. But human? No, that was crazy.

'They're not human, Djedetkha. Most of them are half-animal, at least.'

'They're not human, no,' she agreed. 'Not fully, anyway.'

'What do you mean?'

'There's something coming, Richard,' she said, 'Something terrible.'

'What?' I demanded. Her words sounded dramatic, if not melodramatic, but there was something about her tone that sent a chill down my spine.

'The gods are our future, Richard,' Djedetkha said, putting her cup down. She looked exhausted, and she settled back onto the couch. Her eyelids began to close.

'I don't understand,' was all I could say. And, of course, I didn't. Nothing she'd just said made any sense to me. I don't know why it frustrated me so much, I should have been used to Kemetians speaking in riddles by now. Neferu specialised in them. She was as opaque as you could get.

By way of response, Djedetkha gently rearranged herself on the couch, rested her head on the arm and closed her eyes. Within seconds she appeared to be asleep.

I avoided the strong temptation to shake her back awake and demand she tell me what she meant, in English that I could actually understand. But, I could see she was exhausted, and I honestly had no idea what she'd experienced. She seemed highly traumatised by whatever she'd been through, so it felt selfish to do anything other than let her rest. And, in truth, what real difference did it make whether I knew what was happening or not? Everything else since I'd met Neferu had gone on around me, with the exception of my saving Djedetkha's life. And should I care too much about the future? The only problem was that, if I understood anything of what she'd said, it would appear that the future was messing with the past.

It hurt my head too much thinking about that, so I got up and went and found a blanket. I carefully placed it over Djedetkha, not wanting to disturb her, although she appeared to be in the sort of sleep that that very little would wake her from. I stood over her for a moment, admiring her weary beauty, before going to get another cup of coffee.

Chapter Twenty-Five

When I'd finished speaking there was only silence. I looked around me at the gathered faces, all of which, even Nedjes, registered shock and disbelief. He had known the truth, but had perhaps not dared to admit it to himself. But, now it was out there. This moment, as we sat there in the basement of a dilapidated and abandoned Suchos Corporation building, was a potential turning point for humanity. Well, maybe not humanity. Kemet, certainly.

Nobody spoke for a long time. I could understand that. When your belief system was turned upside down and everything you thought you knew turned out to be a lie, it was hard to know what to say. I had reacted with absolute fury. Incandescent. But everyone was different, and sometimes you needed time to let things sink in before you exploded with rage. But there was no time for emotion now. We had a job to do, and we had to keep cool heads.

'Are there any questions?' I asked, looking around at them all. I knew that there were plenty of questions, but they knew better than to ask anything that wasn't relevant. What I'd just told them raised some serious questions for everyone, but the mission was everything, and they all knew that. And, in reality, I actually knew very little more than what I'd just told them.

'Let's eat and get some rest,' I said, in response to the silence that had enveloped the room. I wanted to travel under cover of darkness, although, from what I'd seen outside, night-time might not appear very different to daytime in Denver.

Nedjes got out some of our rations, and some bottles of water, and passed them around. We ate in silence. After my briefing, no-one seemed to have any taste for conversation. I could understand that. I'd just destroyed beliefs that they'd all accepted blindly since birth, indoctrinated into them by an older generation that had been equally raised on blind faith. And it had been blind, that was very apparent.

After our small meal, we sat down and rested as well as we could, although I'm sure no-one slept. Maybe I should have told them after they'd rested, that might have been kinder. But I wanted them to know. They'd been lied to for long enough. Now was the time for truth. And revenge.

I couldn't sleep, either. Instead, I focused on my life. The one I'd had before Anubis and Sekhemrekhutawy had stolen it from me. It had been happy. I could remember unhappy times, of course. Who couldn't? But the life was easy, at least in terms of what had followed, and good. Kemet was rich and prosperous and we wanted for nothing. My father, Amenemhat, wasn't a kind man, but he was a King of the most powerful and advanced country in the world. A kind man wouldn't have survived. But he was just and fair. As a father, he was hard on his son, but predictably forgiving of his daughters.

My mother, Aat, who was only one of his wives, tried her best to be an authoritarian mother, but failed miserably. Our maids and tutors were much stricter than her, and my sisters and I knew how to get what we wanted from her at a very early age.

My half-brother had been raised to rule, but he died young. It was a great loss for Kemet, and a real problem for our house. He was the only son. No woman had ever ruled in her own right before, but there was little choice after his death. What made it worse was that my older sister, Neferuptah, had been groomed to replace him, but she had died before him. Her loss was a knife blow to us all. She had been strong and resilient, a woman who had been able to command men with ease.

With her death, the throne passed to the next eldest. Neferusobek. Me. Nobody could have been less suited for the role. At least that had been the case when I was twenty-four. I can clearly remember the bitter tears I shed for my brother when I was given the news of his passing. I wept for him and my sister. But not just for their loss, but for what their deaths meant for me.

I was indeed fortunate to have married Senusret. He was both calming and empowering. He saw some form of greatness in me and helped me to tighten my grasp on kingship. If it hadn't been for him, I dread to think what might have happened to Kemet. As a child, I had enjoyed training with my father's soldiers, and, as an adult, I had enjoyed ceremonial events, but I had no clue about the economy or any aspect of running a vast and highly populated state. I owed everything to Senusret. In truth, he would have been a far better king than me. But, to give myself some credit, I did grow into the role. As time went by, I began to feel more comfortable as supreme ruler, more at peace with the demons that had tormented me.

Until Anubis and the usurper stole it all away from me.

When I had returned to Itj Tawy I had desperately wanted to find out the fate of my younger sisters. Hathorhotep, Nubhotepet and Sithathor. There had been a time, when we were very young, when we had been inseparable. However, as we got older that, naturally, changed, and after I ascended to the throne, I barely saw them. I hoped that I might be able to find them, and maybe even take them back to Los Angeles in 2024. But there had been no time, and any hope I may have had of returning again had been dashed when that degenerate creature Horus had destroyed the bridgehead.

My poor sisters. I have no doubt that Sekhemrekhutawy would not have allowed them to live. And, even if he had, their lives would have been more miserable than if they'd died. Of course, I had a device for time travel and could go back, once again, but I was concerned that if I went back another time, there might be significant damage to the timeline. It hadn't mattered before, because I had planned to fuse time together. But now that this was no longer an option, I needed to be careful.

I had often wondered about the death of Sekhemrekhutawy. Even before I went back in

February, he had died in 1799BC. I hadn't been in Kemet then, so I knew nothing about what had happened to him. Was it possible that it had always been my destiny to kill him and reclaim the pschent? Perhaps it was best not to know. Either way, he was dead, and had died a suitably cowardly death. That was good.

I was wearied by these thoughts. Everything in my life had been simple until that fateful day. And now, it was my hope that I could finally reclaim some simplicity, turn my attention to simply enjoying my life. With my husband. I would know whether this was a possibility in the next few hours, and the thought scared me. It's easy to contemplate the endgame when it's centuries or millennia in the future. But when it's so close you can almost smell it, fear comes calling. Fear of failure. I've never contemplated failure in my life, but I failed in California. The prize was in my hands, but it was snatched away again. I really had no idea what I would do if the same thing happened again. It was simple, really. I had to succeed. There were no other options.

I got to my feet, pulled on my backpack and waited for the others to get themselves ready. I nodded to Nedjes, and he led the way back up the stairs and out of the basement. By now, it was dark outside. Properly dark, not just the overcast and gloomy conditions that had surprised me so much earlier. Night had fallen, and as we made our way out of the building, following Nedjes as he led us, via GPS, towards our destination, nothing stirred. It had been quiet earlier, when I'd stepped out into the deserted and decaying street, but now, under cover of darkness, there seemed a stillness that was almost unnatural. No birds, no animals, not even any distant traffic noise. The city seemed dead, although it clearly wasn't.

It took us about twenty minutes to reach the Peiper Institute, a monstrous concrete and glass building that rose out of the distance like a beacon of light as we approached. The area where the Suchos building was situated was simply abandoned and slowly reverting to nature, but the district surrounding the Institute was different. There was visible damage to the buildings and roads here, and I was reminded of the book I'd read, the constant references to war and civil disorder. The future really didn't seem very inviting.

At one point, we had to crouch down behind a bullet-riddled wall, as some sort of police vehicle trundled past. It was a heavily armoured truck, blue and red lights flashing angrily. A big gun of some sort was mounted on top and, despite its armour, it had some significant dents on one side.

Nedjes led us across a field of debris to the back of the brightly lit building. He indicated the track that led to the underground car park and pointed to a dip in the ground on the right. As I peered at it from our vantage point, I could see that it was, in fact, some sort of large concrete pipe, with a large grill across it.

I nodded understanding, and indicated he lead the way. As he crossed the short distance, he pulled off his backpack and searched for something inside.

'What was it for?' I asked him, when we arrived.

'According to the plans, it was supposed to be some sort of waste outlet, but they seemed to have revised the design. It seems they forgot about it.'

How convenient, I thought. There was something to be said for human incompetence. I hid next to the others in the shadows as Nedjes began to cut the grill with the small bolt cutters he had pulled from his backpack. It wasn't easy, the bars being quite thick, but he was persistent and determined, and, within thirty minutes had cut a space large enough for us all to enter through.

As he carefully laid the excised section of the grill on the ground, Soshenq removed a small device from his backpack and set it down next to the grill. His fingers moved across the controls, and after a moment a small light on it began to flash a very dull red. Every security camera inside the building should now have been blocked. That would alert the guards that something was wrong, but hopefully they would simply believe there was a problem with the hardware, rather than it being the herald of an incursion.

We followed Nedjes into the tunnel, which was about four feet in diameter. It wasn't overly cramped, but it was hardly a comfortable experience crawling through it. It was damp, and covered in a combination of mould and mildew. However, it was a blessing that it had never been used for its original purpose.

We made our way forward, one behind the other, crawling on our hands and knees, for what felt like an age. It was dark, and we each had small torches on our heads, held in place by headbands. The tunnel itself was probably less than a hundred yards in length, but, moving as we were, it felt like it went on for miles.

Nedjes finally came to a halt ahead of me, and I could see that there was a grill in front of him. He grasped it and pushed it forwards, holding on to it as best he could, to prevent it from falling to the floor below. It had clearly been secured on installation, but it seemed that the work had been done poorly, and the screws securing it gave way easily.

He lowered himself carefully to the ground, and I followed him out. He offered me his hand, but I ignored it. I was a Queen, I didn't need anyone's help at times like this. I looked around, taking in our surroundings as the others climbed out of the tunnel. The corridor was sterile and white, brightly lit and mostly featureless. Mostly, because there were doors at irregular intervals.

When we were all safely out, Nedjes led the way down the corridor on our right. He opened a door on our left, and we found ourselves in a stairwell. We went upwards, our soft soled boots making almost no noise on the hard concrete stairs.

We reached the third floor, our destination, and were about to exit the stairwell, when the door opened inwards and we found ourselves face to face with what was, presumably, a security guard. He was tall, dressed in a navy-blue uniform, with a gun at his waist and a badge on his chest bearing the name Jones. He looked remarkably strong, his upper body, in particular, seemed ridiculously muscular. His eyes reminded me of Curtis; black, almost formless, a gateway to emptiness.

'Who the fuck are you?' he exclaimed, as he took us in, his eyes roaming over both our dark combat suits and also our very human faces.

Nedjes said nothing, instead instantly lashing out and hitting him as hard as he could in the stomach. Jones buckled over slightly, although his musculature no doubt saved him from real damage. As he straightened up, a look of fury on his face, Soshenq stepped forward and cracked him over the back of his head with his HK416. Jones fell heavily to the floor, and a small trickle of blood began to run down the back of his head.

Nedjes eased himself out of the stairway door, glancing around him as he did so. The corridor seemed quiet, so he gestured for Soshenq and Menkheperre to bring Jones with them. As they searched for somewhere to hide the body, Djedetkha and I made our way down the corridor, towards Laboratory 304. We found it, near the far end, a plain white door with the number emblazoned on it in bold black numbers.

We waited for the others to return, and then Djedetkha opened the door and went in, Glock in hand. In no more than a few seconds, she opened the door again.

'Curtis isn't here,' she said. It was important that Curtis didn't see Nedjes or myself, since he would be seeing us again in the past, and I was pretty sure he would have been less amenable, if he could ever have been described as anything other than disturbing or unpleasant, if he had known that we had visited him in his own time.

The room was large and as sterile and white as the rest of the building. It was full of the most arcane looking equipment and tools, the various work stations and tables strewn with what appeared to be junk. It reminded me very strongly of the squalor that he insisted on living in at La Misión.

However, on the far side of the room was something that I recognised. Something that was the replica of the device that we had used to reach 2105. But, of course, it wasn't a replica. They were actually the same device. I forced myself not to think about the possible complications and inherent paradoxes of the same object being in the same space eighty-one years apart. It was important that they not come into physical contact with each other, but it was my understanding that as long as they weren't touching, we might avoid a serious implosion.

As we stood there contemplating the device, the laboratory door opened and a young woman in a lab coat marched in. She paused momentarily when she saw us, but then continued over to where we were standing. I was surprised that her face didn't register surprise or shock, but, instead, anger and contempt. She was superficially very beautiful, with long blond hair, but there was something in her face that spoke of cruelty, and her eyes were black and cold.

She said nothing, but simply glared at us.

'Where's Curtis?' I asked her.

'He'll be here at any moment,' she said, in a deep and very resonant voice. 'He'll be pleased to see you. We can talk to him about the work you're going to do together. Or, should that be the work you've already done? It's so confusing, isn't it? Time, I mean.' She said all this as if she was discussing a recipe, or something equally banal, with a friend, but as she spoke, her eyes, which were fixed on me, were filled with the worst darkness imaginable

I nodded to Djedetkha, who began to move back towards the door to the laboratory. But she never reached it. The instant she started to move, the woman burst into action, kicking Djedetkha hard in the leg. She fell to the ground. As she did so, a familiar sound began to ring out all around us. The wall behind the woman filled with a vortex, but before it could expand, Nedjes pulled a small box from his pocket and pressed a button, activating it. The vortex stalled, and then faded away.

A look of, first horror, and then full-on anger, filled her face. She lunged for me, but Shoshenq and Menkheperre grabbed her arms, restraining her. As they did so, her whole body shimmered and she transformed, in front of our eyes, into a creature with a lion's head. Sekhmet.

She roared savagely, and lashed out at her captors. Unprepared for her strength, their grasp slipped momentarily, and her arms came free. She turned to Menkheperre and slashed at him, gouging large pieces of flesh from his face. As he screamed in pain, she picked him up and threw him into the nearest wall, head first. He hit the wall with a sickening thud, and slowly sank to the ground, a pool of blood instantly starting to form at his feet.

Djedetkha, who was back on her feet, along with Nedjes and Shoshenq, threw themselves on her, forcing her to the ground. Nedjes pulled some restraints from a pocket and handcuffed her hands behind her back. As he did that, Djedetkha hit her hard in the kidneys, and Sekhmet howled in pain. She hit her again, and again, until she went quiet and stopped struggling.

I rushed across to where Menkheperre had fallen, but he was dead. I glared at the fallen god and kicked her hard in the face. She howled again.

'By the time we've finished with you, you'll wish we'd killed you here,' I shouted at her, struggling to control me anger.

'You are an abomination!' she hissed at me.

I knelt down next to where her head was resting against the hard and unrelenting floor tiles. I pulled it up by her lion-like mane.

'You are the abomination,' I told her, slamming her head down onto the floor. I reached over to where her hands were secured, and pulled the black power ring off her finger. I put it in my pocket and stood up. Nedjes and the others took my lead, jerking Sekhmet to her feet. She was clearly dazed and in pain, and struggled to maintain her balance.

'I've programmed the location, Your Highness,' Nedjes told me, handing Curtis' revamped time travel device to me. 'You know how to get back?'

'I do. There's no need to worry about that,' I told him, although what he probably did need to worry about was whether I would be able to get back. 'But, if I'm not back in five minutes, carry on with the plan without me.'

He gave me a look that said there was no way that was going to happen, but nodded in silent agreement.

'Don't let that thing even breathe,' I said to Djedetkha and Soshenq, and then activated the device. Once again, everything blurred, and then I found myself in a hall filled with the most blinding white light. Before my eyes could adjust to the light, however, I felt a sharp pain in my head and was knocked to the ground. Everything instantly went black.

Chapter Twenty-Six

Extract from the daily journal of Richard Verlice, Friday 15th March 2024:

Djedetkha was asleep for about four hours. She slept soundly and barely moved. While she lay on the sofa, lost in some other dreamworld, I struggled to fill my time. I drank plenty of coffee, and wrote some entries for my journal. There was plenty to note down, although I had wondered what the real point was. Who else would ever look at this, other than me? But maybe that was the point. A chance to reflect on what had happened, to remind myself that all of this had been real, that I really had been the boyfriend of an immortal Ancient Egyptian queen, even if only for the shortest period of time. I wished that I could draw, because it would have been wonderful to have been able to illustrate these recollections. However, the only thing I did worse than drawing was ice skating. And gardening. And quite a lot of other things, in fact, when I thought about it. But I absolutely couldn't draw.

I had kept a journal for as long as I could remember. My parents had a box full of them back home, although I hope they never read them. That would have been super embarrassing. Possibly not as embarrassing as my detailed recollections of my sexual experiences with Neferu, though.

Once I'd written, I'd had some more coffee, and then I'd simply sat and watched Djedetkha. There was something relaxing and calming about watching someone peacefully asleep. Especially someone so beautiful and so nearly perfect. I sat quietly, watching the gentle rise and fall of her chest, hearing the soft susurration of her restful breathing. I wondered what, if anything, she was dreaming of. Did she dream in Ancient Egyptian or in English, I wondered? Maybe another language. I was sure she spoke many. It was very apparent that Neferu believed in maximum investment in her subjects. After all, apart from her accomplishments as a combat-trained soldier, and her bedroom skills, Djedetkha also had a first-class honours degree in law from Harvard. So, it was probably reasonable to assume that her bow had several other strings.

She eventually woke up when her phone started buzzing. She stirred slowly, from what had obviously been a deep sleep, and searched around for it. She appeared a little startled when I handed it to her, having picked it up from the floor, where it had fallen when she'd begun moving. She had presumably forgotten where she'd fallen asleep.

She looked at it, and was instantly awake.

'Get yourself ready, Richard,' she told me, putting her phone down. 'Our Queen is going to address the people in thirty minutes.' She got up, carefully folding up the blanket and handing it back to me, before heading for the bathroom. She'd said nothing, but there had been the smallest of smiles on her face as she'd given it to me. That was thanks enough.

In twenty-five minutes, we were standing amongst a vast crowd of people in front of the Royal Palace, waiting for Neferu's undoubtedly grand entrance. As I looked around me, I saw expectant faces on all sides. Although the whole experience was new to me, it was clear that this wasn't an event that happened too often. However, unlike my own country, where our great leader could always be found pontificating on absolutely nothing of any interest on any number of TV channels, there were no social media outlets on Isla de Gran Esperanza, so the only way of hearing what the Queen said was to actually be in her presence. She was a great orator, that had been apparent when I'd stood with her on the steps of the Royal Palace in Itj Tawy, nearly four thousand years ago. It was ironic that someone who gave so little away should be such a powerful public speaker.

The crowd suddenly hushed itself as a squad of Neferu's guards appeared on the raised platform in front of us. They led their prisoner, Sekhmet, out of the shadows and to the left of the stage. A moment later, the Queen herself, flanked by the ever-present Nedjes and more of her guards, appeared from the other side of the Palace, and crossed to the right of where Sekhmet was being held.

Neferu looked simply stunning. Although it had only been just over two weeks since I'd last seen her dressed in this way, I'd almost forgotten how incredible she looked dressed as a Queen of Kemet. A very modern Queen of Kemet, it had to be said. She wore what was essentially a black sheath dress, with two broad shoulder straps, decorated all over with gold thread and the most colorful beadwork imaginable. The dress was both ancient and modern, straddling four thousand years of history in one powerful fashion statement. In addition, and as you would expect, she wore an array of bracelets, rings, earrings, necklaces and amulets, all appearing to be made from gold, and inlaid with archetypal Kemetian stones like lapis lazuli, turquoise, carnelian and amethyst. I noticed that the images of Sobek and Petbe, which she had worn when I'd last seen her dressed like this, were now gone, and she was modelling fairly standard representations of a scarab beetle, a vulture and a cobra.

Her makeup was her usual blend of traditional and modern, similar to that favoured by so many Arabic women in the modern world. As usual, and hardly surprisingly, she was wearing gold high heels, with her finger and toe nails the vivid blue of lapis. As was her personal taste, she wore no beard and no wig, her own silken and lustrous hair hanging long, swirling slightly in the light breeze that moved through the island. Crowning this almost divine vision of immortal beauty was her crown, the Pschent combining Upper and Lower Kemet, a powerful statement of her eternal power.

The crowd had roared as one when she'd appeared, and from where I stood it appeared completely genuine. There was joy on the faces of those all around me, as they stared at the woman who had ruled their world for longer than any civilisation that had ever risen up.

She raised her arms and lowered them, a sign that the acclaim and jubilation should be reined in, at least for the moment. She had no problem with such mass adoration, she simply wanted her words to be heard. Another hush slowly descended on the gathered masses, and Neferu took a step closer to the front of the platform.

'My people!' she said, her powerful voice loud enough to be clearly heard from every side of the square in front of the Palace. 'I have called you here to share the most important news with you.' She paused for a moment, ensuring all eyes were drawn to her. 'I have news that will change your world, news that will turn what you believe upside down.' She paused again, letting those words sink in. I was drawn in, realising that I was holding my breath as I waited to hear what she was going to say next. 'You will know that I have had all statues revering our gods removed and destroyed. You may have wondered why I would perform such an act of desecration and disrespect. My people, I have done this because I have discovered that these gods are not gods!'

She paused again, to allow the ripples and murmurs that rose in the gathered crowd to slowly die down. When all was quiet again, she continued.

'These gods are false gods, and they have misled us for nearly five thousand years. They have lied to us and manipulated us for their own ends. And not just us. These false gods have appeared to Greeks,

Romans and many other civilisations throughout history.'

She crossed to where Sekhmet was being held very securely. The god hissed at her and struggled against her captors, but, despite her obvious strength, she was unable to gain even an inch of freedom.

'This creature is Sekhmet. I'm sure you all know of her, but this is the reality.' Nedjes crossed to Neferu and handed her a jewelled dagger. She took it from him and stuck it into the side of Sekhmet. She screamed in pain, and blood began to seep from the wound. As the crowd gasped, and some screamed, Neferu turned to face them, handing the bloody knife back to Nedjes.

'This is the reality of our gods. They are flesh and blood, like us. They bleed just like us, and they can die, just like us. I know that we have all been taught to worship and respect them, but they have lied to us down through the ages. I exist now because of their duplicity and corruption. They are not gods. They are the humans of the future.'

The crowd roared at this, the sound a combination of dissenting emotions, some angry, some scared, some simply disbelieving.

'I have been to their world in the future. I have seen their sterile and hopeless world. I have fought them and I have killed many of them. They are an abomination, and they have lied to us for the last time. We have been set free from their slavery.'

She paused again, staring at the bewildered faces in front of her. Some were shocked, some were scared, some were angry. This wasn't what they'd expected to hear, that was obvious. To be honest, it wasn't what I'd expected to hear. The humans of the future? This was what Djedetkha had been avoiding telling me before she fell asleep.

'My people. There is nothing to fear. We are at war, but we will win this war. The only real enemy is our fear. You know that I have never once failed you, so I ask you to believe me when I tell you all this, and when I tell you that we are already victorious. The gods came from dust, and they will return to dust.'

She turned back to face Sekhmet, who was still bleeding, and was staring at Neferu with something beyond hatred.

'This creature bleeds and can die. There is no need to fear anything that is mortal. We are stronger and we are better than them. We are Kemet!' As she said this, she turned back to the crowd and raised her arms, as if in exhortation. At this gesture, the crowd once again erupted with noise, although, this time, it didn't seem quite as jubilant or joyous. Neferu had burst a few bubbles today, there was no question of that.

She turned, and headed back inside the Palace, Nedjes and her guards following her. Sekhmet was led away, back through the door she had entered from. As the platform in front of us emptied, people began to talk amongst themselves. There was too much Ancient Egyptian being uttered for me to be able to make sense of any of it, but I could tell from the faces around me that the Queen's news had created a mixed bag of emotions and feelings. Unsurprisingly. It's hard to imagine how anyone would feel who found out that their belief system had been little more than a blatant lie, perpetrated by inhuman creatures from the future.

I felt a hand on my arm. I turned to face Djedetkha.

'Let's go,' she said. I nodded and followed her away from the Royal Palace.

Chapter Twenty-Seven

I wasn't insensate for long. Those microscopic machines always worked overtime when something happened to my body, and I had revived within a minute or so. Soon enough to be aware of my surroundings as I was dragged through the corridors of the gods. It had been an interesting experience, although that probably was not the right word. Unique, perhaps. I supposed that not many people had ever had the privilege of being inside the home of their gods. Except that being there was no privilege, and these weren't gods. Simply bastardised humans.

Two of Sobek's crocodile warriors had dragged me to some sort of cell, where I had been unceremoniously dumped. It was, like the corridors outside, featureless, bright, white, and completely sterile. It was hard not to draw the conclusion that their architecture and interior décor reflected their personalities and their society. There was no furniture, so I had simply sat on the floor. Not very dignified for a Queen, but I hardly cared. There were more important issues at that moment in time than my comfort and dignity.

I had no idea how long I had remained in that mind-numbingly dull cell, if that was what it truly was. Time was a relative concept for me. Whereas the rest of the human race lived their lives by minutes and hours, a constant race against the clock, my life was measured in an entirely different way. A way that no-one alive would understand or recognise. For me, the passing of time was like a river flowing into the ocean, with no beginning and no end.

So, I could have been in there for minutes, hours, or maybe even days. I was patient. One thing Anubis had taught me was patience. I had been patient since 1802BC.

Eventually, the door had opened and two more of Sobek's guards had entered, grabbed me by my arms and led me out of the room.

They were now leading me through what felt like an almost infinite array of identical corridors, each one as sterile and anodyne as the last.

I glanced briefly at my captors, whose reptilian faces were devoid of any human expression. The last time I'd seen them, they were helping me to restore my husband and regain my throne. I thought about all of that. I had thought that these creatures were hard to understand, but I now realised that they were all too human. Sobek had assisted me in killing one of his own kind, and had helped me go back in time to kill the pretender that Anubis had set on my throne. Just because these creatures pretended to be gods didn't mean that they weren't ruled by the age-old human emotions. I was now only too well aware that I had unwittingly taken part in a power struggle. Sobek had wanted more than he'd been given, and saw Anubis, and maybe Horus, as obstacles. How convenient to let me do his dirty work. And, when you merged the corruption and greed of humanity with the brute instinct of animals, you had a race of creatures who were ruthless and narcissistic. It was hard to see any redeeming features in their brave new world.

The world they lived in reflected all of this. I was taken through sterile, featureless corridors, brightly lit and with no distinctive features whatsoever. There was no ornamentation, no artworks, no embellishments of any sort. From what I could see, which was only a part of their kingdom, these were soulless creatures, whose sole gratification came through the slavish worship of the people they had chosen to torment. Although

Jonathan Peiper had manufactured a path forward through the crisis that had doomed humanity, he had done so at a great cost to the unborn children he'd saved. And that cost had been passed on to the generations of humans who had followed them.

I thought briefly about the crisis. I didn't want to dwell on that right now. All the research we'd discovered had led to one simple conclusion. It wasn't one that I liked or that made me feel better about what had happened, but there were potential solutions. I needed to focus on those, rather than the root cause.

As the crocodile creatures dragged me ever onwards, we passed a large window. What I saw outside confirmed my worst fears. The sky was dark, although it didn't seem to be night. The sky was filled with dark clouds and rain was falling incessantly. It reminded me of the world we'd witnessed in Denver, but all I could see outside was water. It was possible that these false gods had built their citadel on an island, but there was a far more likely possibility. I knew from the readings we'd taken earlier, when we'd detected the presence of time travel, that I was currently in the year 2268 and that I was still in Denver. The fact that all I could see was water told me that global warming had continued unhindered and the world's ice had melted. Our forecasts suggested that this would have raised the sea level by almost three hundred feet. These creatures had inherited a world that was almost uninhabitable, and it didn't seem that they had much interest in doing anything significant about that.

My captors moved ever on, leaving the window far behind. I couldn't be sure how far we travelled, because every corridor looked the same, and some curved inwards. However, I estimated that they'd been marching for around twenty minutes when we arrived at an immense set of double doors. Featureless, gleaming white double doors, which slid apart as we approached, revealing a vast and cavernous amphitheatre inside. They dragged me inside, and took me to an area that, from my perspective, resembled a stage. The room radiated outwards in a large curve, with the floor angling gently upwards, giving the impression of an ancient amphitheatre. It struck me, and it made me feel even more angry thinking about it, that maybe it was these creatures who'd given the design to the peoples of the ancient world. It was certainly a common enough sight in the worlds of Greece and Rome. It was hard to believe the arrogance of these creatures who presented themselves as divine entities, operating in the interests of nurturing humanity, but who were, in reality, little more than subhumans.

I was on the stage, held tightly by the two crocodile warriors, and in front of me, filling the amphitheatre, was an army of the gods. Either my presence had been anticipated, or they all had so little to do that they could attend at a moment's notice. It was, I believed, less than half an hour since I'd arrived in their citadel.

I looked at the creatures facing me, and I could recognise most of them, although even I wasn't fully aware of the identities of every single god. I saw Ptah, Thoth, Bastet, Maahes, Petbe, Nefertum and so many more. I couldn't see either Isis or Hathor, which surprised me, but maybe they were lurking at the back of the crowd. I didn't think that was very likely, given what I knew about them, but it was possible. Maybe they were elsewhere, causing havoc and mayhem amongst my people.

Standing right in front of me, of course, was the god I had been named for. Sobek. Once my rock and my support, now simply yet another corrupt and deceitful creature. I realised now that I had been played, as the Americans like to say. Sobek had known me well enough to know that I wanted more than just the restoration of Senusret. He knew that I wanted revenge for the millennia of suffering that Anubis had inflicted on me. And he knew that he could use this for his own benefit. The evidence was clear, after all. He stood directly in front of me, orchestrating proceedings. Very clever for a crocodile.

'So, daughter,' his deep voice boomed out, echoing slightly in the large space. 'You have decided to visit us.'

I struggled against my captors, and he gestured briefly at them. He knew there was nowhere for me to go, no way that I could hope to kill all of these creatures, no matter how skilled or armed I was. The guards released my arms, and I moved them around a little, getting the blood flowing again.

'What did you hope to achieve by coming here?' he demanded. Despite the situation, it was amusing to witness his showboating in front of his fellow fake gods.

'I wanted to see your face one last time before you die,' I told him.

A strange sound boomed out of his mouth, and I realised that he was laughing. The sound was echoed throughout the room, in a variety of different ways, by the many creatures present.

'Neferusobek, the only person here who is going to die is you,' he told me, when he'd stopped laughing. 'We will drain the nanobots from your body, and we will destroy you.'

'My name is not Neferusobek any more,' I told him.

'Oh? Are you ashamed of being named after me? Have I ever failed you, child?'

'Your continued existence reflects more on my failure, Lord Sobek,' I responded, using his title to reinforce my contempt for him. 'I regret that my naivety has permitted you to master the cruel game that you have been playing.'

'Do not insult me, child,' he boomed, an angry tone creeping into his voice. 'There has been no game. It is hardly our fault if you are too primitive and simple to understand the ways of the gods.'

Now it was my turn to laugh, although, in truth, I found nothing funny in his words. But I wanted to reinforce my contempt and loathing for him and his kind.

'How dare you laugh at me!' he roared.

'Should I not laugh when you give me reason to do so, my lord?' I asked him.

'You are insolent. Anubis should have killed you outright when he had the chance.'

'Anubis. Who you stood by and watched die at my hand,' I reminded him.

'Do not presume to judge me!'

'I do not judge you, Sobek. Your deeds and your words are judgement enough.'

'Have you come simply to provoke us, to incur even more of our wrath?'

'No, my Lord. I have come to kill you. To kill you all.' As I said this, I simply stared coldly at him, letting my deep and infinite hatred soak into his corrupt soul.

He laughed again, as did all those around him. Even my captors, now standing at the side of the platform, joined in.

'You have entered the lion's den, Neferusobek,' he responded, when he'd finished his gloating laugh. 'You will die here, not me.'

'I am the lion's tamer, my Lord. You may call me Neferuhadebnetjer.'

There was silence for a few moments, while he and those around him absorbed this. Neferu, Killer of the Gods. That was how I know wished to be known, how I wanted history to remember me. I was no vassal of this diseased creature, I had become his nemesis. The nemesis of them all.

'You think that we are arrogant, but you are the one who has come here on your own stating you will destroy us.' Thoth spoke, from behind Sobek's right shoulder. His voice was reedy and quite inhuman, as you might expect from a human who had been merged with an ibis.

'I am arrogant, my Lord, but my arrogance is based on my certain knowledge that I am, actually, superior. I have lived for 3,854 years. Your arrogance is based on vacuous conceit. A conceit that will be your downfall.' It occurred to me that everything I had endured, the pain and suffering of all those long years, had been for this moment. Saving my husband was my life's work, but bringing an end to these abominations and ensuring that they never came into being, was my gift to humanity. And my revenge for what they had done to me.

I flexed my arms and retrieved my backpack. I opened it, and quickly placed the device that had brought me here into the titanium case that had been engineered for it, and slipped it inside my combat jacket. I then pressed a switch on the other, far larger device in the backpack. A red light appeared, flashing intermittently, invitingly.

'What are you doing, child?' Sobek demanded, a look of concern on his face for the first time since I'd appeared in front of him.

'I'm preparing to say goodbye, Lord Sobek,' I told him, smiling coldly, enjoying the moment. I wouldn't let it last, but I wanted to savour this very brief instant. The instant before their world ended.

'What is in that bag?' he demanded. He glanced at his soldiers, perched anxiously at the edge of the platform, some ten feet away from me. 'Did you search her?' he demanded of them.

They, for their part, looked guilty, but began to march towards me, hoping to make amends for their predictable oversight. The oversight that I knew these arrogant creatures would make.

'This is how your world ends,' I told Sobek, smiling defiantly at him and his fellow gods, even though I knew that I was about to inflict the most unimaginable pain on myself.

'Stop!' he commanded, as he and the other abominations in the room all began to rush towards me.

I reached into the backpack and pressed the switch next to the flashing red light. For the briefest moment, nothing happened, the world around me moving in slow motion, as the hordes of hybrid humans raced towards me. And then the world exploded. Literally.

The force of the explosion, and the noise it generated, were like nothing I had ever experienced before. I felt myself being torn apart, could feel every atom in my body being ruptured and crushed by the sheer force of the power being unleashed. I could hear myself screaming as the most agonising pain I had ever experienced rushed through my fragmented body. And then, once again, everything went black. Thankfully.

Chapter Twenty-Eight

Abridged version of Chapter Ten, The Global Crisis and its Resolution: How Humanity was Reinvented. Kaddo, R.A. Damascus. 2106:

The wars that followed were crippling (Moss and Patterson, 2098). A world that was in decline could barely cope with the economic and demographic devastation of war. And a series of local wars, built on the fear of the unlike, gradually merged into one large, global conflict. The battlegrounds were the streets of every city, and the sides were simple, yet complex at the same time. It was the pure-blood human, whose blood was now not only not pure but very tainted, against the perceived future of humanity, the human-animal hybrids (Moss and Patterson, 2098).

The Purebloods were never going to win. Aside from the tidal wave of hope that the new hybrids had generated, the Purebloods were at the severe disadvantage of being a dying race, their every member damaged and disabled in some significant way. They fought hard, and with an increasingly bitter resolve, but they really had no future. They wouldn't accept it, but their world was already over.

In the midst of this global conflagration, whose cost in purely human lives has been variously estimated at between one and five billion, the work of Jonathan Peiper continued, given new strength by the fierce support he had received from so many vastly wealthy individuals and corporations who had a vested interest in wanting to survive (Cavanagh, 2102).

The dust from these wars slowly settled, although the wounds created remained open and unhealing. Purebloods remained, despite their profound and damning defeat, but they chose to disappear into the shadows of the world that had once been theirs, a world now severely suffering from the global warming that they and their ancestors had precipitated through their thoughtless and selfish mass production of greenhouse gases over the course of two hundred years (Fernandez, 2095).

Research sped up on the merging of human-animal DNA, and many brilliant minds were created using the new techniques (Peiper, 2097). Minds that were, it has to be admitted, both fragile and something more, and occasionally less, than human. One such mind was that of Dr James Curtis, a man whose personal pedigree merged Human Caucasian with Mandrill. He turned his attention to the disputed area of time travel (Duquesne, 2106), and had made some significant progress when both he and his research work were destroyed in a catastrophic explosion at the Peiper Institute in Denver, Colorado (Duquesne, 2106). His work was abandoned due to fears over the forces that he may have unleashed. Reports that a body matching his DNA profile had been recovered from Zaitunay Bay in Beirut during rebuilding work at the end of the twentieth century remain unsubstantiated (Vincey, 2106).

Chapter Twenty-Nine

When I regained consciousness, everything was black. At first, I presumed that the explosion had destroyed everything, but when I thought about it, I realised that there should still have been some light, if only from the outside world. But it was black. The reason, it occurred to me, was simply because the machines had not yet completed their task of healing me. My optic nerves had been shredded, along with the rest of me, and they had still not been healed. So, I was blind. I also couldn't move. I had no sensation in any part of my body, presumably because it was still being restored.

    I simply stayed in the moment, waiting for feeling and sensation to return. There was nothing more I could do. After a few minutes, I began to sense light, blurry at first, but gradually coalescing into something more solid and concrete. I started to get feeling in nerve endings, that had, until a few moments before, been dead and unresponsive. And, as my whole being slowly came back to life, I realised that I could hear something. I wasn't sure what it was at first, since my hearing had also been destroyed. But, as everything in my body was slowly restored, I understood what the sound was. It was screaming. The sound of a soul in the most terrible torment, a heartbreaking sound of pain and suffering. It took a few more moments before I realised that the sound was coming from me.

I was screaming. Screaming with the pain of death, dismemberment and the most terrible suffering imaginable.

As my body returned to itself, I forced myself to stop screaming. It wasn't easy. I hadn't been aware of what I'd been doing, and it had almost been an instinctive reaction. But, I stopped and lay still and quiet, until I felt certain that I was once again whole. I slowly got to my feet, testing my newly healed body parts to make sure I wasn't going to fall flat on my face. But it seemed that the tiny machines inside me had done their usual excellent job, and my body had been restored. I ached a little, but I knew that would pass in a minute or two, and I would feel in the most perfect health. Which, of course, was my constant state of being.

As I got to my feet, I looked around. The scene was every bit as horrible as I'd hoped it would be. We had planned to cause the most devastating explosion possible, given the device had to fit inside a backpack, and our calculations had been reassuringly accurate. The room had been blown apart, and the amphitheatre was now open to the elements. I was now confronted with the reality of the Earth of 2286, with rain pouring down from all sides, blown around by the howling wind that seemed to come from every possible direction. This entire part of the citadel appeared to have been eviscerated, much like the false gods who had assembled there to witness my demise.

My clothes had been shredded, but the box containing the time travel device remained intact, as we had also planned. That was a significant relief. This was not a place or time I wanted to find myself trapped in. I looked around the room. Body parts were strewn everywhere, and those who had been closest to me when the bomb went off had been almost completely dismembered.

I took a little time to go around the room collecting the power rings that were lying loose on the floor, their owners shredded into non-existence.

There was no sound anywhere, save for the wind and the rain, and the sound of the sea outside lashing the 23rd century coastline. I had believed that these creatures would flock to see my humiliation and destruction, and I felt confident that the only ones who would have survived would be those who weren't physically in 2268. It was irritating and disappointing that any would have survived, but I could deal with a small number of them. It would be relatively easy to seek them out and exterminate them.

I took a last glance around me, wanting to remember this happy scene as it was, before taking the device out of its titanium case and activating it. Once again, everything blurred, and then I found myself back in Curtis' laboratory, Nedjes, Djedetkha and Shoshenq staring at me in surprise. Sekhmet merely glared. Nedjes opened his backpack and pulled out another combat suit and boots, which he handed to me. I'd forgotten I was completely naked, which explained their surprise.

'Mission accomplished,' I told them, as I started pulling on the clothes. 'How long was I gone?'

'About two minutes,' Nedjes told me. I turned to Djedetkha and Shoshenq. 'We'll go back to the building.' I told them. Their task now was to ensure Curtis was sent back to 2017. Nedjes and I couldn't let him see us, for obvious reasons.

Nedjes led the way, and we carefully retraced our steps back to the Suchos building, taking Sekhmet with us. She struggled at first, but a few well-aimed gun butts to her head and kidneys made her more amenable.

As we descended the stairs to the basement, it seemed a little surreal to think that only an hour or so had passed since we'd left there. We travelled in silence, as we usually did. I'm sure Nedjes wanted to know the details of what had happened, but he knew better than to ask, and I really didn't want to talk about it at all. I also didn't want to talk about any of it in front of a false god.

'You will pay for this!' Sekhmet hissed at me, as we secured her to a column in the centre of the room.

'I already have,' I replied, turning my back on her. I felt nothing but loathing and contempt for her. She only existed because we needed her. A live specimen was essential in finding a cure for Zvidsai-Charig Syndrome, as well as to demonstrate to my people just how false their gods really were.

We waited in silence for an hour, and then we heard footsteps descending the stairs. We pulled out our Glocks and took up defensive positions, but relaxed as soon as we saw Djedetkha and Shoshenq framed by the dim light of the basement.

'All done,' Djedetkha told us. 'He came back about thirty minutes after you'd gone. We took him by surprise, and sent him back.'

'It was easy,' Shoshenq added. 'He might be part-mandrill, but he wasn't that strong.'

'Well done,' I congratulated them. I turned to Nedjes. 'Let's go.'

While Djedetkha and Shoshenq took charge of Sekhmet, Nedjes took the device from his backpack, where he'd stored it after my return to Curtis' laboratory, and moved his hands over the controls. Everything blurred yet again.

Chapter Thirty

From the Los Angeles Chronicle Online, Friday 15th March 2024:

'California Catastrophe: The Latest News.

'By Kalandra Straub, Senior Investigative Reporter.

'The news from the Sunshine State doesn't get any better. Every day there is news of more lives lost, and more bodies dragged from the rubble. Unofficial estimates of the dead have now moved above the three million mark. California has been devastated, both in terms of the loss of life and also the loss of land, with so much of the state now being under water.

'And yet the guilty are no closer to being named and shamed. Despite everything that has happened, the government in Washington remains mostly silent, avoiding any discussion on who is to blame and who should be indicted. There is no process in law under way, only endless and meaningless congressional committees, whose sole aim appears to be to avoid coming to any conclusions. While the overpaid and privileged talk in circles, the individual responsible continues to swan around, protected by her wealth and her position, untouched and brazenly continuing with her life, while millions in California have no life beyond the living hell that has been created for them.

'We are no longer allowed to mention names, for fear of prosecution and censure, but the guilty party remains as uncaring and narcissistic as ever. Only this week, the individual who personally payrolled the particle accelerator at La Misión, brazenly used financial privilege and a barrage of bullets to escape the country, when confronted with arrest and questioning by Homeland Security. While this shocking and corrupt situation prevails, there will never be any justice for the millions of victims of this terrorist outrage in the supposed land of the free.

'We call upon the government of this land to take responsibility for its actions, and to surrender the individual it is protecting, so that the wounds so callously and carelessly inflicted on California may be allowed to start to heal.'

Chapter Thirty-One

Extract from the daily journal of Richard Verlice, Friday 15th March 2024:

As Djedetkha led me back to my house, I tried to make some sense of what I'd just heard. Neferu had just dropped a bit of a bombshell, to say the least. I hadn't really known what to make of the gods. I hadn't believed in them at all, other than as a superstitious belief system for a primitive people in awe of their world, and fearful of the apparently arbitrary maliciousness of mother nature. Seeing Anubis a fortnight ago had been something of a shock, something that turned my world upside down, much like everything else that happened then. I had not known what to think, especially as Neferu had killed first him, and then Horus. I hadn't even believed in the Christian God, so it was hard to accept that the gods of Ancient Egypt were real.

However, there should have been some red flags for me in the fact that everything that happened was science, rather than magic, based. Even the restoration of Senusret, which I really couldn't even begin to get my head around, was based on some very arcane scientific principles. I remember what Neferu had said to me, echoing something that one of my professors at college had said many years earlier, that everything we ascribed to magic or the paranormal was simply science that we didn't yet understand. If I invested in that belief, then I could allow for the many unbelievable things that had happened. But, and this was the thing that I needed to absorb, if everything that happened was scientific, including Neferu's immortality, then it was surely safe to assume that there was a scientific rationale for the beings that purported to be gods. There was no supernatural aura to their actions, no divine nature in evidence. So, it stood to reason that they had to be living, breathing creatures. It was just hard to stomach the fact that they were our future.

My thoughts were interrupted by our arrival at my house. It was interesting to think of it as mine. I wondered if that would really be true, when this was all over, whatever this actually was. Would Neferu allow me to stay, if I wanted to? The thought was not without its attractions, Djedetkha included. It was a beautiful island, with the

Kemetian settlement seeming almost like a paradise on earth. If Ceryse was determined to stay in 1982, then maybe this was as good a place as any to live my life. If I returned to the USA, there would undoubtedly be some difficult questions to ask, especially since Homeland Security would be more than aware of my continued links with Neferu.

Djedetkha went in first, which I thought was interesting. She clearly wasn't interested in going to her own home, wherever that might be in the settlement. She went into the lounge, and threw herself down on the couch that she'd only recently been asleep on. I hoped she might stay awake a bit longer this time. I enjoyed her company, for more than just the obvious reasons, and I wanted to talk.

I sat down opposite her.

'Do you want a drink?' I asked her.

'Something stronger than coffee, perhaps,' she suggested.

Why not? I thought. It wasn't every day your world was turned upside down and you were given a small, but terrifying, insight into the future of mankind. And I felt certain that her day had been like nothing I could imagine.

I got up and went hunting in the kitchen area. It didn't take long for me to find a bottle of 2020 Domaine Des Tourelles, from the Bekaa Valley.

There were some glasses nearby, but what did take some time to find was a corkscrew. I hunted through the kitchen drawers, and tried to think what else might get a cork out of a bottle. But, just as I was about to resort to some rather desperate measures, I came across a gold-plated corkscrew, hidden at the back of a drawer full of place mats and an oven glove.

I opened the bottle, grabbed two glasses and crossed back to where we were sitting. I poured us each a glass and sat down.

'Here's to you,' I said, holding up my glass for a toast.

'Here's to our Queen,' Djedetkha said, touching her glass against mine.

'What'll happen when this is all over?' I asked her.

'When what's over?' she asked me, looking slightly surprised.

'When Senusret is rescued and the two of them are ruling together.'

'Life will go on. What else do you think will happen?'

'But Neferu has based her entire life since 1802BC on her quest for getting Senusret back. This whole society has been built on that goal. Surely it won't have any purpose after that?'

'Kemet is Kemet,' she told me, and I could see she didn't really understand my point. 'We will continue as we always have. Besides, we still have work to do.'

'What work?'

'Those creatures,' she said, finishing her glass and holding it out for some more. She clearly had felt the need for something stronger than coffee.

'What do you mean?'

'The war is over. But there is still work to be done. We have to save the future.'

I looked at her as she said this. She sounded very dramatic, melodramatic even, and also slightly pompous. I knew she'd already downed a large glass of 13% red wine, but she really wasn't making sense.

'If the war is over, why do we, you, have to save the future?'

'Because the future is still at risk, Richard,' she said, somewhat patronisingly, as if talking to a child. Maybe it felt that way to her.

'Djedetkha, I don't understand. Can you please just tell me what you mean?'

She sighed, and drank some more of the wine I'd just poured her.

'Richard,' she started, sounding a little frustrated with me. 'Haven't you been paying attention?'

'God, I've tried!' I told her, feeling a little exasperated myself now. 'But neither you or Neferu wants to speak plain English. Every answer is as clear as mud.'

'Okay,' she said, finishing the glass and, again, holding the empty vessel out for a refill. I poured what was left in the bottle for her. I hoped she wasn't going to ask for more. I didn't want to have to deal with her being sick everywhere. 'There is a problem with the future. Okay? In a year or so, babies are going to start being born with congenital problems. As the years go past, this is going to increase exponentially, until by the year 2036 the World Health Organisation will publicly acknowledge that a global catastrophe that threatens the survival of the human race is on its way. Is that clear enough?'

'Perfectly, thank you,' I said. She was now clearly under the influence of the alcohol, and I found her rather didactic, almost parental, attitude towards me quite amusing. And very sweet, although I was less charmed by what she was telling me. 'Was it a disease or something?'

'It was called Zvidsai-Charig Syndrome, after the researchers who first identified it. It affected the DNA of unborn children, weakening it in various ways. As time went on, more money was spent on research, but no-one could identify any pathogens or infection points.'

'So, no-one knew what caused it?'

'They didn't.'

I looked at her closely as she said this. It sounded a harmless enough statement, but she had emphasised her words in a way that suggested that someone else might. And I could almost certainly guess who that someone else might have been.

'But you do?'

'The first cases were detected in California, sometime next year,' was all she said, her eyes fixed on her nearly empty wine glass.

'California?' I said, and paused for a moment, as the significance of her words sunk in. 'La Misión?' I finally asked, a sick feeling in my stomach as I said the name.

'Ten out of ten, Richard,' she responded, her voice slightly slurred, raising her tired looking eyes to meet mine. There was a sadness in them that I couldn't quite fathom.

'So, the destruction of the particle accelerator caused it?'

'Almost certainly.'

I thought about it. I knew nothing about particle physics, but the forces unleashed into the atmosphere by the explosion must have been vastly and unnaturally powerful. I remembered Neferu's new-found ability to sleep and wondered if that had been a by-product of the blast. If that ungodly power could force a change in the machines inside her that had remained unchanged for 3,826 years, then there was really no telling what else they might do. De-stabilising the genetic core of human beings was probably more than likely.

'Shit,' was all I could say. It wasn't very intelligent, but I had no profound or prophetic words for a revelation like that. I'd been exposed full on to the forces unleashed, and I wondered what changes might be occurring in my body, even know.

'It doesn't affect this generation,' Djedetkha said, as if reading my mind. 'But it's all downhill from here.'

'I don't understand what that has to do with the gods, though?' I said, still feeling highly confused about everything.

'Haven't you worked it out yet?' she asked me.

'Obviously not, otherwise I wouldn't be asking,' I responded, a little irritated by her patronising attitude.

'Richard, a man named Jonathan Peiper came up with a solution to the crisis in 2070. He pioneered a technique where human DNA could be spliced with animal DNA, thus stabilising the condition.'

I stared at her, horrified. I could hardly believe what I'd just heard. I thought about the gods. Well, it obviously made perfect sense when you thought about creatures with human bodies and the heads of jackals, crocodiles, falcons and so on. Even fucking beetles. My God, the thought was so disgusting it actually made me feel sick. And then I thought of Dr James Curtis. The scary man with the black eyes. Oh my God!

'You're serious, aren't you?' I asked her, half-hoping she'd burst into laughter and I'd discover it was actually April 1. But she didn't laugh.

'You met Curtis, didn't you?' she asked me. 'He was a human-mandrill hybrid. One of the first. By the time of the gods the whole process had been perfected. Very obviously.'

A mandrill? The most vicious apes on the planet. Well, that explained far too much about him, even those hideous tattoos, probably. I hoped that he'd fallen a long way in time from Ceryse.

'But what can we do?' I asked, a real feeling of panic rising in me. I felt suddenly helpless. What, realistically, could I, a mediocre ancient history academic, do to help the situation?

'There is plenty we can do. Our Queen brought back Sekhmet for a reason. All of our medical and research facilities are now going to focus on finding a cure. Having one of the creatures alive will make that task much easier.'

'So Neferu can save the future?'

'If anyone can, she can,' Djedetkha said, putting her now empty glass down rather clumsily.

'I believe that,' I agreed. If there was one thing I knew about Neferu, it was that she could make things that seemed impossible happen. She'd said to me that she knew that if she could imagine something, it could happen. And I felt certain that if she believed she could find a cure, then she would. I felt suddenly reassured. How wonderful, I reflected, to have a leader, no matter how much of a despot she actually was, whose word actually meant something.

'These creatures,' I said, 'Did you see their world?'

'No,' she told me, 'Our Queen travelled there by herself. We couldn't go with her.'

'Why not?' I asked.

'Because she destroyed it,' she answered, trotting this phrase out as if Neferu had baked a few cakes.

'She destroyed it? How?'

'She took a small fission device with her and detonated it in their citadel. None of them survived.'

I thought about that. Neferu blew herself into what must have been thousands of pieces to destroy their world. If that wasn't a sacrifice, I had no idea what was. And even though she would have been fairly certain she would survive, I knew that every blow she suffered hurt her, even if her nanobots repaired the damage. How brave would you have to be to blow yourself up, knowing that, although you were going to repaired, you'd suffer everything that those who were killed did, and probably more, when you revived? I couldn't even begin to think of words that described how that made me feel. I instantly felt unworthy, and regretted every negative thought I'd had about her. I knew she loathed these creatures with an intensity that I couldn't even imagine, but an act like this went beyond all human understanding. None of us were worthy, I thought.

And then another thought struck me, one that would have had me burnt at the stake in an earlier time. Neferu had died for mankind and been reborn.

'So they're all dead? At least in the future?' I asked, wanting to move my thoughts on from that very unsettling concept.

'We don't think they're all dead, but most of them are. There may have been some in the past when it happened.'

'But Neferu can deal with them, right? We know that.'

'She is our Queen,' was all Djedetkha said.

'So, everything's okay, then.'

'I suppose it is. For you.'

I looked at her as she said this, seeing that sadness in her eyes again. She'd obviously had a day like no other in this world, and had also found her belief system blown out of the water. Everything that she'd grown up believing in was now proved to be a lie. Maybe not everything, but her view of the forces that controlled the world we lived in. There was no Ma'at, and no Ra sailing the Mesektet through the sky, night after unrelenting night. I hoped that she might come to see that it was better to have no gods than to embrace false ones, but perhaps that was hypocritical of me. After all, I came from a world where it was all too fashionable to reject religion and place your faith in the false god that was science.

I stood up and crossed to where she sat, lowering myself next to her. I put my arm around her and pulled her in close. She didn't resist.

'I'm sorry, Djedetkha,' I said, selfishly enjoying the feeling of her warm body next to mine.

'You don't need to be sorry, Richard,' she said, 'It's not your fault. It's nobody's fault, other than theirs. Humans seem even more corrupt and selfish when they're part-animal.'

'What happened to Curtis?' I asked her, remembering that he had actually been an integral part of their plan. 'He didn't choose to go back to 2017, did he?'

'No,' she replied, wrinkling her nose in exaggerated disdain as she contemplated the human mandrill. 'Shoshenq and I ambushed him and forced him back.'

I thought about the fact that the two of them, along with Menkheperre, had not been with Neferu in California. How could they have known, four weeks ago, what they were going to do today? I tried to think about it, but stopped. Time travel really was a mind-fucker. I thought about asking Djedetkha, but there seemed little point.

Her face was close to mine, and I could smell the wine on her breath. I wanted to kiss her, but I realised that the thought was both selfish and tactless. She was both sad and intoxicated, and I knew that was not a great combination for making good decisions. So, instead, I held her close and leaned back onto the couch. She moved her warm body closer to mine, put her right arm across my chest and rested her head on my shoulder. Within five minutes, the change in her breathing told me that she'd fallen asleep.

Chapter Thirty-Two

Extract from the daily journal of Richard Verlice, Saturday 16th March 2024:

As Djedetkha lay against me, her sleep occasionally interrupted by what were obviously troubling dreams, as she stirred and moaned from time to time, I thought about the journey I'd been on, was still on. It seemed a time for reflection, because I knew that when the day dawned, it would dawn on a trip through time back to Beirut in 1982, a mission of mercy to save an immortal woman's twice-dead husband. I wondered how many lives would be lost saving that one. Of course, from what I'd read, as many as 3,500 Palestinians and Lebanese had been brutally killed in the massacre in the Shatila Refugee Camp over a period of about 36 hours. Neferu wasn't about to stop that, but she would happily add to it if it served her purpose. A purpose that had driven her for nearly four thousand years.

If I was going to be honest with myself, I was scared. It should have felt surreal, but it didn't, because I'd already travelled back in time. I'd gone with the Queen to regain her throne from the usurper Sekhemrekhutawy in 1799BC. That was scary, but I hadn't felt threatened. I'd been part of a mini-army, and the gods Sobek and Petbe, accompanied by a squad of crocodile-headed troops, had marched with us.

This time it was different. A small group of Ahati against the Israeli Defence Force and the Lebanese Christian Militia. I didn't even know why I was going. Ceryse had made it plain that she didn't want me to rescue her, so I couldn't see the rationale for wasting one of the few spaces available on an academic who specialized in Ancient Egyptian history. Neferu usually had good reasons for anything she did, but I really couldn't see any rationale for this. And I wasn't going to flatter myself by thinking that she simply wanted me with her. Not on a mission to save her husband.

My life had been turned upside down. I'd been a small-time historian working in a small-time museum with small-time ambitions. The most exciting my life got was exploring the possibilities of a bust of Alexander the Great not being as old as it was documented as being. And having coffee and a regular evening out with Ceryse. Now, it seemed, I was the subject of a Queen who was supposed to have died in 1802BC and whose clandestine Ancient Egyptian kingdom spanned much of the world. That was a turnaround, however you looked at it. My life was crazy. And it was about to get crazier.

I thought hard about the cold reality of what I was about to do. It seemed to me that I was almost certainly going to die. And I'd die in the past. There'd be no grave, no-one to mourn me, other than Ceryse, who, on our last meeting, made it reasonably clear that there was little love coming my way. Even my family would have no idea what had happened to me. I would have just disappeared into thin air, as they no doubt already thought I had anyway.

If I was going to die, then I thought that I probably should to do what everyone else did before it happened. Lying against me, snoring very softly now, was one of the most beautiful women I'd ever met. She was courageous, skilled, highly intelligent, funny, highly sensual, and, most importantly, didn't find the idea of making love to me utterly abhorrent. She was also drunk, I remembered, although I presumed that most of it would probably have worked its way out of her system by now.

I shook her slightly, and her head simply fell further back against me. So, I tried a little harder.

'Djedetkha,' I whispered loudly in her ear, somewhat disingenuously. 'Are you asleep?'

'I was,' she muttered, her eyelids fluttering open slightly, before shutting again.

'I wondered, well, I thought. Or, at least, I wanted to ask,' I fumbled, now feeling very stupid and embarrassed, and realising that my very selfish idea was just that, very selfish. This poor woman had fought demons in the future yesterday, and I had no idea what else she'd done or seen while she'd been away, and here I was trying to wake her for a booty call.

'Richard,' she said, 'Are you suggesting we have sex?' She turned her head to face me, and I could see, even in the near darkness, that her face was very pale and her eyes appeared a little red.

'Well,' I blustered, now deeply embarrassed and ashamed of myself, 'sort of.'

She turned her body to face me, and I saw a pained look appear on her face, although that seemed to be more to do with the movement than the situation.

'Do you think you're going to die tomorrow?' she asked me. She obviously hadn't realised that she'd slept long enough for it to now be today.

'It had crossed my mind, yes,' I told her, feeling suddenly emotional.

'Don't worry,' she said, reaching out a hand to stroke my face. 'I'll keep you safe. It's not your time to die tomorrow.'

'It's today now,' I told her, a little petulantly, not in any way appeased by her soothsaying. 'And how can you be so sure? We could all die.'

'We could, you're right, but you won't. I can't tell you how I know, but there are other plans for you.'

I frowned at her, unconvinced and not really very reassured. It was all very well her throwing these comforting statements at me, but there didn't seem much of a firm evidence base for them. At least, not one that she was prepared to share.

The pained look crossed her face again, and she suddenly got to her feet.

'Excuse me,' she said, 'but I've got to be sick.' She rushed over to the bathroom, slamming the door shut behind her. Clearly, she hadn't actually got all of the alcohol out of her system yet. I tried not to listen as she threw up, I knew she wouldn't want me to hear such a private bodily function. But, it was so quiet in the house that I had little choice other than to listen.

After a while she stopped, and I heard the sound of a tap running, and then, to my surprise, the shower. I wondered whether I should get a drink, but I simply sat back and waited for her to return. I wondered why she hadn't been in California three weeks earlier. Shoshenq, as well, for that matter. But, when I thought about it, it made sense. I was aware that the two of them were the ones responsible for ensuring Curtis turned up in 2017. He would definitely have smelled a rat if he'd seen either of them. The same went for Neferu and Nedjes, I supposed. I understood they had stayed out of his way in 2105, for the very same reason. But then, I realised, it actually didn't make any sense at all, unless Neferu had somehow known what was going to happen before it actually did. Time travel was a mind fucker. It just seemed to create paradoxes and confusion, whatever you did. After her trip back to 1799BC, I wouldn't have been at all surprised to suddenly discover that Ancient Egyptian art had changed to show women wearing high heels. But, it seemed that nothing had changed. Or, at least, nothing obvious. Or maybe it was, but the timeline had changed with it and I couldn't recognise it because it had now always been like that. Time travel was definitely a mind fucker.

My patience was rewarded after around thirty minutes, when Djedetkha finally returned from the bathroom, resplendent in a gold Kemetian bathrobe. She looked better than when she'd rushed off, her beautiful olive skin tone having returned to replace the gray pallor she'd developed before she threw up.

To my surprise, she came and sat down on my lap, her legs straddling mine.

'I've brushed my teeth,' she told me, smiling softly in the dim light. 'I didn't use your toothbrush, either.'

'I'm sorry,' I said, now feeling more than a little awkward. 'I was being selfish. You've just been sick, I'm sure this is the last thing on your mind.'

'I feel much better now,' she told me, 'and you were right. This is the last time you and I will meet, so we should enjoy the moment.'

'The last time? You just told me I wasn't going to die.' As I said this, I thought I realised what she was saying. My face darkened and I began to feel scared.

She saw the look on my face and laughed, her long hair cascading around her shoulders as she did so.

'I'm not going to die, either,' she reassured me.

'So, what do you mean?' I asked, very relieved, but thoroughly confused.

'Our Queen holds you in high regard, you know,' she told me, starting to unbutton my shirt.

'She does?' I said, finding it hard to concentrate as she slipped her hand inside and sought out a nipple. I also found it hard to believe that Neferu viewed me as anything other than an occasionally useful annoyance.

'You have qualities that she finds desirable in a man. Some of them, anyway,' she added, glancing mischievously at me, as she finished undoing the buttons with her other hand, and then slipping that one inside as well.

I was finding it hard to think now, and didn't actually want to.

'And you?' I asked.

She didn't reply, instead pulling my shirt off and sensually moving her hands all over my chest and arms.

I said nothing, instead surrendering to the fire that she was stoking inside me. Some things were far more powerful than words, anyway.

Chapter Thirty-Three

I felt highly trepidatious as I got myself ready for the long day ahead. I wasn't worried about failure. I knew that was not an option, that I would succeed in saving Senusret and returning to the island with him. I simply felt anxious because it was possibly the most important day of my very long life. I had lived through many of the most dramatic and catastrophic days in the history of humanity, and I had also shared in some of the moments of great joy along the way, but nothing would compare to this day, the day I would finally be reunited with my husband for all eternity.

I remembered having had similar thoughts just over two weeks before, and that was why I felt apprehensive. Sometimes my self-belief and arrogance tipped over into complacency and led to disaster, as had happened in the Suchos Building with that abomination, Horus. It wasn't that I'd underestimated the opposition, it was simply that I was too confident in my own success. In hindsight, it was obvious that one of those false gods would try to stop me. I had simply refused to believe that they would dare to enter my domain.

I missed my homeland, the sounds, the smells, the beautiful clean air unsullied by industrial pollution. I missed my people, the relative simplicity of the lives they led. They weren't simple people, which was a common mistake made by the vacuous dumbed down masses of the modern world, they were very sophisticated and erudite. But they were simpler times. There were no smart phones, no tablets, no laptops. There was no question that our people and our culture were all the better for it.

I would never see the rains turning the soil black again. I would never witness the joy of the season's successful harvest, or the despair of a failed one. I would never even drink Kemetian beer again. I might return to Egypt, I might journey down the Nile from the Lower to the Upper Kingdom. But, my Kemet was gone, long since dead and buried beneath the feet of alien invaders. The land remained, but the world had died. And part of me had died with it, no matter how strange that seems, given that it is impossible for me to die. I had forged my own Kemet, had created a world in my own image. But it was a replica, and nothing more.

How could it be? I had my kingdom, but it was a faux kingdom. It was a pale imitation of the real thing, just like all those imitators of Alexander were nothing more than insipid reminders of a spectacular and truly unique man.

I moved my thoughts on. I didn't enjoy being maudlin or morose, and this was a day for celebration, not despair. I turned my thoughts towards Kalandra Straub, the third-rate hack who seemed to have decided to target me. I had put up with her suggestive innuendo in the past, but she had gone too far now. Her most recent article did everything except name me. For some reason, she had decided to stir the pot and bring it to the boil. Well, she might come to regret that. She might find the pot was too hot and she got severely burned. When I returned to 2024, one of my first tasks would be to neutralise her. Permanently. She would learn that if she chose to swim with sharks, then she would be eaten.

After my maids had finished getting me ready, I spent a little time in quiet contemplation. In the past, even the very recent past, I would have prayed to Sobek and invoked his support. But, now, that wasn't even an option. Part of me wanted to pray to someone, and it occurred to me that I should pray to the God of the carpenter, but I couldn't. Maybe I really did feel like an abomination in his eyes. He had certainly made it clear that he wasn't about to help me, suggesting that I had a higher purpose. I had not taken him seriously then, and I wasn't about to now. I had no higher purpose. My only purpose was restoring my throne and saving my husband. I had already achieved both, and then lost them. If I could get Senusret back, then I might consider contenting myself with the imitation throne I currently occupied.

There was a thought, an image almost, on the fringe of my consciousness. I didn't want to face it, or even acknowledge it. But it was hard to avoid. I'd died many times before, but never like that. I'd never been blasted into a thousand fragments, or maybe more, and then reassembled. In truth, I hadn't even known for certain that those tiny machines would be able to fix me. If not, then ridding the universe of those disgusting creatures would have been a price worth paying for my immortal body. But, I'd experienced enough over the previous centuries to believe that little was beyond their capabilities. And I'd been proven right.

However, I believe it was part of the cruelty of Anubis that I was always revived before I was fully healed, so that I not only felt the pain of death, but also the agony of resurrection. And, in the case of yesterday's experience, it went so far beyond simple pain. Who could imagine being revived whilst still dismembered? I couldn't see, couldn't sense anything, but I could feel the agony of my body being slowly reconstructed. No-one who has ever lived could understand that. It wasn't simply painful, it was horrific, distressing beyond my capacity to describe. I willingly paid that price to rid humanity of those abominations, but it was a heavy price. Even now, I didn't want to think about it, couldn't face the memory of those distressing, devastating moments. It made me feel ill to think that the first sound I'd been able to hear was my own screaming. The only comfort was the presence of all those dead, dismembered, hybrid bodies.

There are some things that no matter how much you may wish, you can never unsee or unhear. Some events that you can never forget. It is a tragic human conceit that time heals emotional wounds. It simply is not true. In my experience, time only magnifies the pain of trauma. I have had so much hurt and suffering in my life, and it is the memory of those desperate, devastating moments and events that has kept me going, has enabled me to continue this impossible quest almost to its endgame. I curse the day my mother conceived me, and I curse the day Anubis was given life. Two apparently unrelated events that have caused so much death and misery down through the ages. However, the paradox that is time suggests that, ultimately, it's my fault. That Anubis existed because of me. How is that even possible? Of course, it isn't possible, but, at the same time, it is incontrovertible fact.

I despair of this world, and I grow tired of it. If I failed today, even the microscopic machines inside of me would not be able to mend my broken heart.

I forced myself back into the here and now, into the moment that heralded destiny, one way or another. I was finally ready, and I assembled my guards and maids, and made the short journey to the Research Centre. Of course, I was the last one to arrive. Nedjes, Djedetkha, Shoshenq, Richard, and fifteen M'sha were gathered, all dressed in identical combat suits, designed to resemble the uniforms of the Christian Militia. Once I'd arrived, Nedjes began the briefing.

'We'll arrive at Zaitunay Bay at 4pm on Thursday 16th September 1982. It's just under 4.2 miles to the Shatila Refugee Camp, so we can be there in around half an hour. We'll pass at least one checkpoint. Let me do the talking, and avoid irritating the IDF. When we get to the camp, there is a weakened gate near the main entrance. We'll make our access in from there. We have a witness statement of where our Lord Senusret and Miss Tabrizi were being held, which is not far from our point of ingress. We'll make straight for them, and then, when we've recovered them, we'll leave by the same exit and head back to Zaitunay Bay. You've each got maps and GPS co-ordinates, in case you get separated. There are no mobile networks and there's no wi-fi, so we're going to have rely on old-fashioned walkie-talkies.'

He said this all in a very matter of fact way, as if we were going for a casual stroll on a sunny Sunday afternoon in somewhere that wasn't a war zone. 'Any questions?'

'What do we do if anyone tries to stop us?' Richard asked.

'We kill them,' I told him.

'Neferu,' he said, a pained look on his face, 'There's enough death going to happen. Must we add to it?'

'The only people likely to try to stop us are people who are going to be killing Palestinians,' I told him, letting him work the point out for himself.

'Anything else?' Nedjes asked of the assembled group.

'I thought the device could only transport five or six people?' Richard asked.

'We have more power rings,' Nedjes told him. I had brought back a collection of them from 2268, and, as a result, Psusennes had been able to vastly increase the power output of Curtis' device.

'Any other questions?' Nedjes said, looking around the group as he did so.

No-one said anything, so he started handing out equipment. Everyone was given two assault rifles, as well as a Glock handgun, a Kevlar vest, a steel helmet, and a backpack crammed full of ammunition and percussion grenades.

Richard looked rather anxiously at the guns, but accepted them anyway. He would have been stupid not to. He now had blood on his hands anyway.

As I put on my bullet-proof vest, which I hardly needed, he came over to me.

'Is it true that you're researching an antidote for the Syndrome?' he asked me.

'It is. Having Sekhmet means that we can find it quicker.' I didn't mention to him that it would involve experimenting on her, and that when we were finished, she'd be destroyed. I didn't want to get into a pointless discussion around the ethics of exterminating vermin.

'How will you distribute it around the world?' he asked me.

'I won't,' I told him. I stared at him coldly, knowing what would follow.

'What do you mean?' he demanded, confusion written all over his face. It was a look I had seen so many times.

'I mean that the antidote is for my people.'

'You're not serious?' he said, clearly incredulous.

'I'm very serious. Why would I want to share it?'

'Why? How about the fact that you're still a human being?'

'My kingdom will be saved. Nothing else matters in this world, Richard.'

'But you have a duty!' he exclaimed.

'What duty?' I demanded, although I thought I knew exactly what he was going to say. He was, after all, a historian of Kemet. What passed for one in the modern world, anyway.

'It's your role as Queen of Kemet to ensure Ma'at and banish Isfet,' he told me, as if I didn't know.

'Ma'at is dead,' I informed him, my voice as cold as I could make it. I wasn't interested in this discussion, and certainly not when we were about to step into the past to rescue my husband. 'I killed her. And everything she and it stood for was built on a foundation of lies and deceit. There is no Ma'at, only Isfet.'

'But Neferu, you are a compassionate and caring Queen. This is your world. You've lived amongst these people for nearly four thousand years.'

I simply stared at him as coldly as before. I had nothing to say on the matter. Why should I save the people who had fought against me every step of the way over the centuries? People who still wanted to thwart my plans.

'My Queen,' came a voice from behind me, and I turned to face Djedetkha.

'What is it?' I demanded, the irritation in my voice very clear. This was not a time for talking.

'Please excuse my interruption, but I believe Richard is correct.'

I glared at her, my anger starting to rise. I had expected insolence from Richard, but not from my own subjects, and especially not from Djedetkha. First, she'd let her guard down and been injured, and now she was daring to contradict me.

'You are questioning my judgement?' I challenged her, daring her to continue.

'No, my Queen, I would never question your judgement. You are absolutely right about the outside world. But, there is something else that we need to consider.'

'Which is what?' I demanded. She had chosen her words carefully, emphasising that I was correct to feel the way I did. I knew what she was going to say, though. Her logic was, understandably, impeccable, as I would have expected.

'If you don't provide the antidote for all, then the exact same conditions will arise that first led to the creation of the gods.'

'We can prevent that from happening,' I told her.

'And simply let eight billion people die?' Richard interjected, a look of horror on his face.

'Yes,' I told him. Many more than that had died since my birth. What difference did a few more make? And then Kemet would reign supreme.

'But, my Queen, we were unable to stop it from happening in the future.'

She was, of course, right. I said nothing, but thought about it. My arrogance, as it occasionally did, had blinded me to the truth of her words. I thought about the abandoned Suchos building we had visited in 2105. I knew that, in the future, I would have tried to prevent the spread of Zvidsai-Charig Syndrome and the realisation of Jonathan Peiper's degenerate and disgusting experiments, and I had very clearly failed. I may have accumulated a vast amount of the world's corporate wealth, but I couldn't buy everything. I could purchase favours and protection from world governments, but there were some things that even my money couldn't buy.

I looked at her, and Richard, wanting to be angry, wanting to crush them under a verbal heel, but the point was a powerful one. I should have known better than to doubt her; she was the Golden Falcon. She knew my mind as well as I did. Apart from safeguarding the future, providing the antidote for the entire world made sound economic and business sense, further securing Kemet.

'We'll talk about it after we return,' I said. It would not have been seemly or appropriate for me to concede publicly. She knew that, and would not have expected me to.

'Thank you, my Queen,' Djedetkha said, bowing her head slightly. Despite her having contradicted me publicly, I felt pleased with her. Sometimes I did need to be reminded of the bigger picture.

'Thank you, Neferu,' Richard said, looking relieved.

I simply glared at him. I wished that I didn't have to take him with us, but it was necessary. I had messed with time enough; there was no point in creating any more problems than I absolutely had to.

I looked around at the assembled group. Finally, it seemed that everything and everyone was ready. My guards and maids had retired to near the doorway. They knew that, if we were successful, we would return almost instantaneously.

'Let's go,' I said. Nedjes got out the time device, moved the controls and everything blurred.

Chapter Thirty-Four

Extract from the daily journal of Richard Verlice, Thursday 16th September 1982:

Everything blurred. Just for an instant, and then suddenly there was noise and bright light everywhere. It was hot, although no more so than on Isla de Gran Esperanza. We were standing on a quayside, with the deep blue sea behind us. On our right was a marina, which was completely empty at the moment. Ahead of us were a series of tall buildings. One of them was clearly a hotel, with the name Four Seasons in large letters over the ground floor foyer. On our left, in the distance, was a harbour. The sea behind us was empty, although I could see what looked like warships in the distance on our right. Despite the relative tranquillity of our surroundings, I could hear what I presumed was artillery and rocket fire in the distance. And it didn't sound very distant, either. I could see plumes of dirty grey smoke and dust moving through the air not too far away. At least, it looked as if it wasn't too far away. There were tanks and armored vehicles at intervals in the road that ran along by the sea, and I could make out a checkpoint in the distance. I knew we were near the edge of the Israeli sector, a sort of military tectonic plate, grinding dangerously against the Syrian one.

So this was Beirut in 1982. Zaitunay Bay, to be specific. I preferred 1799BC, without any doubt. It was no judgement on Beirut, which I knew, in happier times, was a beautiful and very cultural city, but the Ancient Egyptians hadn't had tanks or rockets. A khopesh or a spear could still do a lot of damage, but not nearly as much as field guns or assault rifles.

I'd already got my steel helmet on, and the others put theirs on as we started to move off. Nedjes took the lead, for obvious reasons. This was not an enlightened world, and the sight of female soldiers would, no doubt, raise some eyebrows, even amongst the Israelis, who seemed to be happy to conscript anyone who was Jewish and could squeeze a trigger, then and now.

We made our way up towards Al Khantari, leaving the sea behind us. I couldn't speak for the others, but I felt very vulnerable and conspicuous. I was pretty certain that I didn't look much like a soldier, and if I didn't think I did, then no-one else was going to, either.

I saw a checkpoint up ahead and began to feel very nervous. I couldn't believe that the Israelis wouldn't see that we didn't belong here. It suddenly occurred to me that Neferu was being remarkably reckless, and was endangering all of our lives for no good reason. This whole undertaking seemed completely crazy to me, and I began to feel increasingly edgy and anxious.

As we carried on marching, Djedetkha placed a hand on my arm. She had been marching next to me, no doubt deliberately, to keep an eye on me. I glanced at her. The bruising on her face had now faded to a point where it was virtually invisible, unless you were specifically looking for it.

'Don't worry,' she said. 'Just let Nedjes and our Queen take the strain.'

That was easy for her to say, I thought, but, in truth, there was little else I could do anyway. I didn't speak Arabic or Hebrew, so the less I said, or understood, the better, probably. It did ease some of my anxiety to have her there with me. I trusted Neferu, of course, but I also knew that her only real loyalty was to herself. Djedetkha, on the other hand, exuded calmness and reassurance. I liked that. Especially in combat situations.

We drew to a halt at the checkpoint, which was manned by a group of what appeared to be Israeli soldiers. Members of the ironically entitled IDF, the Israeli Defence Force. Ironic, when you considered that they believed themselves to be defending their country when they were in occupation of the capital of Lebanon. That was the Israeli view of defence, though, I thought. Literal overkill.

'Papers?' the sergeant in charge demanded of Nedjes. He produced something from his jacket pocket and handed it over. The soldier gave it a cursory glance and handed it back, which surprised me. He cast his eyes over our little group, and seemed a little surprised when he spotted Neferu and Djedetkha.

'You have women in your squad?' he asked. 'When did you start recruiting women?'

'A woman can kill as easily as a man,' Nedjes retorted, and the Israeli sergeant nodded his head in agreement, clearly admiring the wisdom of these words.

'You headed to Shatila?' he asked.

'Yes,' Nedjes replied.

'You'd better get going then, the party's due to begin.'

Party? I wondered just how more casual you could get about the cold-blooded slaughter of 3,500 people.

He waved us on, and we continued on our way, thankfully leaving the checkpoint behind. We carried on up the road, in complete silence, the only sounds being our feet on the ruptured tarmac and the constant explosions in the distance, from almost every direction.

In my time, 42 years in the future from where we now where, it was no longer possible to criticise the state of Israel without being called Anti-Semitic, which was a little crazy, given that I felt fairly certain the Israeli government was a political, and not a racial, entity. I knew little of the history of this specific conflict, but I knew enough of the general history of the region because of my specialism in Ancient Egypt. I noted that neither Neferu nor any of her subjects had once referred to Israel by its name. She wouldn't be drawn on the matter, refusing to discuss it, her only comment being to acknowledge that these people had once been slaves of Kemet and had notably brutally rejected their own savior, who she, cryptically, always referred to as The Carpenter.

Nonetheless, despite my overall ignorance, I couldn't help but feel it was a sad and very poignant comment on human nature that extreme suffering brought, not compassion, but a brutal desire to survive and flourish at all odds, regardless of the cost to others. The evidence of that was all around us as we marched away from the Mediterranean.

It wasn't really a long march, but to someone as unfit and out of shape as me, it might as well have been a marathon, especially when I was carrying two assault rifles, a Glock, a hefty backpack and a steel helmet on my head. I hated to admit it, but the only exercise I'd had in recent times was that associated with sex. And, until the last month, that had been non-existent. It was interesting to think that I'd made love more times in the last month than I had in my entire life. I'm sure Ceryse would have loved to hear that piece of Verlice trivia.

Ceryse! I had completely forgotten about her, so lost was I in my pseudo-political and self-indulgent moral ramblings. She was here, somewhere. I hoped she was being treated well. She'd indicated that because she was obviously not Palestinian, she had been regarded with indifference, unlike Senusret, who the Israelis had apparently concluded must have been Palestinian. It wouldn't have occurred to them to think about the language he was speaking, not that anyone would have believed he could possibly be Ancient Egyptian. If the whole thing was scary for Ceryse, it must have been terrifying for him. One moment he was being murdered by Anubis in 1802BC, the next he was awake in 2024, and immediately thrown back to 1982 by Horus. I don't know how you would even begin to understand any of that. He was lucky that Ceryse had fallen with him, evidence of the fact that she did actually have some kindness and compassion hidden deep down. He was equally lucky that his wife was Neferu, God Killer.

There was nothing I could do for Ceryse right now, other than to trust her to keep safe, and not to irritate anyone too much. I really didn't think that the trigger-happy people in this city would be even ten per cent as tolerant as Neferu had been. Which was surprising in itself, really, given some of what I'd seen recently.

As we marched, I noticed the various landmarks we passed, trying to focus on the things around me, rather than the pain inside me. The pain of lack of fitness. We passed Haoud Al Wilaya Park on our left, and then the Salim Salam Mosque and the Lebanese International University on our right. There was nowhere that didn't look it had been the scene of fighting or shelling.

We crossed a big junction, bisecting Saeb Salem and carried on south, as heavy trucks rumbled past in both directions, covered in IDF and Christian Militia insignia. There were also some troops hanging around, many catching a quick moment of calm, smoking a cigarette, although their eyes seemed ever attentive. But nobody seemed very interested in us. If they'd looked more closely, seen our HK416's, they might have thought they looked a bit out of place. Which they were, given that they didn't go into production until 2004. That was what Djedetkha had told me, at the same time suggesting I keep both of mine slung over my back, as the others did, to avoid them being too obvious. Casual observers might also have been surprised, as the checkpoint guard was, by the presence of women in our ranks. After all, even in 2024, there were, as far as I was aware, no women fighting in the front line anywhere. And especially not women like the two we had with us.

We passed some more local landmarks, including the Egyptian Embassy and the Camille Chamoun Sports Stadium, before we finally turned to the east, following the winding route of Ghobeiri, past the battered Tahhadi Hospital, until we reached a vast walled area. This, Djedetkha murmured to me, was the Shatila Palestinian Refugee Camp. Today, it was simply a name, a place almost no-one in this world had heard of. By the time the sun rose on the morning of 18th September, only 36 hours in the future, it would be synonymous with one of the most horrific and abhorrent crimes committed by human beings in recent times. It would even lead to the resignation of Israel's Defence Minister. But, right now, it was calm inside, and all I could hear from the camp was the sound of children laughing, shrieking and doing whatever children do when they're locked up in a refugee camp. I felt sick when I thought about what was about to happen to them. It's one thing to know that terrible things happen in this world, it's another entirely to be forced to confront them, and live through them. From my perspective, those poor, innocent, children were already dead, had been so for nearly 42 years.

The situation outside was very different. The closer we'd got to the walled area, the bigger the military presence. Armored vehicles, tanks, even mobile rocket launchers were parked all around us. Troops milled about everywhere, some, who seemed completely detached from the activity around them, were Israeli, others, rushing about, shouting instructions, apparently at no-one in particular, were wearing the uniforms of the Lebanese Christian Militia.

As Nedjes had suggested, there was, indeed, a set of gates that looked well used and battered, not too far from the main entrance, which I could see about fifty yards in front of us. There were two members of the IDF standing in front of them, guns poised. Nedjes led us over to them, and made to carry on past them and into the camp.

'Where do you think you're going?' one of them demanded, not bothering to hide his contempt for our uniforms.

'We're going in,' Nedjes told him.

'That's what the main entrance is for,' the guard told him, pointing a gun at him, his head angled further up the road.

'We're going in here,' Neferu told him, fixing her eyes on his with some intensity. She arched her head slightly, and continued to stare, remarkably intensely, at him. As the other guard stepped forward, she raised her hand and he stopped in his tracks. 'Open the gate,' she commanded, in a tone I hadn't heard her use before. It was powerful, and even from where I was standing, I felt the need to obey her.

'But we have orders,' the man blustered, his tone now very different. Meek, almost childlike. The other guard stared at her, also transfixed, but looking bewildered. As well he might.

'I'm sure you do. But you're going to open this gate for us. Now.' The tone in her voice was dynamic and uncompromising. The guard looked at her, his eyes almost begging her not to force him.

'The orders are clear,' he offered, his voice now weak and apologetic.

'Open the gate!' she insisted, her voice raised in tone.

'Yes, ma'am,' he finally said, clumsily pulling out a set of keys, unlocking one of the rickety-looking gates, and pulling them both open. We filed past and into the camp, as they looked on, shock and confusion etched into their faces.

'How did you do that?' I asked Neferu, as the gats were locked behind us. If she could control people so easily, I wondered why she hadn't done that with me, rather than going to all the trouble of seducing me. Although, I supposed, in a way that was exactly what she'd done, just in a less straightforward manner. I certainly hadn't been able to resist in any way. I hadn't wanted to, but, of course, that was also a part of it. She was enormously powerful, I realised, even more so than I'd believed.

'The baser the creature, the easier it is to control,' was all she said, as she followed Nedjes into the camp proper. Ridiculously, given the situation, I was reminded of the Bene Gesserit in Dune, who had The Voice, and could even kill with it. Maybe Frank Herbert had known Neferu.

I'd never been to a refugee camp anywhere, and it's impossible to really know what to expect. Places like Shatila were not camps as people in the western world understand the term. They're more like shanty towns. There were plenty of Palestinian camps in Lebanon in 2024 that were, really, permanent townships. Areas of segregation, in practical terms.

Shatila had decay as its theme, exuding an aura of permanent impermanence. It was degrading to force human beings to live in such primitive and squalid conditions, but, of course, this was hardly the only place in the world where that happened. There were many governments in my time that forced sections of their own populations to live in areas like that. And, if they didn't always force them, they made it economically impossible for people to move beyond them. Looking around me as we walked, I realised just what a fucked up and terminally sick world I lived in.

Chapter Thirty-Five

Extract from the daily journal of Richard Verlice, Thursday 16th September 1982:

The sun had started to set as we marched up past the squalid buildings on our right, and I glanced at my watch, which I'd reset to the local time. It showed 6.01. Well, I thought, maybe history was wrong, or maybe us being here had changed things, for the better. But, just as those thoughts moved through my head, the sound of gunfire erupted from behind us. It had begun.

We hurried forwards, turning right as we reached the far wall. A set of buildings faced us, and we made our way down past them to the right. As we turned the corner, we came face to face with a squad of Christian Militia. They moved to block our path.

'Where are you going?' their leader, a short, bearded man, probably in his middle 50's, demanded.

'We need to get to the other side,' Nedjes told him.

'All in good time,' the man responded. 'We have to wait. The battle's only just starting.'

The battle, I thought? What battle? The IDF's party line had been that the operation had been undertaken to eradicate members of the PLO sheltering in the camp, but the reality, as history documented it, was that it was a reprisal for the assassination of Bachir Gemayel two days previously.

'Get out of our way,' Neferu told him.

'A woman?' he said, noticing her for the first time. And then he saw Djedetkha, and his eyes lit up. 'Two women? We're going to have a party.'

The goons in his squad laughed with him at this.

'Get out of our way,' Neferu repeated, fixing her coldest stare on him.

'What's your hurry, sweetheart?' he demanded, moving closer to her, moving his right hand towards her hair.

'Don't touch me!' she told him.

'Or what?' he asked her, 'You'll slap me?' He laughed at what he thought was a joke, turning towards his men, who joined him in laughter.

He continued moving his hand towards her, but just as he was about to touch her hair, she grabbed his wrist and twisted it savagely. He screamed in agony and fell to his knees. As he did so, she hit him in the face with her the full force of her right knee, and he collapsed pitifully to the ground, his good hand clutching at his now bloody face.

'Get out of our way,' Neferu repeated, once more, to the armed men in front of us, who were no longer laughing. Like the heroes they obviously were, preparing to murder thousands of men, women and children, they parted. Just like the Red Sea, I thought. Except that Neferu was most definitely not Moses.

We made our way past them, and as we did so, all hell broke loose behind us. The gunfire that had, at first, been confined to near the main entrance, now emerged from all sides. The sound was terrifying and chilling. I'd never experienced anything like it in my life, and I hoped I never would again. The sound of machine guns and assault rifles firing constantly was sickening, but wasn't nearly as disturbing or distressing as the noise made by the terrified and dying men, women and children all around us.

The air was now filled with the sounds of battle. But a battle that was almost completely one-sided. Above us, a helicopter, emblazoned with the markings of the IDF circled, keeping an eye on proceedings. I had read about this before we left, knew how it worked. While their puppets, the Christian Militia, did the dirty work, the IDF stood guard, using flares to light up the night air for those killing inside, and ensuring that no-one escaped. They'd learned their lessons well, I thought. Mind you, they'd had some good teachers.

We carried on our way, and I noticed that Djedetkha had placed herself on my left, to shield me from the open spaces in the camp, where most of the gunfire was focused. From what I'd been told by Djedetkha, Ceryse and Senusret were quartered on the far side of the camp, around two more sets of buildings. They'd been given a tent, some rations and a tiny space on the ground. It wasn't far away, I knew that, but in this atmosphere, it felt like it might as well have been about a thousand miles away.

I wondered why Neferu had chosen to arrive at this time, when the slaughter had begun, but, as we carried on, I could see why. If we'd walked in during the day, in broad daylight, we would almost certainly have sparked some sort of confrontation, have been drawn into something that would have been potentially catastrophic. At least in terms of our planned rescue. But, under cover of the massacre, it would be relatively easy to move around the camp. And, Ceryse had also indicated that Senusret had not been killed until the next day. So, if we hadn't already changed history irrevocably, it was a reasonably sound plan. As sound as any plan that involves going into a one-sided massacre in a war zone, anyway.

Suddenly, I could hear bullets pinging and zinging around me, and Djedetkha pulled me down behind some piles of old boxes and garbage that ran in a line in front of the buildings behind us.

'PLO,' she said, answering my unspoken question. So, the occupants of the camp weren't entirely defenceless, but there seemed little real opposition to the one-sided brutality.

I pulled one of my assault rifles off my back, and held it in front of me, but I had little desire to use it. I'd killed one person, and I didn't want to add to that tally. I was more interested in finding Ceryse and surviving. I had no intention of sending anyone to meet their maker, if I could reasonably avoid it.

We were pinned down in this way for some time. I supposed that it was a delicate balancing act. Neferu had already changed history in some small way by infiltrating the camp and doing what she'd already done. If we started killing people who we'd never killed before, then who knew what effect that might have on the world in the future. And it seemed that Neferu had quite a lot to answer for, in terms of changing the future. And not for the better.

It took about half an hour, but, eventually, the bullets coming our way ground to a halt, and Nedjes cautiously led the force away from our defensive position and closer towards our target. We were about ten feet from the final corner, from where we should have been able to see the village of tents that was our destination, when we were brought to a resounding halt by a loud voice.

'Neferu, God Killer! Stop!'

Every face turned in the direction of the voice. What I saw didn't make any sense. Standing on our left, in front of a group of black-clad armed men, was none other than local LA celebrity journalist Kalandra Straub. I knew she seemed to have a thing about Neferu, seemed to be targeting her, quite rightly, in fact, for what had happened in California, but she was almost the last person I expected to see. And, it dawned on me as I thought about it, how could she be here? This was 1982.

She stood stock still, coolly staring down Neferu, apparently unfazed by the war going on around us. As she stood there, the air around her shimmered and she changed. She was no longer the 21st century journalist, but instead a beautiful

Middle Eastern woman, dressed in the all-too-familiar style of Ancient Egypt. And, on her head, were two horns, protruding as if from the head of a cow.

Isis!

Neferu stared calmly at her, equally still and unmoving, as if completely unperturbed. It occurred to me that she must have known this would happen. Perhaps that was another reason for choosing this time of day to arrive.

'How disappointing that you're still alive,' Neferu said.

'Did you really think you could kill all of us?' the deep-voiced human-hybrid responded, her dark eyes filled with anger and hate. These gods struck me as highly emotional creatures, and it didn't seem that they specialized in positive emotions. Maybe that was the problem with merging yourself with an animal. One of them, anyway.

'I knew some of you would find rocks to hide under, like the cowards you are,' Neferu said, her eyes calm, although it wasn't hard to imagine the anger that lay beneath. She hated these creatures with a passion and a depth that no-one alive could even begin to understand. And with good cause.

'You have gone too far. I could accept you killing Anubis and Horus, even though their loss hurts me, but now you have crossed a line.'

'It is my line, Isis. You should go, while you can.'

'Go? This is our world, not yours.'

While this dialogue had been going on, they had gradually approached each other, until they were almost eyeball to eyeball.

'This has never been your world,' Neferu told her. 'You are an abomination.'

'Of your making!' Isis laughed. And, as she did so, Neferu struck her hard in the face. The fake god fell to the ground, blood streaming from her nose. But she quickly got back to her feet.

'How dare you strike me!' she roared, her anger now almost tangible.

Neferu simply hit her again, with the same result.

Isis leaped up and thrust a leg out towards Neferu, who went tumbling backwards. However, she rolled with the fall, and launched herself back upward. Isis came towards her, and the Queen moved swiftly to one side.

I was aware that the fighting around us had come to a stop, the sound of gunfire now more distant. As I looked around, I could see that everyone in this part of the camp had their eyes on the two fighters in front of us all. I supposed it was quite a sight. A fake goddess and an immortal queen slugging it out in the middle of a massacre.

Isis launched herself at Neferu, twirling in mid-flight and aiming a foot at the queen. But she simply moved to one side, grabbed the leading foot and threw Isis back over her own head. She landed with a crash. She didn't have the advantage of having nanobots inside of her, so she was probably feeling the pain now. Certainly, her face was covered with blood.

Neferu suddenly moved, whirling around and moving a little like a Bedouin dancer, as she rapidly circled Isis, punching her repeatedly. She then swiftly moved out of range as the fake goddess tried to retaliate.

'You are like a child,' Neferu said, coming to a standstill a few feet from Isis. 'I have lived for millennia, but you are barely out of the womb. You don't even know how to fight. You're pathetic.'

Isis screamed and threw herself at Neferu. The queen allowed her to make contact, and they rolled across the ground. As they came to a halt, Neferu kicked Isis in the stomach, and she went rolling back the way she'd just come.

Neferu got to her feet and smiled grimly at the hybrid human, as she slowly, and painfully, got to her feet.

Djedetkha crossed to Neferu.

'My Queen, she is wasting your time,' she said. Neferu glanced at her sharply, but then looked at Isis and her armed men. Some of them were missing.

'You will never win,' Neferu said to Isis. She pulled her Glock out of its holster and simply shot her in the forehead. As Isis collapsed, lifeless to the floor, she emptied a few more rounds into her. Just to make sure, I presumed.

Holstering the Glock, and once again taking an HK416 in her hands she ran off ahead of us, soon disappearing out of sight around the corner. Led by Nedjes, we raced after her.

We were faced with what felt like an infinite line of tents, mostly homemade, but some appearing to be purpose-built. Neferu was running down the line, peering into each one. We ran after her, rapidly closing the distance.

We were about two-thirds of the way down the line, when I heard a sound that made my heart jump.

'Get your fucking hands off him!' screamed a very familiar African-American voice, completely out of place in Shatila.

She was there, about twenty feet away, in the entrance of a shabby, makeshift tent. And there, in front of her, on his knees, was Senusret. A gun at his head.

'Leave him alone!' she screamed at the man holding the gun, one of three guardians who'd raced ahead of Isis. 'He's done nothing to hurt you!'

'Shut up, you fucking bitch!' the man with the gun shouted, looking up at her for a moment. As he did so, his head exploded in a burst of automatic gunfire, blood and tissue showering outwards in every direction. The two men next to him looked in our direction in shock, and were instantly riddled with automatic gunfire.

Ceryse jumped back in shock, some of the Guardians' blood splattered over her clothing. She looked over at us, obviously fearing the worst. The look on her face when she saw me completely melted my heart. There were so many emotions in the one space in one moment, but I could see relief, joy, happiness, anger, and even, I imagined, love. I threw myself towards her and wrapped my arms around her, holding her as tightly as I could.

Chapter Thirty-Six

That creature disgusted me. She dared to think she could best me in battle. She dared to think that she, a mere mortal subhuman construct could outsmart and outfight an immortal queen of Kemet. She was but a child, whereas I had survived on this planet for upwards of fifty modern lifespans. She dared to challenge me to battle, when I had learned every martial art and fighting technique that had ever existed in this world. Her conceit and arrogance had been her downfall, as it had been for all of her kind.

And yet, it had simply been part of a plan. A plan to deny me my husband, to crush my hopes and impose her endgame. And may all of the real gods that exist out there bless Djedetkha for pulling me back into the moment and making me realise the true nature of the game being played. I was so caught up in my anger and arrogance that I failed to see why Isis had decided to fight the unequal fight.

She was sacrificing herself simply to stop my plans. How very human of her.

As soon as I realised that three of her Guardians had disappeared, I killed her, like the animal she was, and raced after them. I hoped that someone amongst my people would retrieve her power ring, but I had no time for anything so trivial. Senusret's life was now in the balance.

I ran as hard as I ever had, holstering my Glock and shouldering my HK416. As I turned the corner, I saw the long, almost endless line of tents, and slowed to peer into each one as I went past, ready to shoot anyone who pointed even a finger at me.

I was halfway down the line when I heard that irritating voice, hurling abuse very loudly. For once, I felt pleased to hear it. Just the sound reassured me that I wasn't too late.

As I approached, my heart beating far too fast, my breathing deafening in my ears, I saw a sight that both terrified and enraged me. I saw Senusret, my beautiful husband, whose face I had only been able to imagine for so many long centuries, forced down on his knees, a handgun pressed hard to his head. I saw the look of terror and fear on his face, the confusion at his complete lack of understanding of the terrible world he now found himself in.

I have felt tremendous anger in my life, sometimes anger that has been so incandescent that it would have burned anything and everything in its path, but nothing will ever come close to how I felt at that moment. If I could have ripped the Guardian apart by hand, limb by limb, atom by atom, I would happily have done so. But, instead, I took my assault rifle and shot him in the head. Repeatedly.

It gave me real satisfaction to see his head explode in a mess of blood and tissue, and his body collapse lifelessly to the ground. As Senusret and Ceryse looked in my direction, Nedjes and Djedetkha took out the two remaining Guardians.

As I reached the tent, sprinting for all I was worth, I threw my gun down and launched myself at Senusret, grabbing him and pulling him in as close as I could. My beating heart felt ready to explode. If I'd let Isis distract me any longer, he would have been dead. How could I have been so stupid? She recognised my arrogance and my anger, and used it against me.

I felt the tears of joy and relief pouring down my cheeks as I held my husband close. I thought about the last time I'd held him, how that monster Horus had come between us and thrown him into the Well Of Time. And now, once again, we were united. I was so completely overwhelmed with my happiness and relief that I couldn't even speak. I simply held him closer than it should have been possible for anyone to be held.

'Ibib,' his beautiful voice spoke to me. 'I can't believe you're here.'

'Where else would I be?' I managed to force out, between sobs of joy.

'What is this place? It's horrific. And who are all of these terrible people?'

'It's a long story. Too long for now. The important thing is that you're safe. We need to get away from here. There's something terrible happening here, something that we have to avoid.'

I didn't want to, but I forced myself to pull away from him. All I wanted was to hold him and have him hold me. But we had to get away. We could hold each other as much as we wanted to when we were safely back on Isla de Gran Esperanza in 2024.

I got to my feet, pulling Senusret with me, and spoke to Ceryse, who was in a similar embrace with Richard.

'Thank you,' I said to her, 'Thank you for everything.'

'Thank me when we're safe,' she said, pushing Richard away.

It was a fair point. I looked at Nedjes, Djedetkha, Soshenq and the rest of my Ahati, who had now caught up.

'The other Guardians are dead,' Djedetkha told me. I was glad to hear that. We didn't need more of those animals turning up in our rear.

I took off my Kevlar jacket and handed it to Senusret, helping him to put it on and secure it. I also placed my helmet on his head.

'But what about you?' he asked.

'You don't need to worry about me,' I told him. I turned to the others, and noticed that Djedetkha had given her jacket to Ceryse. I wasn't very happy about that, but I wasn't going to argue about it now.

'Let's go,' I said, leading them towards the far wall.

'There's no way out!' Richard exclaimed behind me, just as Nedjes threw a grenade past us all. As it hit the brickwork it detonated, blowing a small hole in the perimeter wall. It wasn't big, but it was big enough.

I let Nedjes and Shoshenq go first, and then I led Senusret out, the others following. As we clambered out on the other side, we found ourselves confronted by three members of the IDF. They looked shocked, but before they could raise their guns to protest, Nedjes and Shoshenq shot them.

We ran past their bodies and headed for Ghobeiri and Sabra and, ultimately, the Four Seasons and Zaitunay Bay.

It took us about an hour, running the whole way. We were slowed down by the presence of Senusret, Ceryse and Richard, none of whom were really prepared for a four mile plus run. But we made it safely, avoiding checkpoints and making good use of the darkness that now enveloped the city, although the night sky over the camp was occasionally lit up as the IDF sent up flares. Behind us, slowly disappearing into the distance, we could hear the sounds of gunfire and death, screams and shouts that signalled the massacre that we were thankfully escaping from.

We finally slowed as we crossed the road from the Four Seasons Hotel and made our way past the marina to the sea that skirted Zaitunay Bay. The Bay of Olives.

We got ourselves together, and Nedjes handed out some rations. I wasn't quite sure how it had happened, not being aware at all of the passage of time, but dawn was now approaching, the night sky fading into the brightness of another hot September day. It was Friday, I realised, although that was fairly meaningless. I had one last thing to do, and then we could be on our way.

I crossed to where Ceryse and Richard were in earnest conversation, surrounded by my M'sha, who were listening with some interest. They'd only just been reunited, but already they were arguing.

'I've told you, Rich. I don't want to go back!' she repeated.

'Please, Ceryse?' he begged.

'No,' she insisted. 'There's nothing for me back there. Our future's been stolen. This place is horrible, but I can go back to the States and make a life for myself.'

'But I can't go back without you,' he insisted. He obviously wasn't going to mention that she'd warned him about this forty-two years in the future.

I turned to Nedjes, who reached into his backpack and pulled out a brown envelope.

'Richard,' I said, and both of them turned to face me. They both frowned at me with irritation, as if I'd interrupted something enjoyable. 'This is for both of you,' and I handed him the envelope.

He frowned a little more, looking confused, as well as irritated. He opened the envelope, and pulled out a large number of US dollars, a bank book and two passports. He studied them all, before turning his eyes back to mine.

'Who the hell is Edward Stanhope?' he demanded.

'Don't you recognise the passport photograph?' I asked him.

'Yes, of course, I do, but I don't understand.'

'Of course you do,' I said, knowing full well that he understood all too clearly. 'Ceryse told you she was going to stay here. She told us both that. But I met her husband. In forty-two years' time you're going to bring me a cup of Nicaraguan coffee in a house on James Island.'

His jaw dropped slightly and he looked truly shocked.

'You met me?' he demanded. 'I was Ceryse's husband, the father of her children?'

'Yes, Richard, that's you. Except you should start using the future tense, not the past one.'

'It's crazy!' he exclaimed, 'Crazy.'

'You're forgetting one simple thing,' Ceryse interjected. 'I don't want to marry him.'

'Shut up, Ceryse,' I told her. 'You can't argue with destiny.'

She simply glared at me, but there was no animosity in it. I stepped towards Richard and gave him a large embrace. It was strange to think that I would never see him again. I turned to Ceryse, and threw my arms around her, too. Her face slowly softened, and she fastened her arms around me, briefly.

She looked less happy when Djedetkha gave Richard a very warm hug, their cheeks pressed together, before parting with a kiss.

'I told you,' she smiled sweetly at him. 'We're both alive, but this is goodbye.'

Even Nedjes and Shoshenq crossed and shook him by the hand. For his part, Richard now looked tearful.

'I can't believe this is goodbye,' he said. 'You've all come into my life, turned it upside down, destroyed everything I believed in, and now you're abandoning me in the past.'

I said nothing, instead turning and taking Senusret by the hand. I led him over to where the promenade overlooked the lapping waters of the Mediterranean and waited for Nedjes to get the device out of his bag.

'No!' a voice from behind us suddenly screamed out, disrupting the calm, early morning atmosphere of the seafront. It was Ceryse. I turned instantly, and found myself facing the shocking sight of James Curtis standing about ten feet away, a ferocious look on his half-mandrill face, a gun in his hand.

'Fucking bitch!' he shouted. 'You fucking used me! I hope you rot in hell!'

Before I could even move, there was a flash, instantly followed by a loud crack, and I felt Senusret's hand slip out of mine. I just had time to notice Djedetkha empty her HK416 into Curtis, his bloody and flailing body falling lifeless to the pavement, before I turned back to see my husband hit the ground, his eyes already dead.

Chapter Thirty-Seven

I knelt down, holding Senusret as close as I could, trying almost to force him into me, to give him some of my unwanted life. My tears flowed again. How many times had they flowed for my husband? Once again, I had found him and lost him. But he was dead in the here and now, not the past, and there was nothing more that I could do. My heart ached so much that I thought it would break. I loved him so much, so desperately, and now I had finally lost him. What more could I do? I had worked for nearly four millennia to bring him back to me, and every time I found him, he was taken away again. Maybe this was part of an immutable plan, that when you were dead, you were dead and that death could not be cheated. I had tried so hard, no-one could have tried harder, no-one could have given more of themselves. But it had not been enough. I had failed Senusret.

I held him close and wept. Nothing else mattered; there was nothing else. For me, time had stopped, the world had ceased to spin. I would hold him until there was nothing left but dry bones, until the sun died and my immortal body was frozen for the rest of eternity, my tears stopped in their tracks, icy shards on my cheeks.

Had it been wrong of me to want a life with Sensusret? Had I dared to dream too far? Was it wrong for a woman to want to live in peace and unity with her husband? I had gained my revenge on Sekhemrekhutawy and Anubis, but, in reality, the victory remained theirs. My long, ageless life had been for nothing. Not only was I not a queen of long-dead Kemet, but I was still alone.

Sometimes the pain of loss, the pain of heartbreak, is more than physical. My entire being was wracked with a despair and a desolation that went beyond any words in any language, even mine. I was certain that if I had been able to die, then I would have done. The pain that tormented my soul was more than I could bear. But I had no choice, it seemed.

'Don't weep, child,' came a soft voice from behind me. I didn't turn; I barely heard the words. I hadn't noticed anyone approaching, but I neither knew nor cared who she was. I resented the intrusion into my grief, but didn't want to take my attention away from Senusret for even one second.

'You have suffered as few others have,' the voice continued. At the same time, I felt a delicate hand place itself on my shoulder. As it did so, I felt an incredible wave of relief and release sweep through me, as if a part of my suffering had been lifted.

I looked up, and my heart skipped a beat. I found my attention dragged away from my misery and self-pity by the kind, gentle, and unnaturally beautiful face that gazed down on me. I realised that this was something more than a woman. She positively glowed, radiated really, infusing the air around her with a sense of divine serenity. She was dressed in a traditional, and vividly coloured, tube dress, with a strap over one shoulder, but the aura she exuded transcended everything. And, not insignificantly, she had a cobra wrapped around her right forearm, its hooded head rearing up, staring unblinkingly at me.

'I feel your pain, daughter,' she said, 'As you know, I, too, have suffered in a similar way. And I have also suffered at your hands, as have all of my people.'

'Do what you will,' I said, despairingly, lowering my eyes as I spoke, 'I have no fight left'. It was true; I had caused her much pain and loss, but I felt no guilt about that. She and her kind had manipulated and abused humanity since long before

I'd even been born. I should have felt anger and hatred, but instead I felt nothing. All I could feel was the devastating and overwhelming pain and heartbreak of loss. After all these long centuries, it really did seem that death was stronger than love.

'I have not come to bring more suffering to you. You have caused me pain and suffering, but you were wronged by Anubis and Sobek. You sought redress and restitution. I have come to make things right.'

I looked at her, and wondered just how she could do that. Senusret was growing colder in my arms as every second passed, and I felt desolate. I had nothing left to give.

'You are strong and resourceful, and your love has endured in a way that love rarely does. But it should never have had to,' she continued, 'I am here to release you, to finally set you free.'

At last, I thought, a sense of relief washing over me. After all these lonely, empty, years, death had finally come knocking. Real death, not the mini-deaths that I had suffered with such tedious regularity over the centuries.

'There will be no more despair, no more loneliness, no more suffering. All things are possible to you, Neferuhadebnetjer, and all things will come to you. Those things that you have always wanted, have always coveted, deep in your heart, they will be yours.'

Death. She was talking about death, and that was what I now wanted more than anything else. I barely noticed that she had used the name I had bestowed upon myself. Neferu the God Killer.

'Thank you,' was all I could say, bowing my head in supplication.

'Look at me, child,' she commanded, and I forced my eyes up. I gazed into her deeply azure eyes and she said more in that silent moment than she could have done with any number of words. 'Farewell, daughter,' she said, a sweet smile on her lips. She placed her hand on my arm and I was instantly wracked with the most excruciating pain. Every atom in my body felt like it was being torn apart; I could hear myself screaming in agony.

So, this was what real death felt like, I thought. There seemed very little to recommend it. I began to feel a great heat moving over my body and I felt a terrible nausea rising up from the pit of my stomach. I thought I was going to vomit, something I hadn't done since at least 1802BC. And, just when the pain felt like it couldn't get any worse, everything went black. At last, I thought, as the light faded into darkness, death has come knocking. I opened the door and there was no more.

Chapter Thirty-Eight

Field Report of Colonel Hecht, for the attention of the Commanding Officer, IDF, 17th September 1982:

While overseeing some aspects of the operation against the occupants of the Shatila Refugee Camp by local forces, I was made aware of some strong resistance being offered by unknown forces. To help resolve the difficulties being faced, I took the decision to lead a small team of commandos into the battle zone.

When we arrived we encountered a battle within a battle. While the local forces were continuing their mission, two separate sets of combatants were facing off. One side was dressed in Christian Militia uniforms, although it was very clear they were not part of any known unit. The other side were dressed in simple black outfits, with no regalia or insignia to identify them. They were both heavily armed, but with assault rifles and other weapons that seemed unusual, not like anything being used by Israeli or other local forces at this time. Equally, the forces on one side contained women, which seemed a little out of place.

The unmarked force, which appeared to be the aggressor, numbered about 25, and were commanded by an exceptionally tall woman, who seemed to be wearing some form of head-dress with horns attached. There didn't seem to be any clear reason for this. The opposing force was smaller, but were fighting far more effectively.

What struck me as particularly odd, given the carnage going on all around, was that these two opposing forces stopped firing at each other, while the woman with the horns engaged in hand-to-hand combat with the woman who was clearly in command of the other force.

We tried to intervene, but were met with deadly force from both sides. Many of my men were killed, and we were forced to retreat. We took defensive positions and waited. I also reinforced the standing order that no-one be allowed to leave the camp without authorised paperwork.

After some time, the noise from this battle seemed to have died away, and I led the remainder of my force to reconnoitre. The ground where they'd been fighting was strewn with corpses, including the tall woman. On closer inspection, it seemed that the horns that I had thought were part of a helmet were actually growing out of her skull. She'd been shot through the head.

The situation was concerning. The entire camp was, naturally, in complete uproar. The local forces who had been in this particular area were scared and acting in an unhelpful manner. The figures lying dead would appear to have spooked them, and they were in danger of compromising at least a part of the operation. As a result, I took the decision to destroy all the evidence of this battle, and got my men to douse everything in gasoline and set it on fire.

It isn't my role to speculate on what we witnessed, and who this creature was, but I took the decision to remove any evidence, in case it had been specifically planted to implicate us, or was something that would bring unnecessary attention to what was taking place.

There was no sign of the other force, and there were no reports of any unauthorised personnel leaving the camp, although we did find three dead IDF soldiers outside the camp, next to a hole that had been blown in the wall.

You are aware of the outcome of the rest of the operation, which proceeded as planned, and without the need for our further intervention.

Chapter Thirty-Nine

Extract from the daily journal of Richard Verlice, Friday 17th September 1982:

I felt numb by the time we'd reached Zaitunay Bay. There had been so much violence, so much death, and I had simply stood by and watched it. It had been almost surreal to see Neferu and Isis going head to head, like two prizefighters, I had wondered why Isis persisted with what would obviously be a losing cause for her, but Djedetkha had understood and had told Neferu what was actually happening.

It seemed that Isis had engaged Neferu in hand-to-hand combat simply to divert her, while some of her Guardians went in search of Senusret, presumably to kill him. I felt numb by this point, really. The events of the night had been so distressing, so terrible and so unreal that I hardly knew what to think. And who would ever have believed that the celebrity journalist Kalandra Straub was really Isis?

Hearing Ceryse's angry voice was the first good thing that had happened since we entered the camp. It was so wonderful to know that she was still alive, even though she was clearly unhappy and in trouble. But, as I would have expected, Neferu and her M'sha dealt with the situation very matter-of-factly, simply blowing the Guardians away.

I'd been shocked that, when we began to make our escape, there was no way out. I had begun to feel a slight panic, unable to believe that these people, who always seemed to have a plan, had led us to a literal brick wall. But, of course, Nedjes had simply made a way out, using one of his percussion grenades to blow a hole in the crumbling old wall of the camp. That hadn't quite been the end of it, with three members of the Israeli forces challenging us outside, but they were now dead, probably as cold as the road they were lying on.

We'd run most of the way back to the Bay. Obviously, Senusret, Ceryse and I were not as fit as the others, and it took longer than they probably wanted. My lungs were fit to burst by the time we arrived, but wanting to put as much distance between ourselves and the camp helped me to keep some sort of pace going.

When we'd arrived, Neferu and her people had dished out some rations, and then had prepared to return to 2024. I'd begged Ceryse to come with us, but then, as I knew she would, she'd refused. She told me, repeatedly, that there was nothing left for her in 2024 and she wanted to make a fresh life here, in 1982.

I'd continued to argue, and then Neferu had shocked me. She'd handed me an envelope containing two passports, one for Ceryse, and one for an Edward Stanhope, with my photo. She'd also handed me a large number of US banknotes and a bank book, for an account with the Bank Of America, in Charleston, in the name of Edward Stanhope, to the tune of twenty million dollars.

The name Edward Stanhope, of course, wasn't wasted on me. Lord Carnarvon, Howard Carter's patron, was, of course, really George Edward Stanhope Molyneux Herbert. So, it appeared that the Queen really did have a sense of humor.

I'd rather foolishly talked about Ceryse's husband and children, and Neferu had told me that she'd actually met me as an old man in 2024, serving her coffee when she'd first visited Ceryse. My jaw probably hit the pavement with that revelation. I didn't know that my life could get any more bizarre or surreal, but actually, it could, and it just had.

It all felt like a dream, one that I knew I would never wake from. Neferu embraced first Ceryse and then myself. As she held me close, and I tried to draw her familiar curves as close as I could, I felt an aching longing that dragged my soul down lower than I had believed it could go. I was completely conflicted. Part of me actually felt excited about forging a new life with Ceryse, even if it had to start in such a terrible place. But, a part of me, and it was probably the largest part, felt devastated at the thought that I wouldn't see Neferu's face again for another forty-two years, and that she would look just the same, while I would be an old man.

As this devastating revelation struck me, Djedetkha appeared in front of me, and pulled me in as close as she could, our cheeks gently pressed together. As we held each other tight, time seemed to slow to a standstill, and all I was aware of was the gentle warmth of her breath on my cheek. Eventually, she let go, kissing me as she did so.

'I told you,' she said, smiling at me. 'We're both alive, but this is goodbye.'

While I was getting my head around the fact that I was going to be living in the past, that I would never see these two women who had turned my world upside down again, and while Ceryse was getting her head around Djedetkha giving me such an intimate hug and goodbye kiss, I had glimpsed a movement out of the corner of my eye.

Too late, I realised that the figure I'd glimpsed was James Curtis. How I hadn't seen him sooner, I didn't know. I was fully distracted by the situation, of course, but Curtis hardly blended into the crowd, with his obsidian animal eyes and his freakish tattoos. He didn't look good, not that he ever did. And he simply walked into view, pulled a gun out of his pocket and aimed it in the direction of Neferu.

I'd heard Ceryse scream 'No!', and then I heard Curtis shout a tirade of abuse at Neferu; but before anyone could move he'd fired.

He was no fool, and he hadn't shot Neferu. He'd shot Senusret, who fell slowly to the ground, blood pouring from a wound in the middle of his chest. His body hadn't even hit the ground before Nedjes and Djedetkha emptied the clips on their assault rifles into Curtis.

He'd collapsed, quite dead, and we all just stood in shock. Where had Curtis come from? I knew he'd fallen into the Well Of Time, but it seemed improbable, if not impossible, to think that he might have wound up in 1982 as well. Maybe he had, or maybe he'd made his way here. After all, he was a genius with a specialism in particle physics and time travel. Either way, he was dead, and so, it appeared, was Senusret.

I felt sick. I hardly knew what to think or say. Neferu had come this far, had done so much, had twice rescued her dead husband, and now he was dead again. It was hard to see what she could do now to save him, without completely screwing up time and herself. And maybe, just maybe, it was an immutable law of the universe. If you were meant to be dead, you were meant to be dead.

We all just stood there in shock, hardly believing what we'd just witnessed, as Neferu fell to her knees, cradling Senusret. I could hear the violence of her sobbing from where I stood, some twenty feet away.

I didn't know what to do. I was certain that comfort from anyone, least of all me, was the last thing she would want. I looked at Ceryse, who had tears in her eyes, and simply shook her head sadly.

It was then that I noticed the strange woman walking towards the Queen and her dead consort. At first, I thought nothing of it. And then I realised she was different. Sort of otherworldly. She almost glided over the ground, rather than walking.

It was only when she stood next to Neferu and began to speak to her that I realised who she was.

Which was quite a shock. Especially as it didn't seem that she was about to attack Neferu.

I couldn't hear what they were saying, but after a couple of minutes, Hathor, who had already placed a hand on Neferu's shoulder, touched her again, and the Queen fell to the ground, writhing in agony, before finally lying very still. To all intents and purposes, she appeared to be dead. Which was unthinkable.

What happened next was beyond strange, and I still don't really understand it. Hathor flickered slightly, as if she almost faded out of existence, and then fully returned. As she did so, I realised that my memories had changed. I remembered it all differently. I now had a picture of Curtis being touched by Hathor and dropping dead before he could shoot. I gazed at Neferu, who appeared as dead as Senusret had been, and realised that her husband was now alive again, had never been shot, and was holding her close, a complete reversal of the scene I'd just witnessed.

I glanced at Nedjes and Djedetkha, who appeared equally confused. Djedetkha glanced at me and simply shook her head, as if to say she had no idea what was going on.

Hathor then bent down, once more, and touched both Senusret and Neferu simultaneously. Unlike

Curtis, who was lying dead about ten feet away from me, they simply disappeared, as if they'd never been there. One moment they were there, the next they were gone.

She then turned around, and approached the M'sha, touching them one at a time. They offered no resistance. It was almost as if, without their Queen, all the fight had gone out of them. As she touched them, each one disappeared.

She reached Nedjes, Djedetkha and Shoshenq last. They stepped back as she approached, but she smiled benignly at them.

'There is nothing to fear,' she told them. 'I am returning you all to where you came from.'

All three of them looked uncomfortable, but reluctantly let her touch them. As she did so, one by one, they also disappeared, without leaving the slightest trace.

Hathor then made her way towards Ceryse and me, that same calming smile never faltering. She stopped just in front of us.

'Who are you?' I demanded. 'What happened?'

'Everything will be as it should be,' she told me, her voice a little like music in the early morning air, mingling subtly with the gentle sound of the seabirds all around us. 'Ma'at has been restored.' She paused for a moment, studying us both carefully, and glancing at the brown envelope in my hand. 'Do you wish to return or remain?' she asked.

I glanced at Ceryse, who simply nodded at me. She took my hand and squeezed it.

'Remain,' I said.

Hathor nodded, as if she considered this was wise, and then simply blurred and vanished.

Chapter Forty

I woke to bright light streaming through the windows. I was dazed, confused. Was this the Duat? Was it Heaven? It was unlikely, I thought. The first didn't exist, and I had some strong doubts about the second. I hadn't feared death; without Senusret at my side I had welcomed it, even though I had lived so long that death seemed to be something that only happened to other people. I had died many times, but thanks to the microscopic machines inside me, I had always returned. After living for nearly four millennia I wondered what death might actually be like; what I would transition to, if there was even a transition. Just a few months ago, that would have seemed heretical to me, but now it was the harsh reality of life.

I opened my eyes and glanced around, taking in the bright vista. I looked at the windows, with the vibrant sunshine streaming in, I studied the walls and the furniture. I was in a bed, there were bedside tables, a vanity cabinet, a chaise longue. There were doors leading off in two separate directions, and a set of large glass doors that led outside. As I struggled to rise to the surface of consciousness, slowly struggling against the tides of sleep and exhaustion, it occurred to me that everything was remarkably familiar. I tried to focus my thoughts, to draw myself back from the world of sleep to the world of wherever this was. Although it had felt like I had died, this didn't seem like any interpretation of any version of any afterlife that I could imagine. The pain I had experienced as Hathor had touched me had convinced me that I was going to die, although I was surprised that she had despatched me in such a distressing manner.

I eased myself up onto my elbows and rested my head against the bedhead. As full consciousness finally washed over me, finally bringing me up from the depths of sleep, it hit me. This was not death. This was the master bedroom of my Royal Palace on Isla de Gran Esperanza. How was that possible? Hathor had talked about death, had shown kindness and compassion in ending my miserable, wretched existence. She had shown me such empathy, despite my having killed Horus, her consort. I felt confused and disoriented.

I got up and crossed to the windows. The view outside was stunning, as ever. The sun was high in the sky, and I could see the inner courtyard of my palace, and the mountains of the island's interior in the distance. As I stood there, I put out my hand to rest it on the woodwork. I felt a small, but sharp, pain in my palm as I did so. I looked down at my hand, which was bleeding slightly. I looked at the window and saw the sharp end of a nail that had not been hammered in properly. I'd get Nedjes to take care of that, I thought.

   I turned and made my way back to the chaise longue, sitting down and leaning back; thinking, although not really achieving much. I felt confused. Why had Hathor done this? Why had she inflicted so much pain on me simply to return me to life? My life, at that. And then I noticed something. The little cut on my palm was still there. I held it up to the light and studied it. It remained a cut, with small traces of blood around it. It wasn't healing. I felt even more confused, and I tried to remember exactly what Hathor had said to me. She had told me she was going to set me free, which I had presumed meant she was going to release me through death. But she had also told me that all things were possible for me, and that all things would come to me. She specifically said that the things I had always wanted would be mine.

I caught my breath as I considered what those words might actually have meant. I thought about the pain she had inflicted on me; it occurred to me, now that I considered it, that it had felt very similar to the pain Anubis had made me suffer all those centuries ago. My heart started to beat fast, so fast that my breathing struggled to keep up with it. I looked at the top of my left thigh. And there it was. Something I had last seen in 1802BC, nearly four millennia ago. The small scar, received during combat training with my father's personal guard, and which the microscopic machines in my body had healed properly, was back. I remembered my father had been livid that I had been hurt, but I had been quite proud of my little trophy. And it was hardly disfiguring, it was almost too small to see.

Hathor had removed the machines from my body. I was mortal. After all these long centuries, I was now like everyone else. But why had she done that? Why not just kill me? Unless? I barely dared to complete that thought.

I jumped up and ran out of the bedroom, into the living space next to it. And my heart stopped. I fell to my knees, the tears not just flowing, but flooding down my cheeks. I couldn't help them. My heart, my soul, felt like they were going to explode. Hathor had made me completely whole. I felt as if

I'd been resurrected. Properly resurrected, not the terrible return to life I'd experienced so many times over the centuries.

Sitting on a chair by the window, drinking a glass of water, was Senusret. He looked up as I entered the room, and ran towards me as he saw me crying. He fell to his knees in front of me and pulled me in close, wrapping his arms around me and holding me tight, as I continued to sob.

'I'm sorry,' he said, softly, reassuringly, 'You were still asleep when I woke. I didn't want to disturb you, so I came in here. I was just about to come and look in on you.'

'Senusret!' I managed to say, between sobs, 'you're alive!'

'I am,' he told me, and I could picture him smiling as he did so, although I couldn't actually see his face.

I pulled back slightly, so that I could face him, could stare into his beautiful eyes.

'We're free,' I told him, 'It's finally all over.'

'I love you, Neferu,' was his only response, and he kissed me. Hathor had been right. Everything was now possible. Everything that I really wanted was here, in front of me. And maybe the things that I had dreamed of for Senusret and myself were no longer just a dream.

We slowly got to our feet, and crossed the short distance to the bedroom, our hands and hearts entwined.

'I've missed you,' I told him, as he stroked my cheek and my hair gently with his right hand. He smiled and crossed to close the blinds.

Acknowledgements

These acknowledgements of mine are really a repetitious series of thank you's to the people who make my life happy and worthwhile.

So, as ever, I would like to thank my great friend Ziad and his wonderful wife Carole. Thanks must also go to my brother Tony and his wife Pauline, my son Jamie, and my friend Luan and her mother Susan.

My usual planet-sized thank you goes out to Emilija of www.emilysworldofdesign.com, who continues to produce cover designs that are consistently better than the best I could hope for.

I also need to thank Neferu and Djedetkha, without whom the book in your hands wouldn't exist. And, of course, it goes without saying that I have to thank the divine Haifa Wehbe, always an inspiration in so many ways. And not just for me.

The biggest thanks, of course, go to my family, specifically my son Mudiwa and my wife Fungisai, who have also come to realise that they are living in a small adjunct of Kemet.

For those who are interested, the events of 16th to 18th September 1982 in the Shatila Refugee Camp in the Sabra district of Beirut did take place as reported by Neferu and Richard, although they were only present for the first few hours of the massacre. If you would like to know more about what happened, check out the entry on Wikipedia.

Author Biography

Martin Dench keeps writing books and they keep being published. He is extraordinarily pleased about this. He'd also like to point out that the books in this series should be classified as non-fiction.

This is, by his reckoning his sixth published book. There would appear to be many more on the not-so-distant horizon.

He lives in a small outpost of Kemet, with an African Queen and a little African Prince.

Printed in Great Britain
by Amazon